This critically acclaimed collection was selected by the editors of *Saturday Night* magazine as the first work of fiction to appear under the prestigious Saturday Night Books imprint.

FEVER

Sharon Butala

Saturday Night Books

 HarperPerennial
HarperCollins*PublishersLtd*

This collection was written with the assistance of the Canada Council.

"Babette" appeared in Sky High, Coteau Books, 1988; "Dark of the Moon," in Canadian Woman Studies/Les Cahiers de la Femme, Fall, 1987; "The Metric System" in Canadian Forum, January/February 1989; "Discord" in Wascana Review, Spring, 1989; "Dinner on the Edge of the City" in Briarpatch, May, 1986; "The Prize" in Canadian Fiction Magazine, No. 64, Fall, 1988, where it won the Annual Contributor's Award.

The stories from Richard St. Barbe Baker's life in "Healer of the Earth" are paraphrased from his books; "Healer of the Earth" is fiction.

First Paperback Edition

Canadian Cataloguing in Publication Data

Butala, Sharon, 1940-
Fever

"Saturday Night Books".
0-00-647143-9

I. Title.

PS8553.U6967F49   1990   C813'.54   C90-094964-3
PR9199.3.B8F4   1990

91 92 93 94 95 JD 5 4 3 2 1

For Sean and Carol

Contents

FEVER

Fever

Cecilia had slept well the first part of the night, but later she was dimly aware of a restlessness on Colin's part that kept pulling her up from the dreamless depths of her heavy sleep to a pale awareness of something being not right. She remembered feeling hot and must have thrown off all her covers, an act unusual for her since she was almost always too cold, and often resorted to a flannel nightgown even in summer. About two-thirty she came fully awake, shivering because she was uncovered, and in her gropings for blankets, found that Colin was hugging all the bedcovers tightly to himself.

She woke him, pushing against his shoulder, then touching his cheek and forehead with her palm, puzzled and then alarmed by the hotness of his skin and by the dry heat radiating from his body.

"I'm sick," he mumbled, with a mixture of fear and irritation in his voice that woke her further.

"What's the matter?" she asked.

"I'm sick," he repeated, a whisper this time, and gave a little moan, involuntarily it seemed, as though he had been stricken suddenly with pain.

She fumbled for the bedside lamp, its location forgotten from the evening before when they had checked in, exhausted from their long flight and the delay when they had changed planes in Winnipeg. The lamp on, she blinked, staring down at him, trying to tell if his pallor was real or just the consequence of poor light or her grogginess.

"I'll need a doctor," he said, his eyes closed, and he clenched his jaw as if against the chattering of his teeth, or pain.

Cecilia was confused, vague pictures passed through her mind, vanishing before she could catch them. She sat up in bed, put both hands over her face, and tried to make sense of things. They had arrived in Calgary, Colin was sick, he said he needed a doctor. She put her hands down and was disconcerted to find him staring at her with an expression that was — surely not — beseeching. But yes, that's what it was. He was beseeching her to do something, and his eyes were the eyes of someone in extremity such as she sometimes caught a glimpse of on the news on television, frighteningly dark, holding depths she had never guessed at before.

She wanted to close her eyes again, to sink back into sleep, to wake in the morning to find him well, or gone.

Colin grunted once, softly, and she got out of bed, went to the desk, and opened the phone book.

"It's my stomach," he said, and his voice was strained now and pitched too high. She looked back at him, saw he had raised his head off the pillow and that his black hair, always neatly trimmed and short, was pushed by his restlessness into spikes like a punker's. She wanted to laugh. "Call the desk," he said, straining to say it loudly enough for her to hear, then his head fell back on the pillow. But the way his head dropped like a stone as if he had fallen that suddenly into unconsciousness made her dial zero.

They drove the short distance to a hospital in an ambulance, down deserted, icy streets, the siren senselessly screeching. Almost at once Colin was taken from the emergency ward to a bed in a ward three flights up. It was a small room across from the nursing station, and it was equipped with valves, dials and tubes attached to the wall at the head of his bed that the other rooms Cecilia had glanced into as they went down the hall, didn't have. This, and his proximity to the nursing station, alarmed Cecilia. Or rather, these facts registered, she knew this meant he was seriously ill, and that she should be alarmed. But she found she felt no fear, or at least, she didn't think she did.

It was four a.m. Cecilia stood by his bed looking down on him while a nurse on the other side, for at least the third time since their arrival, took his blood pressure, counted his pulse, and listened to his chest.

Colin's eyelids flickered open. Closing them, he said to Cecilia, "You came." She wondered if he had forgotten that she had come with him to Calgary, that he wasn't alone on this business trip as he usually was, and if he thought, in his fever-distorted mind, that she had flown in to be with him when he was taken ill. She drew in a breath to explain, but the paper-like sheen of his eyelids, which looked now as though they had been sealed shut and not merely closed, silenced her. She looked to the nurse but the nurse seemed to be avoiding looking at her.

"He's not likely to be awake much," she said to Cecilia in a tentative tone, casting a glance at her that Cecilia couldn't interpret. "The doctor wants to talk to you." Cecilia went out into the hall where the doctor was leaning on the counter and sleepily making notes in a patient's chart. When he saw her, he stopped writing. Cecilia approached him slowly, and waited for him to speak.

"He's a very sick man," the doctor said to her, solemnly. For a second Cecilia thought she hadn't heard him correctly. When she didn't reply, he said, "I know it's a surprise, since he's so healthy and strong looking, but whatever is bothering him has hit him hard. We'll have to watch him closely." He said something further about vital signs and some medical jargon that she didn't listen to. She interrupted him.

"But what's wrong with him?"

"We have to wait till the lab opens in the morning to get the results of the tests and to do more," he said, "before we can pinpoint the problem, but we've got a nurse with him full time for now, and if we need to, we can have him in the O.R. in minutes." He seemed used to the bewildered silences of relatives, because he filled the pauses when she, her mind crowded with not so much questions as dark, empty spaces that refused to form themselves into words, could only look up at him in silence.

"I think you might as well go back to your hotel and get some sleep," he said, looking vaguely, with red-rimmed eyes, down the empty, polished corridor. "Mrs. Purdy will call you if he should get worse." He said good night and left her standing there, holding tightly onto the nursing station counter with one hand.

She looked in on Colin once more, the nurse was taking his blood pressure again, before she took a taxi back to the hotel. It was when she was in bed that she began to wonder if he would die. Her mind shied at the idea, it wasn't possible. And what could be the matter with him? The doctor had given her no clue, at least she didn't think he had. She wondered if she had done the right thing by coming back to the hotel, or if she should have stayed at the hospital. Did the nurses think badly of her because she had gone? This worried her for a while, but finally, she fell asleep.

When she woke it was only three hours later. Light was streaming in around the curtains and she could hear traffic in the street below. She was at once fully alert and knew she wouldn't be able to go back to sleep. Before her eyes had opened she thought of Colin, remembering what the doctor had said and how Colin seemed to have gone away even from behind his sealed eyelids, and she felt momentarily angry with him for deserting her and then for spoiling their trip.

She phoned the hospital and was told that he was not awake, that his condition was pretty much the same, and that the test results wouldn't be back from the lab for a while yet.

"I'll be there in an hour," she said, feeling the need to assure them of her interest, and then, because it seemed to be important to do the normal thing, she bathed, dressed, and went downstairs to the hotel restaurant to order breakfast even though she was neither hungry nor thirsty.

The restaurant was almost empty. While she waited for her coffee she noticed a tall, thin man who looked a little like Colin, although he was not so dark, sitting at a table near the window eating breakfast. He glanced up and caught her watching him. She lowered her eyes quickly, but when he passed her table on his way out of the room, he smiled briefly, wryly at her, indicating by this the oddness of them finding themselves the only two people in such a big restaurant. She observed that his eyes were blue, not brown like Colin's. She recalled then that he had checked in just ahead of them the night before.

She drank her coffee and her orange juice and ate a piece of toast politely, carefully, not tasting it, then went back to the hospital.

As she arrived two white-coated women were wheeling Colin, bed and all, out of his room and down the hall in the direction where the labs were. The empty room, with intravenous and oxygen tubes connected to nothing, and the silent dials on the wall, gave her such a peculiar feeling that she went into the TV room to wait for them to bring him back. When he returned he was still drifting in and out of consciousness. Nurses, aides and lab technicians hurried in and out of the room, speaking in loud voices to Colin and softly to her, as if she were the sick one. They took his pulse, his temperature and blood pressure and poked him with needles, then measured his blood into little glass vials. The doctor came alone and nodded good morning to her, then left. Later he came again, this time with two other doctors. In the hallway they murmured in soft voices to her, speculating about the cause of his illness, enumerating the results of tests, and commenting on what each one might mean.

"But will he be all right?" she asked. The doctors looked at their feet and mumbled some more, while she stood too close to them, lifting her head to hear better, trying to understand what they were saying, or rather, what they were not saying.

In the afternoon Colin spoke to her.

"This will be all right," he said, in a new, high-pitched voice. Although his eyes were directed to her, she had a feeling that he was actually looking at something beyond or behind her. "I am frightened." Having failed to show any sign of fear, he closed his eyes. It was such a contradictory, puzzling message that she discounted it entirely, blaming it on the drugs they were giving him for pain and to control his fever.

Not long after that she began to wonder if the doctors had been trying to tell her that Colin might die. But she could not believe that Colin's death was in the cards for either of them at this moment, and after a pause, she dismissed the thought.

By nine in the evening his illness had still not been identified. Talk had gone from appendicitis or food poisoning to a malfunctioning gall bladder to a kidney ailment or bowel dysfunction to every possible virus from influenza to AIDS. Cecilia went back to the hotel, hesitated for a second in the empty lobby, since she still didn't feel hungry, then went into the restaurant anyway.

There were a few more people scattered around at the tables now, talking quietly, drinks on their tables in front of them, or cups of coffee. The hostess seated Cecilia, then left her. As she was picking up the menu, she realized someone was speaking to her.

For the last few hours she had had a steady, quiet hum in her head that put a distance between her and the voices of other people. She tried to make it stop by shaking her head, by concentrating very hard on anyone speaking to her, and then by reciting to herself her own name, Colin's name, the names of their children and their street address at home. None of these had helped and eventually she had given in and allowed herself to be lulled into the hum.

She turned her head slowly in the direction of the voice, expecting to find that it wasn't she who was being addressed. But the man she had seen at breakfast was leaning toward her from the next table where he was sitting.

"Pardon?" Cecilia said.

"I said the hostess seems to think we should talk to each other, since she placed us so close together." Cecilia glanced around. It was true. In a room three-quarters empty, the hostess had placed them at adjacent tables. How had she not noticed him? "I believe I saw you check in with your husband," he remarked. "I suppose he's off doing business."

"Yes," she said, "I mean, no." It was hard to talk through the hum. "I'm sorry, I haven't had much sleep. He was taken ill last night. He's in the hospital."

"I thought there was something wrong," he said, and leaned toward her again. "You looked," he paused, "sort of in shock. I hope it's not too serious." She hesitated, not sure what to say. There was a warm intensity in his blue eyes that calmed her.

"Yes," she said. "It's very serious. He's unconscious most of the time. I left because," she felt herself frown, "I was too tired to do anything else. I wanted to get away," then was embarrassed at what she had said. She had a quick mental picture of Ingrid Bergman being torn away from the bedside of her dying husband by well-meaning friends — No! No, I don't want to leave! Let me stay! — and managed not to laugh.

He seemed to be absorbing her remark, mulling it over, and now he nodded briskly, a quick acceptance or agreement.

"Yes," he said. "You need to get a perspective."

"I guess that's it," she said, a little dubiously. He smiled at her quickly, impersonally. They didn't speak again for a while.

"Please don't think I'm being too forward," he said after several minutes had passed, "but I'd enjoy it if you'd have your dinner here, at my table. It's lonely, all this eating by yourself." Cecilia found herself standing, then awkwardly sitting in the chair he held out for her. Some part of her perhaps regretted this action she was taking, but she found no will to resist what seemed to be her inclination.

"It is lonely," she agreed, in a serious tone.

The waitress came and took their orders. If she was surprised to find them sitting together, she gave no sign.

"I don't want to intrude on your privacy," he said carefully, not looking at her, "but do you know anyone in Calgary? Are you alone in this?"

Cecilia told him how Colin was thinking of opening a branch of his sporting goods business in the city if it looked like it would be profitable, how they had talked about maybe moving West if things went well, how she had come with him because she'd never been west of Winnipeg before, and now this had happened. And no, she didn't know a soul in Calgary.

"I've told our children he's sick, but nothing else, and I told his sister not to come ... yet."

"Then let me be your friend," he said. Cecilia was overcome with embarrassment. She took a sip from her glass of water. "I'm a representative for a chemical company," he said. "I make regular rounds through southern Alberta, among other things, selling chemicals to the dealers who sell them to farmers. I have a wife and three kids in Edmonton where our head office is."

He was touching his cutlery, moving his hands with precision and a certain amount of tension which she couldn't read, but when he finished speaking he lifted his head and smiled at her in a way that was almost embarrassed. "And I liked you as soon as I saw you standing in the lobby last night with that same puzzled look on your face while your husband checked you in."

"I saw you too," she said, finally, and noticed that the hum in her head had lessened and that the room was a pleasant temperature, not too cold as she usually found restaurants. She relaxed a little, then thought of Colin.

"If you're worried, phone the hospital again," he said. "There are pay phones in the lobby."

When he left her at the elevator, he paused, and leaning in the open door, kissed her gently, not quickly, on her mouth. Thinking about it later as she lay in bed, she told herself, I knew he was going to do it and I didn't back away or try to stop him. I wanted him to kiss me. And she felt a burning through her body, even in her arms and the palms of her hands, a burning that she recognized as sexual longing. She who had never been unfaithful, who had never dreamt of such a thing, and Colin so sick.

She passed another restless night and was at the hospital before eight. Several doctors were standing around Colin's bed gazing silently down on him while the head nurse stood by tensely. She noticed Cecilia in the doorway and spoke in an undertone to one of the doctors.

"Ah," he said, turning to Cecilia.

"I'll stop in at noon," the second doctor said. He and the third doctor walked out of the room past Cecilia and down the hall.

"I'm Dr. Jameson," the first doctor said to her. "Dr. Ransom asked me to have a look in."

Colin lay motionless on the bed, his eyes closed, an unnaturally red spot of colour high on each cheek. His lips too, were more vividly coloured than usual. Dr. Jameson took her arm and said, "Let's just sit down and talk this over." He guided her into a small office behind the nursing station, held a chair for her and sat down himself.

"Now," he said, "your husband is very sick. But you know that."

She said, "Have you found out what's wrong with him?" He didn't reply directly, but instead, not looking at her, began to list the different tests they had done and the result of each. He remarked on certain possibilities and dismissed them with a gesture or left them open. Cecilia tried to listen to him, but her mind wandered to Colin's strange colouring, to the fact the head nurse was a different one, and to wondering who Dr. Jameson was and what might be his field of specialty.

Gradually it dawned on her that Colin was worse, a good deal worse, and that was why Dr. Jameson had brought her into this room and why the nurses and aides at the station or passing down the hall had avoided looking at her as she followed him.

She tried to get a grip on this idea, to admit, to force it to penetrate the shield of her own bewildering indifference. She repeated to herself, Colin is desperately ill, but still no shiver of fear passed down her spine. Dr. Jameson stopped talking and went away. Cecilia went back to Colin's bedside.

At noon he opened his eyes and spoke to her.

"They are coming with flowers," he said. "They want to speak to us. Be ready."

"Yes, Colin," she replied, and bent to kiss him on his hot, dry forehead, but as her lips touched his skin, he turned his head fretfully away from her much as a cranky, feverish child might, and screwed up his face before he lapsed back into unconsciousness. Later he said, "It is very big and there is an echo like silver."

They were keeping the door to his room closed now and had hung a 'No Visitors' sign on it. Nurses moved swiftly, silently in and out of the darkened room, staring down at Colin with pursed lips before they went away again.

"I don't understand it," Dr. Jameson muttered to Colin on one of his several brief visits.

At eleven that night the head nurse came, put her arm around Cecilia's shoulders and told her to go back to the hotel and try to sleep.

"I know you want to be here, but you don't want to collapse when he needs you. Is the rest of the family on its way?" Cecilia shook her head numbly, no.

"His parents are dead," she said, "and I don't want our children here. If he isn't better by morning, I'll tell his sister to come."

"Go back to the hotel," the nurse said in a kindly way, "if you are carrying this alone. I'll call you at once if I think you should be here."

Cecilia obeyed and took a taxi back to the hotel. Just as she entered the lobby the doors of the elevator opened and the man she had talked with the night before stepped out as if he had arranged to meet her.

"You look so tired," he said to her, without any preliminaries or surprise. "Come and have a drink with me before you go to bed."

"I don't think I could sleep anyway," she said. They went together into the bar across from the restaurant and Cecilia had a glass of scotch. She inhaled its fumes, finding them delicious, she let them rush into her brain.

"He's worse," she said. "He may not live through the night," but her own words carried no meaning, she frowned with the effort to feel them, but they seemed to be as on the other side of an impenetrable glass wall. Finally she abandoned the effort; she was too tired. "I guess I shouldn't be here," she said, meaning that she should have stayed at Colin's bedside, not that she shouldn't be in the hotel bar with a strange man.

He was thoughtful for a second, then shook his head.

"No," he said. "There comes a moment ... If it's his fate ... " She studied him. He had such bright eyes, so blue, and the intensity in them fascinated her. She remembered Colin's eyes the night he had gotten sick, as if, behind their transparent glistening surface, they opened into worlds she hadn't been to, hadn't known existed, didn't want to know about. He took her hand and held it tightly.

"Hold on," he said. "You're not alone. I'll stick with you." At that moment all she could feel was the pressure, almost too hard, and the warmth of his hand around hers. And then he put his other hand on the side of her face. She turned her head into his palm and breathed in the smell of his flesh, she opened her mouth and touched her tongue to his palm, tasting the faint salt taste. They sat that way for a moment, she with her eyes closed, until he loosened his hold on her hand, and slid his other hand down to her shoulder.

"Better?" he asked. Yes, she was better. Surprised, she opened her eyes. He was staring at her with a slight frown, his blue eyes burning with a steady light.

He walked with her to the elevator and this time, instead of letting her get on alone, he got on too, and pushed the button for his floor which came before hers. The elevator stopped, the doors opened, he got off and began to say good night to her in an oddly formal, unsmiling way, when she stepped off the elevator beside him. He stared at her, perplexed, not speaking. She touched his arm in a tentative, supplicating way, holding her eyes on his face.

He hesitated, then took his room key out of his pocket and led her down the hall.

His room was identical to hers except that it was less tidy and he had left a lamp burning. The desk was covered with papers he had evidently been working on, and his pyjamas lay across the foot of his bed. She closed her eyes again and after a pause, he kissed her.

At one moment, finding herself in a posture both undignified and profoundly arousing, she had felt a second's horror at what she was doing. For she had never consented to such behaviour — or even thought of it — before in her life. She was reminded of the ugly grappling of pornography, and for a second she was filled with distaste at where her body had taken her, as though she had wakened now, but only to the flesh, to the room, to the rug on the floor and the bed and the walls and the dusty TV set in the corner, and to his hands and mouth on her, and hers on him; she was filled with amazement.

And my husband sick, dying, she thought.

She told him what Colin had said, about the big room with the echo like silver.

"Maybe he really is somewhere else," the man said. "Maybe he's somewhere in a big place and it has an echo like silver. It sounds beautiful," he added. "It doesn't sound like you should be worried about him."

"I didn't like the sound of it," she replied. "So remote, so cold." She shivered, lying in his arms, and was glad of the warmth of his flesh against hers.

"We thought it might be his pancreas," Dr. Jameson said to her in the morning, "but now we've ruled that out, too." She had given him their family doctor's number so that Dr. Jameson could consult with him about Colin's medical history. She could have told him there was nothing: flu, colds, a broken bone in his foot.

At noon the head nurse who had been on duty when Colin was admitted came in and read the record of his vital signs and intake and output of fluids that lay on the stand by his bed.

"That's better," she murmured, then went out without saying anything more. Cecilia meditated on this till the nursing shifts changed at three and the new nursing team came in and clustered around Colin's bed. She was about to ask if he was improving when the new head nurse said to the others, "A slight improvement here." Cecilia could see no difference, except perhaps that the unnaturally bright colour in his cheeks had faded.

After they had gone, she stood beside his bed.

"Did you hear that, Colin?" she asked. "They say you're getting better." Colin's eyelids flickered and he looked at her with that same well of darkness behind his eyes.

"The blueness of things," he said, in a voice that might have been awestruck, had it not been so faint.

"The antibiotics are working," she said. There was no response. She wanted to reach down and shake him. She was his wife, she had been his wife for fifteen years. They had children. What right had he to ignore her in this way? The doctors and nurses whisking in and out of his room barely glanced at her, spoke to her only occasionally, waited politely for her to leave the room before they pulled the curtain around his bed to do some unspeakable thing to him. Was she of no account at all? But Colin had become a stranger, while the man she had gone to bed with the night before was not. She tried to summon some remorse for what she had done, or sympathy for Colin lying so ill and in pain, but all she could feel was anger.

At six the nurse who took his vital signs replied, when Cecilia asked her, that Colin's fever was still elevated, and she smiled at Cecilia in a commiserating way.

"A little change this afternoon," she said, "but now he's much the same."

Around seven Colin said loudly, in a clear voice, "Let me sleep," then, more quietly, "I'm tired and the music lulls me." Cecilia put her hand on his forehead. It was damply cool now, and beads of cool sweat sat on his upper lip. He didn't respond to her touch and after a moment, she took her hand away.

At nine she went back to the hotel. The man she had slept with wasn't in the lobby or the restaurant. She went directly to the bar, stopped in the doorway and peered from table to table through the smoky gloom. He was seated on a stool at the bar and when he glanced back and saw her standing in the doorway, he stood at once, put some money beside his half-full glass, and came immediately to where she waited for him. They went to the elevator, got on, and went up to his room.

This time their coupling was less dramatic, less violently experimental than it had been the night before. Lying beside him on his rumpled bed before she returned to her room, she said, "Today when I tried to talk to him, he said, 'the blueness of things.' What do you suppose he was dreaming about?"

"Or thinking," he said. "Or maybe he was somewhere else."

"Do you think he's trying to tell me something?" Cecilia asked. "No," she answered her own question, "I don't think he is. But what did he mean?"

"Maybe he'll be able to tell you when he wakes up," the man said. "You should write down what he says so you can ask him."

"If he wakes up," she heard herself say, and refused to amend or qualify what she had said.

"Do you love him?" he asked her. In the same unemotional voice she replied, "Yes, or I did when I married him and we've been married fifteen years, so if I don't love him anymore, I don't think it makes any difference."

"Tell me then ... " he said carefully, and paused. "Tell me. Do you ever wish that ... " He paused again. "Do you ever wish that he would die?"

"No," she said. "Why would I wish that?"

He shrugged, was perhaps a bit embarrassed. "To free you."

She started to ask him why he thought she wanted to be free, then realized where she was and what she had just done. She got off the bed and gathered her clothing.

"No," she said. "I don't wish that." When she had dressed she left the room without saying good night. He didn't say anything either, although she had glanced at him before she closed the door behind her and saw that he was watching her steadily across the shadowed room.

In the late morning Colin opened his eyes

"You're here," he said to her and his expression seemed almost amused.

"Yes," she said softly and rose from her chair in the corner to stand by his bed.

"I feel like I've been on a long journey," Colin said, looking up at the ceiling, "and now I'm so tired."

His words, his tone of voice were so obviously normal that her stomach turned over. He closed his eyes slowly and seemed to fall asleep. Cecilia went to find a nurse to report this turn of events to and the nurse was so surprised that she came with Cecilia, setting down the tray she was carrying on a trolley as they passed it. She took Colin's blood pressure, his pulse, and then his temperature.

"I think there might be some difference," she said cautiously.

Colin didn't wake again or speak until Cecilia was preparing to leave for the hotel. His voice was very faint as he asked her about the children and the appointments he had missed. Then he began to shiver so violently that Cecilia rang his bell and got a nurse in at once. The nurse came in, took his temperature, went out of the room and returned with a thick white wool blanket. She covered Colin and in a few moments he had stopped shivering. Cecilia waited a little longer and when it seemed clear that this had passed, she went back to the hotel.

Her friend was waiting in the bar for her and when he saw her coming toward him, he stood quickly and reached in his pocket for money. She crossed the room and sat on the stool beside him.

"I'll have a scotch and ice," she said to the bartender.

"Bad day?" her friend asked, after a moment.

"Good day, I think," she replied, and told him that although Colin was still very weak and sick, he was sometimes awake now and lucid.

"Have they figured out what was the matter with him?" the man asked.

"A rare tropical disease picked up off a toilet seat?" she suggested, and began to laugh. She put her hand over her mouth and bent her head, while her torso convulsed with spasms of rolling laughter that she couldn't stop. She couldn't catch her breath, she couldn't see anything for the tears of laughter filling her eyes. Alarmed, she made a great effort and managed to stop. She took a few deep breaths, wiped her eyes, and blew her nose. A giggle burst out and she caught it and stifled it. Her friend sat beside her looking at her in a way that was concerned, yet faintly amused. He didn't touch her.

"Come on," he said, and Cecilia rose and followed him to the elevators. They went to his room and he began kissing her hungrily, pressing her body roughly against his, holding her so tightly she could barely breathe.

"What?" he said, into her hair, sensing some coolness in her that had been absent before. He began to fondle her with less ferocity and more tenderness. They made love again, and Cecilia dressed and went to her room immediately after.

She found that she couldn't sleep and sat up in bed watching a long, silly movie, then lay in the darkness with her eyes open till very late. She was later than usual going to breakfast, too, and the man she had been spending her nights with wasn't there, had probably already left on his day of driving out to the nearby towns.

Colin was propped up in a half-sitting position when she arrived at the hospital.

"I think I remember getting sick," he said to her, as if she had been in the room with him all along, "but I don't remember the hotel room and I can't remember the flight here at all." After a pause he said, "Calgary," as if to remind himself. His voice was still weak and his eyes kept closing, as if he was too exhausted to keep them open. She bent to kiss his lips, but he turned his head away so that she met his cool cheek.

Off and on during the day he woke to tell her something as if he were reconstructing, for his own instruction, as much of the past week as he could.

"I came here in an ambulance, right?" he said, looking out the window to the even blue of the winter sky.

"Yes," she said. "I had to convince the doctor who came to the hotel that ... "

"It must have been late," he said. She opened her mouth to reply, but he had already moved on. "One-thirty, I think. I think I remember those numbers in red on the clock."

It went on like that, a monologue. A soliloquy, she thought, and gave up trying to converse with him.

Dr. Jameson came in, and after he had studied Colin's chart and examined him, he took Cecilia out into the hall.

"He seems to be mending," he told her. "His fever's down, he's fully conscious, no longer complaining of pain."

"But what was wrong with him?" Cecilia asked.

"If he keeps improving, I'd think you could take him home in two or three days."

"But what made him sick?" Cecilia asked again.

"A good question," he said, and turned his back on her to walk briskly away down the corridor.

That night when she returned to the hotel she slipped quickly past the entrance to the bar, and waited nervously till the elevator came. She thought she had caught a glimpse of her lover sitting in his usual place at the bar, but she went past so quickly, she couldn't be sure.

He was waiting for her at breakfast the next morning.

"Where were you last night?" he asked.

"Nowhere," she said, embarrassed. "I was tired."

He got up from his table, bringing his coffee cup, and sat down at hers.

"I missed you," he said, and she noticed again how very blue his eyes were, and his manner of fixing them on her so that she seemed to be the sole object in the room. "Meet me tonight."

"Colin's getting better," she said, suddenly, running her words into his. "He's conscious and clear-headed. I'll be able to take him home in a couple of days." He set his cup carefully into its saucer.

"To tell the truth," he said, "this is my last day in this district. I leave in the morning." She glanced quickly at him and noticed that the intensity in his eyes had faded, that he was not even looking at her.

"Your wife will be glad to see you," she said.

He gave her a wry look, then glanced at his watch and said, "I'd better get going if I want to finish up today." She said, "I'm late, too," although she wasn't particularly.

At the door they stopped and faced each other. Cecilia was stricken with embarrassment, muttered a short, "See you," and hurried to the elevator. She didn't think he had said anything. Just before the door shut, blocking her view, she saw him buttoning his overcoat and reaching for his briefcase which he had set on the floor by his feet. He wasn't looking at her. The elevator doors shut.

"We've moved him," a nurse said gaily to her as she neared the nursing station. She pointed to a door down the hall, almost at the end.

Colin was awake, his intravenous apparatus had been taken away, and this room had no gadgets attached to the walls. It looked like a bedroom.

"They've started me on clear fluids," he said, and his voice was stronger. "They're going to get me up this afternoon."

"Oh?" she said.

"But I can't sleep," he complained, like a child. "I try to sleep, but I just lie there."

"You slept for a week," she said, cheerfully. "Maybe you don't need to sleep anymore."

"Of course I need to sleep," he said irritably. "I wasn't asleep before. I was ... "

"What?" Cecilia broke in sharply. "What were you doing all week? What?" She went close to the bed, but didn't try to kiss him or touch him. He looked up at her, disconcerted, and she saw that the blackness had gone from his eyes leaving them a translucent, yellowish brown. He blinked several times.

"What are you talking about?" he asked, his peevishness returning.

"All week," she said, patient now, "you said things to me. You said you were somewhere. You said ... " His expression was growing puzzled, was there an edge of panic creeping into his voice?

"What do you mean?" He squirmed away from her, like a small child.

"You said you were somewhere big. You said there was an echo like silver. You said ... "

"Don't, Cecilia," he said, and the sound of her own name stopped her, brought the blood rushing to her cheeks. Colin looked away again to the rectangle of pale blue that was all he could see from his window, then turned his head slowly till he was looking at the wall at the foot of his bed.

"I've been sick," he said, and the distance returned to his voice and his eyes. "I've been sick," he repeated, while she waited. "It's hard ... " She leaned closer, his voice had grown so faint. "To come back." His eyes closed, and gradually his face smoothed.

How thin he had grown. Now his nose was prominent, even hawk-like, and his eyes seemed larger. She found herself wanting to put her hands on each side of his face, gently, to kiss his thin, fever-cracked lips, to lie sleeping beside him, pressed against the warmth of his sickness-wracked body. She stood quietly, looking down on him as he slept.

She wanted to tell him that she too had been gone, that she had been exploring, lost, in a wild, violent country, that she had narrowly escaped, that she had had to tear herself away, lest the swamps and bogs and blackness claim her forever.

She stood looking down at her sleeping husband. His eyelids twitched, his lips moved, he winced as if the pain had returned, and out of the corners of his eyes, a few tears came and crept slowly down his temples to disappear in his hair.

Discord

My husband always says that from my stories about my childhood, it appears to him that my father was guilty only of a sort of generalized bad judgement. But when he says that, I always wonder what the nature of bad judgement really is, how an intelligent person acquires it, and why. Why did he have bad judgement, and our mother, by default, apparently good, leaving the way open for recriminations, accusations and the bitterest regrets? Why did he invariably make the wrong decisions time after time, so that as a family we were always poor, and always in turmoil?

It may be too, that our father was an alcoholic, but if it was so, I have never blamed him for it, although, of course, our mother did. But he used to say, to her, to us, when they were quarrelling, that she had stolen us from him, his children, that she had turned us against him so that he was not a part of his own family. And that was true too, and I always knew it was, even when he said it when we were still only children, and even though our mother always denied it with all the considerable scorn she could muster.

But we were ordinary, an ordinary family: mother, father, ill-matched and quarrelsome but together, and children, all girls and too many, but a family. We lived in a cramped house in a small prairie town, our father went to work everyday with the municipal road crew, our mother stayed home and cooked and cleaned, we girls went to school. What could be more ordinary.

In those days I would often come in from playing at six or six-thirty in the evening, so tired that even now, without any effort, I can close my eyes and feel again the exhaustion that burned through all my limbs like a fire without heat, so that I could barely drag myself the two blocks home from the playground. I would come quietly into the house and say to my surprised mother that I was going to bed. I would take a book and lie there in the bed I shared with my older sister, reading through the long summer evening, till the tiredness, soothed finally, would overcome me and I fell asleep hours before my older sister crept in beside me.

One evening when I was lying peacefully reading, a wind came up. The lower pane of glass in the window beside the bed was cracked and the wind blew so hard that it rattled it and finally shattered it, scattering shards of glass all over the floor and even onto the bedspread where it covered my feet and legs.

Nothing was ever done about my unnatural and inexplicable fatigue, nor did I expect anyone to. In fact, I loved the solitude of those hours upstairs, the noises of the house distant and dimmed through the closed door, the feeling of being remote from all demands and requests that might burden me.

Often my older sister, Gwen, and I woke in the night because our parents were quarrelling. They quarrelled often during the day, too, but the important fights took place at night, when we were all in bed upstairs, the two middle sisters sharing a bed in the room next to ours and our youngest sister asleep in her crib at the end of our parent's room. Then our parents quarrelled in voices that rose above a whisper, at least our father's did, and it was from him that we learned what seemed to us to be our parent's worst, most terrifying secrets.

Our mother had caught our father kissing Mrs. Markham. Aside from everything else, this was appalling news since none of us liked her, including our mother, although they were considered to be friends. Mrs. Markham had heavy, lustreless brown hair that she wore pulled back from her face and hanging in a page-boy down her back, and when we visited there, she was always trying to repair my sisters and me, offering to sew on a loose button that apparently our mother hadn't noticed, providing a little unasked-for salve for a pimple that was just starting, or resetting a barrette in our perpetually untidy hair.

Mr. and Mrs. Markham lived across the street from us and Gwen and I babysat for their boy and girl who were the ages of our youngest sisters. They were richer than we were, they owned a piano, and their house was always tidy and so dustless and polished that everything seemed to shine, while at our house there were only the barest of necessities for furniture and things were never in place for more than five minutes at a time no matter how hard our mother worked nor how desperately she railed at us in her frustration.

"You're still my girl," our father declared in the night, not even bothering to whisper, as if our mother, the five of us notwithstanding, had declared that she no longer was. Gwen and I, lying in the darkness, must both have thought of the times we had seen our parents embrace and kiss, standing in the kitchen or the hall, their arms around each other, their bodies pressed together. We must have wondered if that was how our father had kissed Mrs. Markham. I remember being torn between a desire to giggle wildly and horror at the treachery to our mother; both of us were struggling to keep from being swept into the black and bottomless wave of emotion that our parents were drowning in, that we could feel rolling out from wherever they happened to be. But we pretended to be asleep, and for days after we pretended we didn't know the other had been awake and heard, until I, younger after all and not so sophisticated, couldn't stand it any longer and brought it up to my sister.

"Shut up," Gwen said, before I could finish whatever I'd been going to say, and there was something so frightening in her eyes that I shut up at once and went away, and never mentioned it again.

They were too different, I suppose, and even though they loved each other, they should never have married. Our mother's father was a professional man, a family man, she was raised with dogs and horses for pets, while to our father, dogs were nuisances that snarled and bit and horses reminded him only of the hard labour he had done on the subsistence farm where he was raised.

I believe our father was a gentle man, though he hit our mother, and once during a quarrel I saw him kick her, carefully, as if he didn't really want to hurt her. Certainly he drank too much and once Mr. Markham had to help our mother bring him home because he was too drunk to walk, let alone drive. The black eye my sisters and I saw for the first time the next morning was never explained, despite another long, half-whispered quarrel in the middle of the night that Gwen and I heard in our usual way, lying rigidly side by side, our eyes open, not touching or looking at one another, each acquiescing to the fiction that the other was asleep.

Once I said wearily to a Mennonite friend when we were talking about what had made us the way we were, "The truth is I had a father who liked to drink and dance and chase women."

"How lucky you were," he said, with such longing in his voice, that I could imagine the details of his childhood. But all through mine I'd wished for a father like his. One who stayed home, who never raised his voice, I would even have tolerated the endless church-going for what I imagined to be the calm and peace of his home.

My childhood and Gwen's were punctuated by verbal onslaughts and hysterical crying on our mother's part and by shouting, swearing and door-slamming on our father's, by dreadful, horrifying days when he hadn't been paid and we were out of groceries and there was no credit to be had, so that we ate porridge for all three meals and didn't have to be warned by our proud and disappointed mother not to tell anyone.

And, too, Gwen and I have our pool of secret, never spoken-of memories of a kind of wrestling match their quarrels would sometimes disintegrate into when our mother, tears blinding her, her teeth clenched with passion, words at last failing her, would move close to him to strike him and he would catch her wrist in his big hand, twist her arm down and hit her, clumsily, experimentally, as if he didn't quite know how to do this, on the shoulder or the side of her head.

"Stop it, Mom!" we'd both beg, when she'd reached a certain point in her attack, her voice growing louder and more hysterical, her accusations bitterer and more cruel. We knew it would end in this, because with the clear vision of childhood we could see that our father was helpless against the things she said, had no other idea how to stop her.

Even though we lived in an atmosphere of disorder and unhappiness, my sisters and I were famous among our parents' friends for being well-behaved. In public we never spoke unless we were spoken to, we never ran when we'd been told to sit, or cried, or whined or begged, while the Markham kids were just as famous for being unruly, troublesome whiners.

I was babysitting for the older boy once, while Mrs. Markham took her little girl, a toddler, downtown with her while she shopped. She came home early and instead of paying me and sending me home, she went straight into the bedroom where she and Mr. Markham slept and through the closed door I could hear her crying and the rustling of tissue.

Later she told our mother that Connie, her daughter, had crept into the display window at Janet's Ladies' Wear when Mrs. Markham was trying on a dress and had knocked over the mannequin, spilled a vase of real flowers, which soaked the rest of the display, before Mrs. Markham had climbed in and pulled her out, and that the owner had ordered her in front of everyone never to set foot in his store again unless she left her children at home. No doubt our mother thought it served her right, since she disapproved strongly of badly-behaved children. This must have happened before our mother caught our father kissing Mrs. Markham.

It was, I suppose, a certain period in all our lives: the oldest child about to enter high school, the youngest child ready for grade one, our parents in their early forties, and their lot by then laid irrevocably out for them — poverty as long as we were all at home and meagre working class existence after that. Still, it was several more years when I was turning fifteen and our youngest sister was eight, before our father left us.

What I mostly remember about that time after he left, at least the first while, was not his absence — we barely missed him — but the sudden whirlwind of activity, my mother putting on lipstick, getting ready to go job-hunting as soon as we'd all left for school, cheerfully, as if she'd been freed from something,

Gwen abruptly leaving school before she'd finished grade twelve to get a job.

I remember too, the helplessness I felt because I was only fifteen and small for my age and nobody would hire me. But then there were new arrangements at home which fell mostly on me, with sporadic help from Marilyn, the next sister down the line, once our mother got a job clerking in the dime store. Someone had to look after the two youngest, Charlene and Linda, when they weren't in school, and keep the house fairly neat, the grocery shopping done, the meals cooked and the dishes washed.

We managed though, and when, after two years, most of which I recall only vaguely — our mother pin-curling her hair in the evening, Gwen putting on red nail polish sitting barefoot at the end of the couch under the lamp — our father came back again, he had become so irrelevant to Gwen and me that she left home the same week and immediately got married, and a month later, as soon as the school year was over, I left too. Or perhaps both of us wanted to get out of there before the fighting started again.

The years after that, though, I hear from my three younger sisters, were the best of their childhoods. Our parents lived peacefully, each going to their jobs everyday, not bothering to quarrel. There were family outings then, picnics, ballgames, and on weekends, even the occasional trip to the city. With both of them working and two of us gone, there was more money and the household grew a little more elaborate and comfortable.

But at the reception after her oldest son's wedding, I talked with Marilyn about those few years, the ones between our father's return and his sudden death from a heart attack.

"It was like nothing one of them did could matter anymore to the other," Marilyn said. "They'd stopped connecting, if you know what I mean. It seemed like they didn't fight anymore because they didn't care enough." She paused to survey the wedding guests as they moved out onto the polished dance floor. Our second youngest sister was there in a floor-length pink dress that was too girlish for her, dancing with her son who had just had his sixteenth birthday. I can never look at Charlene without seeing our mother, that pale blonde hair, that smile that was once so sweet. Linda, the youngest, and Gwen were both missing, busy with other things.

They hadn't come to any of the weddings, although all of us had been present at both our mother's and our father's funerals.

Marilyn pursed her lips and frowned faintly. "The peace, the whole atmosphere, it made me uneasy. I kept looking over my shoulder to see what was creeping up on us from behind. We were raised on discord," she said, turning to me, "we didn't know how to cope with harmony." She glanced over to her volatile, dark husband who, drunk on wine, was dancing too close to the bride's mother. I saw a red flush creep up her neck to her cheeks, and she laughed suddenly, a little explosion of sound quickly stifled, as if she had just had a thought that embarrassed her.

I was in my thirties before I married, and had just about concluded that I never would, when I met Robert at the university where I was teaching. He was a teacher of English literature in the same department, and we were drawn to each other at once, both of us quiet, serious scholars, misfits in a department full of drinkers, party-goers and -givers, who wrote novels or poetry on the side and who seemed to suffer from some deep and bitter disappointment about where their lives had taken them, so that apart from Robert and me, the department was always steeped in disgruntlement, argument and confusion.

"Stop fighting!" Gwen or I would shout at our parents once we were old enough to understand that a fight between them had parameters and might not be a universal, biblical catastrophe, but not old enough to realize that nothing we said could possibly make any difference in the sum of their relationship.

Now that I'm getting older and even the sharpest pictures from my childhood have blurred, I think that I don't drink, or enjoy society or parties much because I haven't the energy. It seems to me that the quarrels of our parents, the air of our home continually thick with emotion, sapped all my energy, stole my strength from me, so that as a child I was often worn out by six in the evening, and as an adult I have to horde it carefully to have enough just to get through my daily duties.

And yet, sometimes they did stop. They would look at us with surprised expressions, then they would look at each other, and one of them might laugh in a strange, mirthless sort of way, or one of them might turn and walk away.

Gwen's hasty marriage turned out badly. She divorced, then travelled, took interesting jobs that the rest of us envied her for, and married again. It was no more happily than the first time, but this man was rich, or at least his belongings, way of life and income surpassed our wildest childhood dreams, which consisted variously of owning a bicycle, wearing an evening gown, having a reversible plaid skirt, taking a holiday at a beach. I rarely see her anymore and when we do meet, we look at each other and have nothing to say. We share a world beyond and beneath words. Looking into her eyes I can tell that at night we must inhabit the same dream world, we must even dream the same dreams.

"You're still my girl," our father declared in the night to our crying mother, and in fact, he didn't leave with Mrs. Markham or anyone else. He simply went to the city and got a job as a mechanic and lived as a bachelor in a rooming house. He bought himself a new car and if he drank or chased women, we never heard of it. Missing us, he finally returned.

Not wishing to dramatize my childhood, that was after all, full of trivial incidents and minor calamities, I said we were an ordinary family, but now, reflecting on that time, I see beneath our surface ordinariness, something darker, much worse. Lives were shaped, twisted and thwarted. Hearts were broken. We don't even have a family portrait. Not one. And from every single snapshot, one of us is missing.

Justice

The worst thing about the breakup of my marriage, the part I found the hardest to bear, even worse than the loss of my husband and first love, Lucas, was that it seemed to me that there is no justice. By this I meant that there was no one who would say, yes, you were badly treated, there was no one who would take my part and in my desperate need for support would say, whether it was true or not, that I was blameless. I no longer had any friends who were exclusively my own and even my mother, to whom I hadn't been able to bring myself to talk at all about my divorce, could only watch me with puzzled eyes and no matter how she could see it hurt me, couldn't stop herself from laughing and joking with my former husband if he phoned or came around on family business, because she liked him, everybody did, and I had told her of no reason to stop liking him.

But worse than the lack of support was that I could see that Lucas would go blithely on through his life and never accept any blame for any of the countless miseries he had inflicted on me, would never suffer for the suffering he had caused me, possibly would never even comprehend what he had done to me. And so I tried to carry on as if life could still go on, tried to swallow the knowledge that seemed unavoidable to me, that in human life there is no justice.

After our divorce I kept on at my job, our children finished high school and moved into their own places, I got over my depression, sold the house and moved to a smaller one, and eventually I met and married Gary. Gary hadn't been married before, which was a blessing it seemed to me, because I was lugging around enough emotional baggage from my first marriage that I did not then expect ever to get rid of, and I knew our marriage would have been impossible if Gary too, had been carrying a burden of unresolved problems and unfinished arguments. Not to mention the load of pain, so heavy that no matter how I thought I had subdued it, and in most practical ways actually had, it still emerged in my dreams.

In the first years of my marriage to Gary I would dream of Lucas night after night for stretches of time that seemed endless. I wouldn't dare speak of it to Gary. Waking in the mornings and catching a glimpse of myself in the bathroom mirror, seeing a pale, anxious face, eyes still sunk in the dreaming's darkness, I'd say to the face in the mirror, ridiculous. You'll get over this, one of these days you'll put that internal feeler out to test for the pain and the pain won't be there, and no matter how you poke and prod, you won't be able to find it. Then you'll be free. Eventually your life will be new again.

But it wasn't just the dreaming. I couldn't keep my mind off Lucas, not even after Gary and I moved into a big apartment overlooking the wide treed park that stretched along the river-bank. We could see from our windows the far bank billowed green with trees that rose up to meet the grey stone of the university buildings, a view radically different from the one Lucas and I had seen from the windows of our suburban house, of a street of similar houses, and another street behind it much the same and beyond that, more streets, more small, clean houses.

Gary would make some remark, or he would touch me, or I would pick up something so ordinary as a can opener and I wouldn't be married to him anymore, steeped in the gentle ambiance of our life together, but sucked back into the passion of my marriage with Lucas. In those moments the very texture of the air in our marital home surrounded me. I saw the brocade gleam of the new sofa we bought that we both loved but couldn't afford, I saw again the way his shoulders rounded, grew comfortable when he was deep in a book, and the creased denims and faded blue air force shirts he always wore at home that would forever spell masculinity for me. I could even smell his skin.

These were not merely memories, they were the texture of my soul made evident to me. And it occurs to me that marriage perhaps, is soul-making, and if it is so, then my soul is made of love and hatred and anguish in equal parts, and I have Lucas to thank for that. And this, it pains me to say, leaves Gary no place in this soul of mine, although he would be glad, because Gary disowns soul, which is probably why I found it possible to marry him.

I couldn't stop feeling I was living in the middle of two marriages at the same time, an internal and an external one, and at any moment the internal one might be the more real to me. It continued to be the one on which I spent the most emotional energy, although I don't think that Gary ever really noticed, much less understood why I suddenly tossed down the paper as we sat together reading by lamplight in the evenings with the curtains open so we could see the lights of the university shining steady gold across the river from us, beneath the colder silver light of the stars.

I couldn't call them memories because they were as real to me as the first time they happened and I was lost in them again. One minute I would be sitting by Gary reading the paper with my feet up on the shared footstool, dimly aware of the subdued roar of traffic far below our apartment, and the next I would be back in Lucas's and my house reliving some episode from our marriage: the night he got so drunk at a party that he sat on the floor in our living room in front of everybody and necked with the visiting very pretty niece of one of our neighbours, who didn't know who he was. While I danced in the dining room with neighbours' husbands and pretended I thought it amusing, as the chasm that was becoming familiar inside my abdomen grew deeper and blacker, even while I smiled. Coming back to the present with an inner gasp, I would toss aside the paper and jump up, hurry to the kitchen and make coffee and occupy myself by polishing the fridge and stove while I waited for it to perk.

Lucas's chief crime against me was that he was unfaithful, although I don't believe I ever told my mother that. I was in such turmoil for those three or so years it took to make the decision to divorce, to do it, and then to recover from the immediate shock and misery, that even though her pleasantries with my former husband cut me to the quick and made me confirm my conclusion that there is no justice, I still couldn't bring myself to talk to her about what he had done to me. So perhaps indeed she did go to her grave wondering what had broken up her only daughter's marriage. Maybe she even blamed me.

Lucas's infidelities were legion, they were probably dull, no doubt they were banal and silly too, but they were no less painful to me for all that. They began in the first six months of our marriage and they went on year after year, growing more reckless and more pointedly open while, although with wifely intuition I suspected them as soon as they began, I refused to acknowledge what was happening, even to myself. And went on refusing year after year. Ridiculous, I'd tell myself in my new life, watching the food processor spin my cake batter around. I could even smile wryly at myself, for the greatest mystery continued to be not why he did it over and over again, but why I chose not to know, why I refused to admit his affairs to myself even secretly, even in the face of the most blatant evidence.

And yet, occasionally, I remember, I would tempt fate. One Sunday Lucas and I and another couple had taken our kids tobogganing and when we returned to our house four of the five kids quickly threw off their outdoor clothes and rushed up the stairs to some computer game in Steven's room. Michael, our youngest and Lucas's favourite, was still struggling with a knot in his scarf. The other husband, Karl, hung up his parka and went into the bathroom. Only Florrie, Lucas, four-year-old Michael and I were left in the entryway, and knowing but not admitting that Florrie and Lucas were in the middle of an affair, I deliberately went ahead into the kitchen to begin making cocoa, leaving Michael behind with them as a witness perhaps, as my agent, for what I was fairly sure would happen as soon as I left Florrie and Lucas alone. It was a test, I suppose, of the accuracy of my intuition, or to see if Lucas would sink as low as I suspected he would.

A moment passed, then, as I'd been fairly sure would happen, Michael began to wail and came running to me where I stood waiting at the kitchen counter, and threw his arms around me. Lucas called him back in a voice I remember as surprised and chagrined. "Mikey, Mikey, what's the matter," but he didn't follow him into the kitchen for another moment. But I knew, oh, I knew perfectly well, even as I held Michael to me and soothed him, exactly how his father holding Florrie and kissing her had frightened him. It's a miracle the things kids know of treachery and cruelty.

Yet I went on calmly making cocoa and served it to all of them, Florrie too, and never once said to Lucas, stop having an affair with my friend, or even asked him if he was.

There must be two of me, I often thought, because even while I was steeped in that long-ago moment, suffused by my old misery and shame, I noticed when the cake batter was mixed, I poured it into a prepared pan, I set it in the pre-heated oven. Some part of me continued to do all those things, even as it did them then, when the phone rang and it was Lucas saying something had gone wrong with the car, it had stalled in downtown traffic and he'd be home late because he'd managed to find a mechanic who was willing to fix it then. I'd serve supper to Steven, Karen and Michael, supervise their homework, get them into bed, and all the while be imagining which woman Lucas was with and where and what they were doing, while the other person in me worried about the cost of Lucas's imaginary repairs, which at that moment I believed to be real, and wondered if I should keep his supper hot since he'd be hungry from standing around for hours in a cold and gloomy garage.

Lucas, of course, having learned that his actions would go unchallenged, grew more and more reckless. He became cruel to me in everyday ways, he taunted me about my failings, he ridiculed my remarks. In public he claimed never to have said the words or held the opinions I had just quoted as his which he might have said to me as recently as breakfast of that same day. Time and time again he left me stumbling through the wreckage of my self-esteem. His affairs grew stupider and more pointless, the women younger, increasingly naive. I chased them away when they came to our house hoping to see more of Lucas by becoming friends with me. One of them even came to me in tears to tell me she had slept with my husband and wanted me to forgive her.

He had, by this time, apart from our older mutual friends, a circle of younger friends of his own. I rarely had anything to do with them, because around me they were sullen and hostile, any other attitude toward me would have forced them to face the situation they were a part of and that they didn't wish to admit to. So Lucas always saw them alone. I had become more and more isolated, I had no strength left for friendships of my own, and I finally began to realize that in all the world I had no allies. That was when I first began to muse on the nature of justice.

Eventually my self-delusion had to end. There was no great revelation, no conscious decision, the subject of Lucas's infidelities simply leaked slowly into the open and then became a flood, unstoppable. But even after the pretence was over there could be no peace between us. I was too full of chaotic love and rage, simultaneous, inseparable, that paralyzed and silenced me, and Lucas, seeing at last the hopeless state our marriage had sunk into, could with relief leave the blame at my door and depart.

I read an article the other day, sitting across from Gary as he chatted on the phone with his sister in Edmonton — it was their weekly call and I envied them both that closeness and unquestioning affection — written by an American officer who had been a P.O.W. in Vietnam where he had been starved, beaten and tormented. The only wisdom that bewildered military man had been able to gain from those years of suffering was simply that life is not fair, that terrible things happen to some people whether they do anything to deserve them or not, and like Job, those victims can only wonder why and try to bear their fate. I felt a kind of amused sympathy for the man, that it took that much to shake him into wisdom, then was faintly ashamed of myself for equating our experiences.

These last few years were peaceful ones, the first in my adulthood that went on in a pleasant way day after day without calamities, disasters, or even minor blow-ups to destroy them. I had almost forgotten about the kind of suffering most people go

through day after day all their lives. And when I thought of
Lucas, which was seldom, I could find almost no pain. Those
unbidden moments from the past had stopped dragging me
down into them, it was rarely anymore that I came back to my
life with Gary with a sense of shock. I felt as though a cure was
possible after all, as though I really might live a life that was new
in more than appearance.

One day a letter came to me from Lucas. Gary handed it to
me and waited while I nervously opened it. For years Lucas's
only communications had been waspish, complaining letters
about the children. I had got so that I could barely bring myself
to open them, and yet, in the name of our years together and our
ineradicable, shared parenthood, could not prevent myself. But it
had been a long time since his last letter and I didn't even know
where he was living when this one arrived.

As I read it I had to sit down. Gary listened to my few stumbling phrases of explanation, then tactfully went into the other
room. I couldn't stay seated though, I rose, put on my coat,
stuffed the letter into my pocket, and went out to walk in the
park under the tall, old poplars, through the rustling yellow
leaves that lay scattered across the curving asphalt paths. I thrust
my hands into my pockets and held tightly to the letter.

Lucas had written to ask my forgiveness. He had written to
tell me that he was filled with remorse, tormented by it, for the
way he had treated me and that while he didn't blame me if I
couldn't forgive him, he wanted me to know how sorry he was.

Justice at last, I thought, and I threw back my head and
opened my arms to embrace the trees, the park, the wide, swift
river, the endless, burning blue of the fall sky.

In my initial wave of emotion I thought I had been released
at last, and all my old love for him came flowing over me, and
tenderness for him, the one who was suffering now. This is too
much, I thought, *this* I can't bear, to be able to love him again
when I had for so long allowed myself only hate.

But I had not walked far before I came to see the hopelessness of loving him again. I was married to another man whom I
also loved. I had no wish to hurt Gary by leaving him and anyway, (I found myself using a crisp, legal-sounding language even

in my head), an apology from Lucas did not constitute a desire
to renew our relationship.

Eventually I went back home to Gary who had made a pot of
coffee and was sitting at the kitchen table drinking it while he
waited patiently for my return. I handed him the creased and
wrinkled letter and waited while he read it. When he had finished, he stood and got the coffee pot and filled the cup he had
already set in my place.

"Well," he said in his quiet way, unsmiling, "how about that."

That night I lay awake tossing in the darkness, one moment
filled with tenderness for Lucas and the next angry that a few
words scratched on a piece of paper could make me forget the
anguish, the misery of those years. All the scenes of his cruelty
came flooding over me: Lucas entering the house at breakfast
after being out all night, the kids, Karen especially, rushing off to
school as soon as he entered the kitchen; me walking into a
friend's house unannounced for coffee and finding him there;
him disappearing from a party with a woman so that I had to
catch a ride home with the next-door neighbours.

Finally I got out of bed and went to sit in the living room. I
didn't turn on the lights, but sat in the big chair by the window
and stared out across the blackness of the river at the myriad
steady lights shining above the wide, soft shadow I knew to be
trees. The night Lucas left me: coming into the house after midnight when I was alone reading in our bed, the kids asleep in
their rooms, not speaking to me as he tossed his clothes into
suitcases, his friend who was driving him, (he was leaving me
even the car), coughing gently as he waited in the hall, me sitting helpless in my nightgown, smelling the musky scent of the
marijuana he had been smoking, not realizing for years that the
marijuana wasn't another insult aimed at me, but his way of gathering his courage to come and make the final break.

No, I said to him in my head, I don't forgive you. Some
things are not forgivable.

Gary came to find me then, took me back to bed with him,
and I at last fell asleep curled up against his warm back.

What does he think he did that was wrong? I had pondered,
walking slowly up and down those winding paths. What was his

conception of his sin? Was I to forgive him for the women? For his casual and deliberate insults and the way he so often shamed me? Was it for taking my love and abusing it? Was it all of these, or only some, or something else I hadn't remembered or thought of? I found I could not imagine for what he was asking forgiveness.

I wrote him a reply. His letter had seemed genuine and I couldn't bring myself to let him suffer anymore. I forgive you, I wrote. It wasn't all your fault, and I told him how I used to think there was no such thing as justice, that justice was an artificial, man-made and childish concept that had no place in the history or psychology of humankind. I wrote, I guess I was wrong and I have you to thank for that, but then I crossed that last line out and scribbled over it so he couldn't read it, and thought with pleasure how he would puzzle over it and try to decipher what I had written and then decided I didn't want him to see.

I had even thought, walking up and down those paths, that I would say to him in reply, your apology is too late, I forgave you long ago, but that seemed cruel, a trivializing of his anguish which I believed to be real.

But now I see that words like justice and forgiveness have nothing to do with anything, they are only words. I see now that whatever happened between Lucas and me was only life, and while neither of us will ever know why it happened, I know now that neither will I ever recover, as I had always expected to, from what it did to me. Nor, I suppose, will Lucas. If you are in an accident with your new car and are hurt, no matter how well you heal or how much time passes, you always have twinges to remind you of what happened, and though you may get the car's motor running again, and its body hammered smooth and freshly painted, it is never quite a new car again.

Dark of the Moon

Janet and her friend, Livie, and Livie's boyfriend, Nathan, get out of Nathan's car and then stand uncertainly, listening to the faint laughter and occasional muted shriek coming from the darkness on the far side of the parking lot, across the space that must be grass, between them and the tall black pines whose uppermost silhouette they can see hard against the starry, luminous sky.

"No moon tonight," Livie says.

"The dark of the moon," Janet says softly, and shivers. The summer night is cool at this altitude, out here on the edge of the forest.

"Can't see a goddam thing," Nathan says. "Well, let's strike out. They aren't going to come for us." Crickets, or is it frogs, are singing loudly and steadily with an immediacy that the human voices don't have. The three of them stumble across the gravelled parking lot behind the row of parked cars, trying to find their way in the dark. When they reach the slowly rising sweep of grass — they hear it against their sandals and feel it on their bare ankles — they suddenly see firelight not so far ahead, just inside the forest's edge. It flickers and glows between the straight black trunks of the lodgepole pines. There must be a clearing ahead. It's been so dry up here that open fires are forbidden except where the park attendants have dug pits and circled them with rocks.

"Those stars are incredible," Janet says. The others don't answer her, which doesn't surprise her, she's used to that, and Nathan walks straight into a metal barbecue stand that the park people have fixed in cement in the grass.

"Uh!" he says. "Damn!" The bottles in the case of beer he is carrying rattle alarmingly. He backs up and feels his way around the stand.

"Oh, look," Livie says, excited now. "There's Brian and Annie."

"Did you think we had the wrong party?" Nathan asks her, amused, but they are all walking faster now toward the bonfire which has grown larger as they near it and the people standing or sitting around it with bottles in their hands, their faces rosy with firelight.

"In this blackness we could still have the wrong party," Janet says, "and none of us would ever know." Her voice rises lightly at the end, but neither Livie nor Nathan pay any attention to her.

"Hey, somebody's coming," a voice ahead of them says, and a few people turn to peer into the darkness through which Janet, Livie, and Nathan are walking. Then they are in the circle of dancing light, saying hi, exchanging the case of beer for three opened bottles.

"How come you're so late?" Brian asks, one hand thrust into his trousers' pocket, the other holding a beer bottle that is wet from the tub of melting ice that must be sitting somewhere nearby.

"I had to work till eleven," Livie says.

"Where's the food?" Nathan asks. "I skipped dinner. I'm starving." Brian points behind them, deeper into the woods, past a cluster of pines.

"Back there."

There is an awkward moment for Janet and Livie when Brian turns back to the people he'd been talking to and Nathan leaves them to circle the fire and squat, talking, beside somebody he knows. They are still looking around, trying to adjust to the scene, but everywhere people seem to be locked into conversations. The couple on their right who have been talking quietly, their faces close together, begin to kiss, and laughter breaks out among some others they can' t see, who are standing far back in the forest.

"Come on, Janet," Livie says. "Let's go over to where they're cooking." They circle the fire in the path between its radiance and heat and the cool darkness of the night, behind the backs of the people who stand or sit facing the fire. Janet doesn't know anybody here. They walk a few feet through absolute black toward the metal barbecue stands on the other side of a ring of huge pines and find another group of people, all men this time, standing together talking, occasionally reaching out with their long-handled forks to turn pieces of meat which are cooking on the barbecues in front of them.

"Hey, Livie," a man says, sounding pleased to see her. She moves around the barbecue to hug him and he bends to brush her cheek with his lips. "Glad you could make it," he says, holding his fork lightly in both hands, balancing it.

"I had to work late," she says. "It smells terrific."

"I figured that," he says. "Won't be much longer till we can eat." He turns his head to look questioningly at Janet who still stands on the other side of the barbecue.

"Oh," Livie says. "I'm sorry. This is my friend, Janet. I talked her into coming with us tonight. Janet, this is . . . " But a conversation next to them which suddenly grows louder, drowns out her voice so that Janet hears only his last name, which is Baker.

"Hi, Baker," she says, and when he grins at her, interested because she has unexpectedly called him by only his last name, she sees how the glow from the charcoal fire in front of him — even through the smoke that drifts upward from the cooking meat — makes his eyes glint. She moves around the barbecue toward him.

A woman is calling Livie, at first she doesn't appear to hear, then, without speaking again, Livie turns and goes through the night toward the voice.

"Look at the stars," Janet says to Baker. "Just look." He lifts his head and looks. They stand together staring up, while the meat beside them drips juices which hit the hot charcoal and sizzle. High up, above the pines which are unexpectedly, gently swaying at their black, mysterious tops sixty or so feet above them, in the vast distance beyond that, there are the stars, shining with a pure, brilliant light, a hard brilliance that takes Janet's breath away. She almost falls, and puts her hand out on Baker's arm, apparently to steady herself, but really because she is afraid.

She feels the wrinkled softness of his shirt and his hard, warm forearm under that, and amazingly, he sets the fork down, draws her to him, and holds her against him with both his arms around her, his head still raised to the stars.

Janet is on top of Baker, leaning over him so that her long, dark hair sweeps along his chest. She's laughing. Tonight there is some moonlight which the curtains can't fully shut out and she can see how his eyes and teeth gleam as he looks up at her, smiling. She lets herself fall gently toward him till their chests meet. She puts her arms under his neck and her mouth next to his ear.

"For some reason I keep thinking of this movie I saw. 'Heartbreaker'? Did you ever see it?"

"I don't think so," Baker says. His hands are on her waist, resting there gently. He slides them down over the curve of her hips and then up to hold her rib cage tenderly between his palms.

"Peter Coyote and Nick Mancuso, or something. They're these best friends in New York. Peter Coyote is an artist and he has this model." Baker begins to turn his hips slowly to the right. She realizes he wants her to turn so they can lie on their sides facing each other. She knows he isn't really listening, but this doesn't silence her. Even as she turns with him, sliding her leg down by his longer one, she is thinking of how to tell him the next part in an interesting way.

"And his model is really a nice girl, but she's a call girl, too. And she loves him, the artist. But he doesn't love her." She pauses a moment. Baker has found her mouth and is kissing her so that she can't speak. It's almost as if he is trying to stop her from talking. "So one night the two friends and the model wind up in bed together. You know how things like that can ... happen ... "
She pauses, knowing that for a second, at least he is listening.

"Yeah," he says, his husky voice rising attentively.

Encouraged, Janet goes on. "And then, later, she sees all these artists and people around him and she's really sad, and she says, 'I know I'm not interesting or smart. The only interesting thing about me is my chest.' She has these big breasts, you see."

"Are you just about finished this story?" Baker interrupts to ask, but he's laughing and he takes a handful of her long hair and gives it a teasing tug. Janet kisses his mouth, then whispers, "And then she says, 'The other night?' " She kisses his forehead. ".'You loved being inside me ... ' " She kisses his chin, and she knows by how still he is that he's listening again. She remembers how the actress spoke, her intonation, the pain-filled way she turned her head away from the artist to deliver her next line. " 'You're a heartbreaker,' she says."

Janet waits. Baker says nothing. "I don't know why I keep thinking of that." Or maybe he hasn't been listening. "It was a good movie," she says.

He rolls over so that he is on top of her, spreading her legs with his, and puts his mouth, hard, over hers.

"Who was that?" Janet asks. She never, not in a million years, meant to ask him that question, but the look on his face as he returns from the living room where he has been talking on the phone so takes her by surprise that the question is out before she quite realizes she has spoken.

"My wife," he says. Janet stops chopping the celery, the quick, hard crack against the chopping board ceasing abruptly, then beginning again. "My ex-wife," he amends, opening the cupboard where he keeps his pots and pans.

"I didn't know you'd been married," Janet says.

"Yeah, two kids." He sets a glass casserole on the stove beside him.

"Does she live here? In the city?" She tries to sound casual, and, in fact, succeeds.

"No," he says, "in Vancouver. She married again. She phones sometimes about the kids."

"Should I chop the almonds?" Janet asks. Sometimes, when they are together in his apartment the phone will ring and he will talk a little longer than is polite. Somehow she always knows when the caller is a woman. Is it his manner then?

"I bought slivered almonds," he says. "Bad form, I know." They smile at each other in a playful way, suddenly intimate again, and a little shiver runs down Janet's back.

"I've never been married," she says, leaning on the cupboard still holding the knife, watching him as he works. "I wish I had been."

"Hah!" he says. "Don't wish that."

"Why not?" she asks, teasing, setting down her knife. He is working with the chicken now, stripping the skin off the pieces and setting it in a pile to one side.

"Because," he says slowly. "Because it's ... pretty hard, to be married."

Janet reflects on this, on the way he has spoken so carefully without looking at her, keeping his voice light, stripped of emotion, which reveals to her all too clearly, how deeply he feels, although about precisely what, she doesn't know. He glances at her then, and smiles again. "Time to put it all together," he says, stretching out his hands to take the celery, and now he speaks in an entirely different voice, the one she is used to hearing.

"So," Livie says. "You've been getting it on with my friend Baker." Her voice borders on unfriendliness, so that Janet looks up from her salad and studies Livie cautiously, who doesn't look up from hers. Janet can't think what to say to Livie in response. Yes?

"I like him a lot," she says, finally. "I think he's a nice man." She eats a little salad. "How are things with you and Nathan?" This seems like a strange thing for her to say, and she can't think why she did, except because of that funny tone in Livie's voice.

"Yeah, he's a nice man," Livie says. "Nathan and I'll probably get married one of these days." When Janet looks up, surprised, smiling at her, Livie adds hastily, "Well, it's no big deal. We've been living together for almost a year. You know that. And we've both been married before, so it isn't exactly first love."

"I suppose," Janet agrees after a minute. For some reason she finds herself feeling like crying. Livie suddenly relents, or else the emotion that Janet has sensed her to be full of today, ever since they sat down to eat, can't be contained any longer.

"I ... we'll get along fine. We really care for each other," Livie says, "and I ... he ... he's a nice man." The two women smile tentatively at each other, although Janet is thinking that Livie had meant to say something else.

"A nice man," Janet says, and laughs. "Well, he is," she says.

"Nathan or Baker?" Livie asks in a careful tone. She is looking at her salad again, and Janet can't figure out what's the matter with her.

"Both of them," she says, shrugging, not smiling now.

"Nathan for sure," Livie says. "Baker, not so sure." But she refuses to explain or elaborate when Janet questions her.

"I think you must have had an affair with Livie," Janet says to Baker. They are driving somewhere in Baker's old car through the late fall evening, and Janet thinks that now and then she can smell the old dead leaves, like smoke drifting through the silent air.

"Didn't you know that?" Baker says, surprised.

"No," Janet says.

"I took it for granted she would have told you. Don't women always tell each other things like that."

"Yes," Janet says, and sighs. She cannot imagine why it is whenever she gets news she'd rather not hear that her whole insides go dead. Her bowels feel as if they have turned to cement, her stomach loses all hope of sensation, and she feels as if she will be forever unable to rise from wherever she is sitting. "But she didn't tell me. I ... just ... figured it out."

"Clever," Baker says. His voice has changed again. That lightness she has heard every once in a while is back, his unconscious way of hiding what he is really thinking, which, of course, reveals to her that he is upset. Angry? Sad over the loss of Livie? Or is it something else? What else could it be?

"Are you angry with me for mentioning it?" she asks him, finally.

"No," he says. "You have a right to ask."

"I don't think I asked you," she says.

"It felt like a question to me," he says. Janet watches the

steady place ahead of them where the road meets the night sky. Now her hands, resting palms up on her lap, feel dead, too. She forces herself to turn her hands over so that her palms are touching the warm wool of her skirt and don't feel so unprotected, bruised even, by the air in the car.

They arrive at the house they have been travelling toward. The hostess, opening the door, glances swiftly at Janet, whom she has never seen before, then her eyes move to Baker, she breaks into a smile and reaches up to receive his hug. Janet is reminded of the way he hugged Livie in the park months before.

Oh, well, she thinks ruefully, what can you expect from a man you meet in the forest in the middle of the night. This thought delights her so much that she smiles with what appears to be an eagerness and warmth at the roomful of strangers.

Baker is sitting on the side of the bed holding a cigarette in one hand and an ashtray in the palm of the other. The smoke drifts past his bare arm to curl across Janet's naked hip where she lies with the lower half of her body curled around him. It is cold in the room, but neither of them seem to feel it. She lifts herself and puts her arm across his thigh, her palm on his knee and then runs her hand down the back of his calf following the contours of the muscle.

"I like your leg," she says. Her hand reaches his ankle and she pushes it on to feel his long instep and even his toes. "I like your feet, too," she says. He flicks the ashes from his cigarette into the ashtray which he moves away from her head. "I love men," she says. "Despite my mother teaching me that I should hate them." Baker laughs briefly, but doesn't speak.

Janet sighs and lies back again, straightening her legs and not touching him. He glances at her, then goes back to staring at the wall across from him. She looks up at the ceiling.

"Did you ever see the movie, 'Heartbreakers?' " she asks. Her voice is dreamy, far away, as though she has forgotten who it is she is talking to.

"No," he says, still staring at the wall.

"It's about these two men, good friends, and one of them's a painter. Peter Coyote and Nick Mancuso, I think." She pauses, takes a long strand of her dark hair, pulls it around in front of her eyes, then lets it go. "Peter Coyote plays a painter, I think, and he has this model. She's a call girl ... "

"I have to go right away," he says.

"Just let me tell you this," she answers. Her voice has returned to its normal tone and quickness. The air in the room, she notices, suddenly feels colder and more taut somehow. She thinks how if there were a fire here, it would pop and crackle now.

"All right."

"One night the two friends go to her apartment for dinner, and something happens, you know how things happen ... " She waits. He nods. "And they all go to bed together." She lies back again, thinking about the blinking red light on his answering machine in the other room. 'The call girl, his model, is in love with him, but he doesn't love her. And she says to him ... something, um ... " She looks at Baker's smooth back curving up and away from the concave line of her abdomen and touches him with her fingertips, on his shoulder, then drops her hand. "She says, 'You loved being inside me. You were so ... hard.' " Baker turns his head to look down at her, his eyelids flicker, then he looks away again. 'Then she says, 'You're a heartbreaker.' "

She touches him again. Her voice has trailed away and in the silence the furnace begins to hum down in the basement. She wonders what time it is — three, four o'clock? And when he leaves, she has to go, too, because it's his place they're making love in. He sets his ashtray down on the floor.

"Is that what you think I am?" he asks. "A heartbreaker?" But she doesn't reply. Only looks at him.

The Prize

I can't look through the window behind my desk to those hills to the west without thinking of the dinosaur skeleton that I know lies buried, a few bones exposed by the icy spring runoff, at the bottom of a decaying coulee, its grave a secret all the incomprehensible length of sixty-five million years. To see it I have only to walk a half-mile out onto the prairie, up a sage and cactus strewn slope, around a thinly-grassed hill or two, retreating further and further from civilization into that gorge where only coyotes, deer and rabbits come, till I reach the place below an abandoned eagle's nest where the pieces of bone protrude from the yellowish clay.

When I was an obscure, barely-published writer filled with dreams of glory, I had made a solitary pilgrimage around the prairie provinces to the few small towns and farms where writers of talent had once lived: to the homestead of the Icelandic poet, Stephan Stephansson in Alberta, to Margaret Laurence's family home in Manitoba, and in Saskatchewan I had searched for what had been the farm where Sinclair Ross was raised.

For a month I spoke to almost no one; I remember the feel of the steering wheel under my palms, day after day, the green countryside passing by the open car windows, the heat, the perpetual prairie wind, the undercurrent of loneliness that I could never quite shut off, and my determination that never wavered in spite of it. I felt propelled by some compulsion over which I had neither control nor desire for control. Was it only that I wanted to be close to the intimate, personal lives of writers who had achieved what I only aspired to? Not exactly that — I was searching for something I hadn't been able to name even to myself. Although I don't know why this happened, nor any reason for it, the truth is, I was in the grip of the conviction that I had been chosen for greatness.

In southern Saskatchewan I had found the village written about by an American writer who had lived there during his childhood. It was small, not more than seven hundred people lived there, but it was a pretty town, and the shallow river with its steep, grassy banks that wound its way through it, added to its charm. Rows of cottonwoods grew down the streets, probably planted by the first settlers at the beginning of the century, and they had grown so tall that their boughs met overhead to provide welcome shade in what I could see were summers so hot and dry they were barely endurable.

I remember I had no trouble finding the house. Knowledge of who its original owners were seemed to be part of the local folklore, and when I asked where it was, it was pointed out to me with a sort of casual pride that obviously didn't extend itself to concern about the house's preservation. It was in a sorry state of disrepair, but I could see that with its gables and its meticulously crafted wooden trim around the eaves, it had once been handsome. I remember that after I had seen its exterior — nobody answered when I knocked — I stopped to eat lunch in the town's only café, and then I drove on into Alberta.

Not long after that journey my first novel won the top literary prize in the country, and I was abruptly thrust from my impatient obscurity into a measure of fame. Where I had been ignored, I was suddenly in demand, the object of endless interest, of affection and jealousy. I was invited to give readings, lectures and workshops all across the country. I attended meetings, conferences, and parties where I talked too much and drank too much and took full advantage of any woman who showed interest in me.

But as the year after the prize passed, it grew harder and harder to find time to write; I began to feel more and more uneasy. I was afraid I liked the attention too much — people who had never said hello before the prize now hanging on my every word, everyone suddenly having time for me — I was ashamed, and a hollow was growing inside me. I was afraid I might not write again.

Now, lying in the morning in my rumpled, seldom-occupied bed, aching with dissatisfaction and the desire to go back to what I had been before the prize, I thought of that small, decaying house in that distant village. I thought, if only I could live far away from all this, be solitary, and remote from this craziness I'm mired in.

Eventually it came to me: I would use the advances I had received from the publishers of my novel in Britain and the United States to buy that house, I would restore it and I would make it my home. There, maybe, in the surroundings of the famous writer's childhood, where the great artist in him had surely been born, I would be able to finish my second novel. Maybe it would even be as good as everyone had said my first had been.

I got out of bed, I checked my calendar and then ignored it, I packed a suitcase, got into my car, and drove for five hours from Saskatoon south to the village where the house was. During that long drive my certainty grew that I was doing the right thing — the volume of work the man had produced well into his old age, the way that it echoed again and again, explicitly, implicitly, of his boyhood in that village he had made miraculous, the startling clarity of his vision, as though his puzzling, half-deprived, half-blessed childhood in that place had perfected in him a vein of prophecy even the best of us in our smoother lives had missed.

When I reached the village, I didn't pause on the short main street, but drove through puddles of melting ice down its length, made a turn, and pulled up in front of the writer's house, finding it as easily as if I went there every day. I parked, got out, and I marched up the sidewalk, the front door looked as though it hadn't been opened in years, to a door on the side, near the back of the house.

I knocked loudly, there was a thumping inside as though

someone might have knocked over a chair or banged against a piece of furniture, and then the door opened.

"I want to buy your house," I said to the big, bulky old man who stood in the doorway blinking into the sunshine of the bright, biting, early spring day. He studied me for a minute out of deep set, small eyes.

"You come inside," he said, and stood back so I could pass into the house. I entered a small, cluttered room that smelled of bacon fat and grime.

"I pour you drink," he said. "Sit," indicating an old wooden chair with a burnt-wood design in the backrest. It was splattered with white paint, but the seat, where the paint hadn't touched it, was worn to a pale gold satin. I sat in it at the table in front of a window, he reached into a cupboard and brought out a whiskey bottle and two small glasses. He filled the glasses with the thick, purple liquid from the bottle.

"Chokecherry wine," he said. "You got to get berries when just right," and he made a delicate, pinching gesture with his thick fingers. "My name Nick Esterhazy," he said. "You?" I told him my name, and silently resolved to wait for him to mention again the selling of the house.

He began to talk about his life, some roundabout way, maybe, to lead up to naming a price. He was a bachelor, a big, powerful man in no way broken by his years of hard labour as a section hand with the C.P.R., in a country that still remained, for him, foreign. He paused now and then in his telling to peer out the window where it was possible to see part of the sidewalk and the street. He all but slavered at the sight of the teenage girls, their books in their arms, passing by from the nearby high school. He waved his still muscular arms, his small, deep blue eyes gleaming darkly.

"Forty years," he whispered, leaning close to me so that I couldn't look away. "Forty years section hand. Work! I tell you we work." He held out his thick, gnarled hands as evidence. He made a fist, he bent his arm at the elbow and touched his bicep, looking meaningfully at me. He was about to go on, but someone knocked on the door. We had been so intent on each other that neither of us had noticed anyone passing the window. He rose hastily, his chair rocking noisily from his hand thrusting against its back as he stood, and opened the door.

A small, grey-bearded, slightly stooped old man peered up at Nick. He was dressed in a creased black suit that appeared to be made of a heavyweight cotton. The jacket had no collar and his plaid shirt was buttoned up tight against his wrinkled throat. He wore heavy black boots and a black hat too, and he was grinning, exposing a row of strong-looking, yellow teeth.

"So, Benjamin!" Nick boomed. "I not see you for long time! You sick?" I'm sure they heard him at the post office, two streets over.

"Want to buy chickens? I got good chickens," the old man said. Without waiting for Nick's answer, he turned to go back to the big van I could see idling at the curb, in front of my car. "I show you," he called over his shoulder.

"Make damn sure they got both leg!" Nick bellowed. I couldn't tell if he was teasing or not. "I don't want no more busted chicken!" The old man hurried down the narrow sidewalk, flapping one hand behind him as if to say, don't be silly. Nick stood in the open door, his body blocking out all but a halo of light above his shoulders and around his head. The old man passed the window again. When he stopped, I could hear him panting.

When their transaction was finished, I watched Benjamin go back down the sidewalk and climb awkwardly into the van. As soon as he had shut the door it pulled away.

"Damn Hutterites," Nick muttered, but without rancour. He took the two dripping, plastic-wrapped chickens into his bedroom, and I could hear the opening and closing of a fridge door. He had closed off all the rooms except the kitchen and the adjoining room which appeared to be his bedroom. He came back into the kitchen wiping his hands on his pants.

"What's the matter with them?" I asked. He shrugged.

"Always selling," he said vaguely. "You want to buy my house?" My heart gave a leap against my ribs and sweat broke out on the back of my neck. I took a drink to cover my nervousness.

"I'd like to talk to you about it," I said, setting down my glass.

"Have more," he roared, and filled my glass again. His mood changed abruptly and he sighed heavily, the lines around his mouth turning down. "I want to die in Old Country," he said. "Have brothers, sisters there. I go home." He looked sadly at the wall behind me where a small window between the cupboards gave a cramped view of the hills on the western edge of town. "I die with my people."

I doubted his honesty, he doubted mine, but we managed to strike a deal in a fairly short time. I knew I was being reckless, but I didn't care. I was desperate to have the house, to live in it, as if some hidden part of myself that my conscious self didn't have access to, had taken over my will.

I declined his offer to stay the night with him, I had no idea where he thought I might sleep, and went to the hotel. The next day I drove him to the neighbouring larger town where there was a lawyer, we drew up the papers, I wrote a cheque, and the house was mine.

Nick asked for a month to sell his furniture, which I had said I didn't want, and to make his arrangements. I hoped privately that a month would be enough time. I didn't like his size with its hint of brutality, his abrupt swings of mood, and his way of narrowing his little eyes at me as if assessing the depth of my depravity.

There was running water in the house, but no bathroom. Nick had used an outhouse during the summer and a chamber pot in winter, so before I left the town that day, I made arrangements with a carpenter recommended to me by the café-owner, in whose café I had eaten my meals, to begin converting an upstairs bedroom into a bathroom. As I drove back to the city I was filled with an elation that I hadn't felt since I'd received the phone call about the prize, a deep satisfaction that things were going as they should, that puzzled me and disturbed me a little, at the same time as I enjoyed it.

"Don't bother to visit," I warned all my acquaintances. "It's too far away, and anyway, I'm going there to write. *I vant to be alone.*"

"No danger," Will, my closest and oldest friend said. "You'll be back by fall, if you last that long. Anyway, Cheryl and I will be in the East till late June or July." His manner was joking, but I

detected an undertone that bordered on cheerful contempt. I
didn't reply, a little surprised, faintly hurt.

I went back to packing my books and clothes and dishes, to
sending out change of address notices, arranging to have my few
pieces of furniture moved, and to paying a few farewell visits. I
debated, then decided not to call my ex-fiancée, Louise. My frequent, prolonged absences during the past year, and what I
swore to her was only her overactive imagination had broken
our relationship. Anyway, I knew she was involved with a recent-
ly-divorced English professor. No doubt she'd hear about my
move through the grapevine, the same way I'd heard about her
new relationship.

At the end of the month I drove through a greening countryside back to the village, climbing slowly over many miles to that
high plateau, and at last descending into the deep valley with
the town spread out below me where my house waited for me. It
was a soft spring twilight as I descended that long hill, the few
lights in the town winking orange, and I had the sensation of
sinking into some warm, dusky dreamworld. At the bottom of
the hill passing the newly sprouting hayfields on the outskirts, I
was seized by a wave of loneliness, so powerful that for a minute
I thought I would have to pull over. I slowed, and as the outlines
of the first houses grew sharper under the streetlights, the sensation diminished, grew less keen, till only a faint memory of it
lingered.

Nick was gone, leaving me, for some unaccountable reason,
with the beautiful old chair I had sat on during my first visit, a
few other broken remnants of furniture, and a twenty-year accu-
mulation of dirt. I hoped that the other old man, the writer, was
still present somewhere in those dusty vacant rooms with their
fading, stained wallpaper and their worn, linoleum-covered
floors. Although what I meant when I thought that, I didn't try
to articulate.

While I scrubbed the floors and carted out and burned old
rags and ancient, mouldy Eaton's catalogues I found lying in the
back of closets and in the crumbling cellar, I thought of the writer, that serious, book-ridden child, a misfit in a community of
work-obsessed, silent people. I found myself looking for his

ghost in the bedrooms with their slanted ceilings, and in the decaying front porch where he had sat with his mother on summer evenings, and listening in the night for a hint of his child's voice echoing through the long years.

I began to convert the other back room opposite the kitchen into my study. I set my desk squarely in front of the big, old-fashioned window where I could lift my head and see the hills across the little river and the opening into the more distant coulee where I would one day find the relics of a dinosaur. I took paint remover and scrubbed away the white paint that marred the Golden Oak chair Nick had left me. Perhaps it had been there since the house had belonged to the writer's family.

I had been warned about small towns: how they were hotbeds of gossip, innuendo and outright lies, of deep-seated prejudices and antiquated attitudes, also, of the most disgusting hidden vices. But some had told me of their warmth, and of the concern of villagers for each other's welfare, of their appreciation of the past. What the people of the village thought of me didn't matter to me; I didn't expect to fit in, nor want to; I hoped only to find solitude and anonymity, to be better able to hold at bay all the temptations that accompanied fame, for I was sure they would ruin me as an artist.

I want to be a writer. I murmured the incantation to myself over and over again. I want to be a *good* writer. And silently, so silently that I never formed the words even in my own head, something in me murmured steadily, like the sound of the wind in the trees that lined the streets: I want to be a great writer.

The woman from the neat new bungalow next door came to visit. I was at my typewriter when I heard the front door close and a woman's voice calling, "Yoohoo," down the hall. Startled, wondering if somebody had arrived without warning from the city, I hurried out to see who was there.

A short, middle-aged woman in a print housedress, the kind my mother wore when I was a child, was advancing down the hall, peering to the left and right, holding a cake still in its pan in front of her.

"Oh, there you are!" she said when she saw me. "I'll just put this in the kitchen," and disappeared into it. I followed. "Have you made a difference in here! That old Nick was so dirty! And when I tried to clean up for him, he got downright grabby, if you get my drift, so I had to leave him to stew in his own juice, if you know what I mean." She set the cake on the counter, turned, and seeing me standing in the doorway, she said, "I'm Palma McCallum. I live next door. I thought it was high time I came over and introduced myself."

"George," I began.

"Barrett, I know," she said. "You wrote that book. I read it," she added, and went no further. She began to peel plastic wrap from the cake pan. "I didn't mind it," she said. "Heaven knows, there's lots worse than that."

"Would you like some coffee?" I asked, deciding to ignore her remarks about my book.

"Just the thing," she said. "We'll have some of my cake."

Palma had a husband, but I rarely saw him. He was always out at the farm seeding or summer fallowing or spraying or hauling wheat. I soon realized that she would be in my house everyday washing my dishes or dusting, if I didn't make it clear to her that I wanted few interruptions. I was a bachelor, after all, and she assumed that I was like all the others in the district, a man whose socks always needed mending, whose buttons were perpetually popping off and needed sewing on and who would starve if it weren't for the occasional casserole or pie fresh from her oven.

"That rug needs vacuuming," she'd say. "I'll just run over it ... " but I would quickly intervene, "Now Palma, I'm not helpless. I can vacuum my own rug. Come and have a cup of coffee with me. I was just going to take a break." She would meekly follow me into the kitchen, checking behind me for dust on the windowsills, then sit while I made the coffee, chattering about her husband and her relatives and our other neighbours. Her sharp eyes took in everything, and I knew what she saw in the morning was all over town by afternoon. She kept bustling in without knocking until I took to turning the key in the door so that when she decided to drop in, she had to knock.

I had quickly recovered the regime I had maintained before my first novel was released: up at six, write till ten, then out for a long walk across the river, over the prairie and up into the hills behind my house, then back to my desk. The pile of pages by my typewriter grew thicker with each day that passed. It seemed to me, though, that my original idea was changing slightly, and I wasn't sure whether to wrench the novel back to that, or to follow this subtle new tone to wherever it might lead. I decided finally to let the writing go to where it seemed to want to.

When my writing had temporarily stalled and I had tired of scraping off old wallpaper or mending wiring or painting, and I found my thirst for human company too strong to resist, I strolled down to the café for a cup of coffee and a hamburger.

"Evenin', how's the carpenter?" Harry, the owner, always asked as I sat down. Then he'd pour me a cup of coffee without asking if I wanted one.

I soon began to see that the café was the centre of social life for a certain strata of local society: the retarded people who lived in the old peoples' lodge on the riverbank, the men who had never married, Hutterite men in town on business, strangers passing through, outsiders like myself — in short, everyone who was left after all the circles of friends and relatives had been cast. I found too, that because the town was located in the heart of what had once been dinosaur country, any scruffy-looking stranger might turn out to be a distinguished paleontologist from a distant university.

Occasionally, when I tired of my own company, and the café held no appeal, I went to the bar, which was in the old hotel, where, even if there were only a few old-timers nursing their warm draft beer or a familiar face or two from the café, there was at least loud rock music playing and a pretty barmaid to look at. Later, I knew, the place would fill up with a stray oil crew or two and young farmers and ranchhands and their girlfriends, and the bar would grow raucous with a palpable current of violence that often erupted into fights.

One night I was surprised to find three middle-aged Hutterite men sitting quietly together, each with a glass of beer in front of him. I wondered if this was allowed, or if they were breaking rules. After I had been there for a while a pair of young Hutterite girls came in the outer door and put their heads around the corner of the entryway. They looked to be about sixteen or seventeen and they were grinning broadly and giggling so loudly that everybody, a dozen or so people, turned to see what was going on. Everybody except the Hutterite men who seemed to know without looking, who it was making the noise.

"What's that all about?" I asked Denise, the barmaid, who had come to ask me if I wanted another drink. She was only a few years older than the girls giggling in the doorway.

Denise laughed, turning her head toward them. She had a wry, flippant way about her that wasn't pleasant, but that intrigued me because it contrasted so sharply with her perfect pink complexion and her face with its small nose and sensual mouth and large blue eyes, all framed by her long, pale-blonde hair. She had a way of standing holding her tray that emphasized her full young breasts in the tight shirt she always wore. I had wondered if it was meant especially for me, but I had soon seen that she stood like that in front of all the men, as if she believed that a casual parading of her charms was part of her job description. Once or twice I'd thought of taking her home with me, I thought she could have been persuaded, but something held me back. The welcoming calm of my house, the sense of a presence that was always there, so that I never felt alone — I felt she would disrupt all that, that she might dispel it, and I wouldn't risk its loss.

"I guess they want to go home," she said. "Everything in town but the bar is closed." One of the old men who were waiting at the door each morning for the bar to open, and who sat in his usual place near the door, lifted his unsteady head, his greasy cap stuck on sideways, patted the seat beside him, and called to the girls, "Why doan youse come and sit with me?" The girls dodged back around the corner and their giggles reached such a pitch of hysteria that I thought surely the men would have to get up and tell them to be quiet or shoo them back to the van I had seen parked down the street.

When they didn't move, I said to Denise, "It doesn't seem to be bothering them much," nodding my head in the direction of the three Hutterites who were talking quietly together. She made a sour face and shrugged one shoulder so hard her breast bounced.

"I bet they'll catch hell on the way home. The men aren't

supposed to be in here, so the girls know they can get away with it." She took my empty glass away without looking at it, her eyes meeting mine in a too-frank gaze that she practiced on most of her customers. "Hutterite women don't have much to say about anything."

I looked back to the two apple-cheeked girls in the doorway — I had never before seen anyone that description fitted — and studied their costume, the black and white polka-dotted scarves they wore over their hair, their ankle-length bright plaid dresses with the long aprons over them, and I saw that their faces shone with a childish innocence, unabashed as they were by the attention they were provoking from the audience that, except for Denise, was entirely male. I hadn't known there were still teenagers in Canada like that. I wondered if I could find a place for them in my novel and then dismissed the idea as silly.

Ten more minutes passed, the girls didn't tire of their game, and the three Hutterite men, one of them very drunk, slowly stood up. As soon as they began to rise, the girls let out a couple of delighted shrieks, pulled open the outside door and pushed each other out into the street. When I went out a half hour later, the van was gone.

Other than Palma only canvassers for the Heart or Cancer or Lung associations knocked on my door. And, of course, the Hutterites, who came selling freshly killed ducks and geese, frozen chickens, and fresh vegetables from their gardens which must have been vast. It was always the old man with the thin grizzled beard, Benjamin, who came, too old to work on the colony anymore, I guessed, and a young man who drove the van, carried the heavy sacks of potatoes or carrots and any large orders of birds.

I never bought much, but I always bought something. I even placed an order for some pairs of hand-knitted wool socks, in my case, good for nothing but wearing inside my winter boots since they were so thick and bulky. But I had first seen Benjamin when the house was still Nick's and I felt leery about disturbing a tradition.

One day they arrived at noon as I was taking a small roast out of the oven. It was too much for me, I had cooked it in order not to have to cook for a few days, and on impulse, I asked him and his driver to have lunch with me. Although he barely knew me, Benjamin accepted without a trace of hesitancy or surprise. I realized that such an invitation was in keeping with the communal tradition he lived by, and I knew too, that if I arrived at the colony at mealtime, it would be taken for granted that I would eat there.

Benjamin said grace before I had even thought of it, and then dug in with a good appetite.

"You should come visit us at colony," he said. "Our women cook you good meal."

"I'll have to do that," I said, although I had no intention of ever doing any such thing. I hadn't even any sure idea, beyond the direction, where the colony was.

"What you do for living?" he asked.

"I'm a writer," I said. "I'm working on a book." He put his fork down and looked hard at me, his dark eyes sharp.

"About this town?" he asked. I had to laugh.

"Heavens no," I said.

"Why not?" he asked, returning to his meal. "Lots here to write."

"I'm sure there is," I said, "but ... " and couldn't think how to finish my sentence. "I'm finishing something I started before I came here."

The young man with him, William, hardly spoke at all, but he ate with ferocity, not lifting his eyes from his plate. Despite Benjamin's frail old age, it was plain he was the boss.

"Is William your son?" I asked.

"No," Benjamin said, "grandson. My boys men now, have sons of own."

"They live on the colony, too?"

"Two in Manitoba," he said, then gave me that sharp-eyed glance again. "Sure on colony. All on colonies. How else to live?" He gave a little laugh, more to himself, and I glanced at William, wondering why he never spoke. Benjamin must have seen me looking at William, because he said, apropos of nothing that I could tell, "It's hard to keep young ones on colony. They want to go. Some of them. Gets harder all the time."

"Oh?" I said.

"They want to see world," he said. "Television, cars, women." I kept silent. "They want to see world," he repeated, giving his old head a shake and reaching with his knife for the butter. "I tell them, the world!" He flapped his free hand as if to make the world vanish. "On colony we keep out bad things."

William kept chewing, his eyes on his plate, but red was creeping up his neck to disappear under his short, white-blonde hair. "We get him wife," the old man said, winking at me. "He settle down then." William swallowed hard, but still refused to look at us.

"You married?" Benjamin asked me.

"No," I said.

"Man needs woman," he pointed out.

"Oh, I suppose I'll get married one of these days."

"Have little ones," he suggested. "Not good for man to live alone."

When the two of them had gone, I thought about what Benjamin had said about me living alone. I realized then that although I had been living alone for a couple of months, I didn't have that empty, alienated feeling that being alone had always raised in me in the past. I felt as though someone was with me. It was peculiar, and I found myself wandering through my house thinking about it. It had to be the house, there was something about it, it exuded a warmth, I actually felt it welcomed me, it wanted me in it. But that's silly, I told myself. It's only your imagination. But there it was. Perhaps, I thought, it's the writer glad to have a kindred soul living here.

Still, I reminded myself, if it really were the dead writer, surely my work would be going better. My first novel had poured out of me, but this one seemed to be going in fits and starts. Often a couple of days would pass without my writing a line, and yet I couldn't quite put my finger on what the trouble was. I knew my characters; I knew where I wanted my characters to go; the setting was as familiar to me as the city I had grown up in. Oh well, I thought, you hit a bad spell every once in a while. You can't expect it to be always easy and smooth.

Palma dropped in unexpectedly about five o'clock one afternoon when I was lazing around with a new novel an acquaintance
had just had published. It wasn't very good, I didn't think, and I
was wondering what I would say in my letter to her.

"Let's have a glass of wine," I suggested to Palma, glad to put
down the book.

"Heaven's no! I don't drink," she said.

"Come on," I teased her. "One little glass won't set you on the
road to ruin." She looked as if she was about to give me a lecture,
then relented.

"Oh, all right," she said, "but you have to promise me, I mean
promise that you won't tell anybody." The village was full of
female teetotallers, all innocent and pious women who must
have felt that not allowing a drop of liquor to pass their lips
would somehow redress the cosmic balance for the kids who
drank too much beer and rolled their trucks, the old reprobates
nothing would ever change, and those ranchers and farmers who
drank whiskey to soothe their aches and to forget their bankers
breathing down their necks.

Soon Palma was on her second half-glass, her cheeks were
flushed a becoming pink, and her tongue thoroughly loosened.
She sat across from me at the kitchen table and chattered away.

"I see those Hutterites coming to your door all the time," she
scolded. "Can you afford to buy so much? Don't be afraid to tell
them to buzz off if you don't want to buy."

"Are you suggesting they aren't honest?" I asked. She hesitated, then nodded sagely.

"The young ones steal." When I looked surprised, she hurried
on.

"Nothing big or expensive, just little things, fasteners for
their hair, cheap costume jewellery, things like that."

"I wonder why that is," I said.

"Well, then, it's what they believe," she said, pursing her lips
smugly.

"What they believe?" I prompted. Behind her in the back
yard the June sun was shining warmly on the one tall cotton-
wood that was left — the others had had to be cut down, sawed
into manageable pieces and hauled away before the dead

branches could blow down on the house. I wondered if the dead writer's parents had planted them. His mother, I thought.

"That you can't own anything," she said, surprised at my ignorance. "They can't have rings or earrings or necklaces, they think that's sinful, and since they can't have money, they steal. You can't keep a young girl away from pretty things, you know. It isn't natural. Betty in the Co-Op has to keep a weather eye on them whenever they come into the store."

I was trying to decide whether this was true, or merely local prejudice. "Do you know they don't want their kids educated? They've got their own school on the colony, but if they get educated, the first thing they do is leave, and the elders can't have that. So they make it hard for the teacher. They're forever taking their kids out of school to help kill geese or babysit during harvest or whatever, anything to keep them out of school. And they all stop going as soon as they're old enough."

"Do ... " I began.

"And they won't allow television or music except religious singing or even pictures on the walls. Now I ask you, how can you teach school without even pictures on the walls? Or tape recorders or radios?" She would have gone on and on, I saw no hope of stopping her if I had wanted to, but the phone rang and I went to my study to answer it. When I came back, she was rinsing our wineglasses in the sink.

"I can't think why I stayed so long," she said over the noise of the running water. "It was that darn wine. I never should have taken any. Now remember, you promised."

"A little wine won't hurt you," I said. "But I promise." She seemed to think I might put up a notice on the bulletin board in the café!

She set the glasses on the drainboard and wiped her hands vigorously on a paper towel. "I don't understand it at all," she said. "The men drive tractors and big, expensive combines,but the teacher can't even have a record player." She looked up at me, frowning, her lips pursed, as if I might be able to explain it.

"I don't understand it either," I said, finally. She went out into the hall and stood by the door. I followed her. "My sister taught on one of the colonies for a couple of years. That's how I know."

She went out without saying good-bye, shutting the door clumsily so that it banged, leaving me standing in the hall watching
her figure, muted and wavering through the frosted oval glass of
the door, disappear down the sidewalk.

I had lived in the town about three months. I should have
been finished with the first draft of my novel, but there it sat, a
thick enough pile of pages, but no longer the novel I had
planned and begun in the city. I wasn't wholly lost, but neither
was I able to find the tone I wanted and to hold it steady.
Instead, it fluctuated from the driving, energy-filled narrative of
the first novel with its wry, angry tone that the critics had loved,
all the way to the other extreme — a calm, almost meditative
voice that I didn't recognize and that was becoming harder and
harder to break free of.

I picked up the stack of pages sitting beside my typewriter.
They weighed satisfyingly heavy in my hands. I sat down on the
old oak chair and flipped through them. There it was, that quiet,
removed voice that made me think of the small river that flowed
past my house — at night, when the moon was shining on it.
Mixed in with passages of prose that might have come straight
from my first novel.

I lifted my eyes from the pile of paper and stared out the window at the hills that were deepening into blues as night drew
down over the countryside. I could see now that while in my
first book I had dealt with every conceivable problem of urban
life — the constant hurry, the obsession with matters of style
and taste, the driving passion to get ahead, the unspoken urge to
transcend it all — what I had not dealt with was the possibility
of any other way of life. It was as if I had been so involved
myself in that life that I couldn't even imagine any other way of
living.

The more I wrote, the more it seemed to me that I was actually losing interest in that rich, perpetually exciting world. It had
lost its urgency, had begun to seem dreamlike. I was having more
and more trouble conjuring its colour, its sensuality, its speed. I
even had moments when I felt I simply couldn't be bothered.

I sat for a long time looking out the window behind my desk

at the moon-washed hills and the high, winding coulee eroded back into them, a deep shadow now, and I saw two deer moving haltingly down the slope, going to water at the river. Abruptly I pulled down the blind, blocking out the scented countryside, pulling the small room back into itself. I sat a while longer, then I went upstairs to bed.

It was after that I found the dinosaur bone. I felt I had been spending too much time in the café in the evenings and I vowed that when the urge to go for a mindless chat with Harry and a cup of his foul-tasting coffee came upon me, I would instead, cross over the small footbridge at the end of the street and go for a walk across the prairie and up into the hills. I knew that once I was well away from the town the glimpses of deer or rabbits, hawks or even the occasional eagle, and the calm and beauty of the landscape would work its spell on me and I would forget how much I had wanted company. On one of these walks I went further than usual into the coulee, and spotting a white rock at the base of a steep clay cliff, I went closer to it to see it. I could tell at once that it was bone and of an animal so large there was nothing on the prairie to rival it for size. A femur, perhaps. The piece newly exposed was not big enough to identify definitely, but I knew if I chose to dig I would find more, much more. I stayed out till dark that night and when I returned across the little footbridge, the coyotes were yipping and howling in the hills as if to mourn what I had uncovered.

Summer came, and I had begun a second draft. I went occasionally to the café again, where absolutely nothing seemed to have changed in my absence. One night when I was there Benjamin and a young companion were just finishing supper in a booth near the back, across from another booth where four farmers were lingering over cups of coffee. Otherwise, the café was empty.

"Did you hear about what happened in Black River?" Harry asked me, leaning close over the counter and lowering his voice. I said I hadn't. "The council tried to stop the Hutterites from getting any bigger or starting another colony in their municipality. They passed some bylaws that would keep them from building on any new quarters of land they bought, so nobody could live on that land. Stopped 'em cold. But the Hutterites went to court and the news just came out today. They beat 'em. Unconstitutional, the court said." He sighed. "To tell the truth, they don't bother me none."

"Funny they wouldn't want them around," I said. "I heard they're good neighbours, that they'll go help anybody who's in trouble."

"Oh, yeah," Harry said, still keeping his voice down. Benjamin and his companion came and paid their bill and left. Harry came back from the till and leaned on the counter beside me again. "They roll onto the place with their big equipment and all that help and they have that whole damn place seeded or combined by noon. It's really something to see." There was a roar of laughter from the booth where the farmers were sitting. One of them, still laughing, stood up, a toothpick in his mouth and his bill rolled in one big brown hand. He came up to the cash register.

"What's the joke, Dave?" Harry asked as he accepted the man's quarters.

"I was telling 'em about old Ben. He came up to me on the street in Mallard the other day. He was all upset. Saw a sign that said there was strippers dancing in the bar there." He had to stop talking for a minute because he had begun to laugh again. He shifted his toothpick. "So I said, 'What? Naked women dancing? It can't be true!' I get a kick out of teasing them Hutterites," he explained. "Especially old Ben, he's so serious. So Ben said, 'It's true, you see?' He was shaking his head he was so shocked. 'It's crazy,' he said. So I said, 'Ah, I don't believe it.' And I took his arm, pretended I was going to get him to come with me to see. I said, 'It can't be! Come on, let's go see!' " He had to stop again to get control of his laughter. "But old Ben, he took me serious. 'No! No!' he says, and he pulls his arm away. 'I ain't going over there! It's crazy!' Christ," the farmer said, "I couldn't stop laughing." He went out of the café shaking his head and chuckling.

I paid for my coffee and walked slowly home through the soft summer twilight. There was nobody on the street or in the yards, everyone had gone indoors, and lights splashed out across the sidewalk now and then, from rooms where families sat talking or watching TV. I thought of the life I had left behind, and I was overcome by a longing for my old apartment in the city, for my friends and our familiar haunts, for the busy, full life we led, for the laughter we shared, and the talk, and the love.

When I got home, instead of going straight to bed, I went into my study. I turned on the desk lamp and sat down not really intending to work, but not yet ready to go to bed either. There was a passage, though, that I hadn't been able to turn to my satisfaction, that was what had driven me out to the café, and I picked up that page again and looked at it. I began to cross out phrases and re-write them in the space above the line of type. Slowly the futility of what I was doing swept over me and I tore up the page and threw it down.

It was no good. For months now I'd been wrestling with this book, fighting to keep it true to the concept I'd developed in the city. I'd twisted passages and ideas, I'd compromised, I'd left in what I couldn't bring myself to leave out even though I knew it didn't quite belong.

And now I knew it was no good, it didn't work, in my desperation to match my first success I'd been kidding myself. Would I ever again write anything that was worth reading? Was what I had accomplished so far worth what everyone said? At this moment it seemed of little consequence, and all the world of art, of great achievements, lay spread out ahead of me, on the other side of a transparent wall that I knew I had not yet even breached. Perhaps, I never would. If I had been chosen, as I had believed, it was not in the simple-minded way I had thought, and the prize I had won meant nothing.

I moved to my armchair and fell into it. My eyes lit on the stained patch on the wall, high up, that spilled over onto the ceiling. I had tried everything to remove it, but it had resisted every effort, and now it was coming through the water-base paint I had applied over it.

I remembered then how the writer whose home this had once been, had written in an autobiographical essay about that very stain, how it had come to be there as a result of a chemistry experiment he had tried as a boy, that had exploded. And I knew then that my vision, or my revelation, or whatever I might choose to call it, had come from that dead writer. And I felt, with a certainty that settled in my bones, that this was why I had come here. And I was filled with dread, and an overwhelming sense of the implacability of my fate.

I sat in the armchair in the shadowed corner of the room and sweat broke out on my forehead and ran down my backbone. To stay here for the rest of my life, to struggle day after day alone, with nothing but the hills and the wind for company. I can't do it, I said, over and over again. I can't do it. I won't, I won't do it. There has to be an easier way. And then, I can leave if I want to. I can leave.

When I had calmed myself I went upstairs to my bed and escaped into sleep.

In the morning I woke late to the ringing of the phone. I stumbled downstairs to my study to answer it and stood in a patch of sunlight spilling in from the hall that faced the east while I talked. It was Will, phoning from the city to say that he and Cheryl had gotten up this morning and decided, without any warning, that today was the day they would drive down to see me.

"Fine," I said, heavily. And then, with a little surge of pleasure, "Fine," for I had remembered what had happened the night before and I felt wholly lost, as if the floor could no longer be trusted to hold me, or the entire house might float away, like a hot air balloon that had lost its anchor.

Later in the day I was vacuuming when I felt somebody was in the room with me. Turning, I saw Palma McCallum standing in the doorway. I hadn't bothered to turn the key in the lock.

"Hi," she said, and then, a little timidly, "Are you working?"

"Just housework," I said. "Want some coffee?"

"I'll just put the kettle on for tea," she said, and disappeared toward the kitchen. I pushed the vacuum cleaner out of the way and followed her. "Thurman and I are going to visit his sister in the city," she said, over her shoulder, as she ran water into the kettle. "I had a few minutes while he's out checking things at the farm. I thought I'd drop over and see if we can pick anything up for you."

"No," I said, "I don't need anything, but it was nice of you to ask." "What's a neighbour for," she said, taking my teapot out of the cupboard and setting it on the counter. "You got any cream?"

"Cream!" I said, "Where would I get good farm cream?"

"Darn! I got some from the Hutterites that'll just go bad when I'm away. I was going to bring it over."

"I'm having some friends come from the city later today," I said. "They'll be staying a couple of days."

"And I'm going to miss them!" she wailed. For one awful moment I thought she might try to persuade Thurman to postpone their trip.

"You wouldn't like them," I said. "They're trendy city folk."

"I might like them a lot," she replied indignantly, so that I had to laugh.

Cheryl and Will arrived about five o'clock. I was watering the front lawn when they drove up in their big, old seventy Ford. I hurried to turn the hose off while Will got slowly out of the driver's seat, untangling his long legs, and stretched luxuriously. Cheryl jumped out, and before I could say hello, called, "Wow! This must be the ends of the earth! We've been driving for hours!"

She hugged me, brushing my cheek with her lips, my nose in her hair, and I smelled that good, womanly smell, perfume or whatever, that I hadn't smelled for what suddenly seemed an eternity. Will came around the car and we slapped each other on the shoulders and shook hands.

Later, when I served the whipped cream on the saskatoon pie that Palma had claimed was only going to waste in her freezer, they were ecstatic.

"I've never seen anything like it," he said. "It's like mayonnaise."

"Why can't we get cream like this in the city?" Cheryl asked. "Where does it all go?"

"I guess this is one advantage to living in the country," I said.

After dinner we went for a long walk through the town, up one street and down another, while people in their yards stared at us or said hello.

"Can we walk out there?" Cheryl asked, pointing across the river to the hills. So I took them across the footbridge and out onto the prairie, and eventually, up into the coulee where not long before I had found the partially uncovered skeleton of a dinosaur.

"How did you find it?" Cheryl asked, kneeling and gently brushing away the earth from around it. I remembered that she knew a little about archaeology. I wondered if that included old bones, or was it just cities?

"Pure luck," I said. "I was out walking and I just happened to spot what I thought was an unusual colour of rock. It must have just been eroded out because it was still white and chalky to touch."

"That's absolutely incredible," she said. "All the people who must come out here and you're the one to find it. I can hardly believe it."

"How long ago was that?" Will asked. He was kneeling too, bending to study the piece of exposed bone. "Aren't you going to do anything about it? I mean, phone the Museum of Natural History or the University?" I shrugged, then knelt too, a little embarrassed.

"Oh, yeah, eventually," I said.

"Why don't you take these little pieces home?" Cheryl asked. She held something in her palm and blew gently on it. "I think this is a tooth, or a part of one."

"Maybe I will," I said vaguely, but I didn't touch the piece she held. She set it down again and brushed a little dirt over it.

It was growing dark, but there was a gold half-moon riding the hills to the south. Cheryl gave me a puzzled look, then stood up, brushing her hands on her jeans.

We sat in my living room drinking scotch. After a while Cheryl stood up and said, "All this good country air is making me sleepy. I think I'll go to bed." She yawned and stretched, unconscious of how desirable she looked with her round breasts pushed against the light cloth of her shirt. I had to drop my eyes before Will noticed me looking at her.

When she had gone, Will said, "So, this is where the great

old man lived." Will taught English Lit. at the university, specializing in modern American. Come to think of it, I was surprised he hadn't come before. "It's not much, is it," he said, "to have produced a genius."

"They were poor people," I said. "But I think the house must have been comfortable enough, especially when it was new."

"Have you had any visitations?" Will asked, grinning.

"Not exactly," I said. "I mean, there haven't been any manifestations or any weird noises in the night, if that's what you mean." He raised his eyebrows questioningly and waited for me to continue, but I felt I didn't want to talk about it, at least, not yet.

We talked about people we knew in the city, about what was going on in the publishing world, about Will and Cheryl's plans to spend Will's sabbatical travelling in Europe.

"Louise had a one woman show at the campus gallery," he remarked, not looking at me.

"Oh?" I said. "Has she made any progress from that series of dances or whatever it was she was doing?"

"I didn't think so," he said. "The show was a disappointment, I think that was the general opinion."

"I'm sorry to hear that," I said. Her long back turned to me in the dim light of the bedroom, her dark hair falling over her shoulders.

"How's your writing going?" Will asked softly, and I could hear in his voice how long he had been waiting to ask me that.

"It isn't going very well," I said. It had cost me something to say that, but Will was, after all, my oldest friend, the one who had encouraged me most in my desire to write, who had stood by when nobody would publish me, and who hadn't deserted me when I went off the rails after the prize. "It keeps changing on me," I said.

Will set his drink down and leaned back, staring up at the ceiling.

"How?" he asked.

"I set out to do one thing and it slipped away from me. It turned into something else." I wasn't sure anymore that this was the problem, but I didn't know what else to say. "It ... I've ... lost my way, at least, I've lost the old way, and I'm not sure what the new way is, or if there's a new way." There was a long silence while both of us thought about this. "I mean, I think I'm, maybe, just at the beginning of something new but it's not what I was doing before."

"Maybe what you're doing now is better," Will said slowly.

"Better?" I thought about this. "Are you trying to tell me you didn't like my first novel?" He glanced at me, then quickly looked away, and I realized that he hadn't.

"No," he said carefully, "that's not necessarily what I meant. But you must have known you couldn't keep doing that forever."

"I wasn't planning to," I said, annoyed. But of course I was.

"I know there's a tremendous amount of pressure on a writer, once he's had a success, to duplicate it the second time."

I thought of how sweat actually broke out on the back of my neck and how my stomach tightened whenever I thought of how the critics who had so praised my first book, would meet my second. I shuddered. A coyote far out in the hills behind the house had begun to yip, and a wind had risen. We could hear it blowing softly around the eaves and through the open windows of the house. I began to tell him how my life was, in this house, and what had happened to me the night before in my study.

"No wonder your work is changing," he said. "But what does it mean?"

"It means that I wasn't a writer before," I said. "I think it means I had to undergo some kind of ... profound change ... before I could go on." I shook my head, then fell silent. I could hear the papers in my study scattering across the floor as the wind grew stronger. Let them blow, I thought.

"You'll be coming back to the city then?" Will asked.

The next day we went for a longer walk in the hills, this time carrying with us a few sandwiches and a bottle of wine that Cheryl and Will had brought. When we were far from the town, or any signs of civilization, we sat down on a grassy hillside and enjoyed the sun and the breeze and the scent of sage that was on the air all around us. Watching Cheryl lying on her back in the grass, one arm thrown across her eyes to shield them from the sun and her blonde hair spread out around her head, I thought again of Louise, and regret swept through me.

"By the way," Cheryl said, taking her arm down, "that thing Louise had going with Bob Stewart is over."

"They were always fighting," Will said. "It was downright funny." Cheryl rolled over onto her stomach and grew silent, looking up at me where I sat above her on the hillside.

"Are you happy here?"

"I'm not unhappy," I said.

"Isn't it awfully lonely?" she asked.

"I only started to get lonely lately," I told her. "I swear I wasn't before."

"Nobody's even seen you for four or five months."

"I've been to the city a few times," I admitted. "But I didn't go to Saskatoon. And I had to fly to Toronto for a few days last month. I haven't been here the whole time."

"Just avoiding your friends, eh," Cheryl said, laughing.

"No," I said. "I was avoiding something else."

"The scene of the crime," Will said.

We decided to have supper in the café, which, for a change, was more than half-full when we arrived. We found an empty booth next to the row of stools at the counter and Harry came over to say hello, then left us to go back to 'chewing the fat' as he put it, with a couple of farmers in a back booth. Benjamin, the old Hutterite, was there, too, with a different companion, this one a tall, skinny twenty-year old in a black suit that was too short in the sleeves. They were eating supper in their usual booth near the back.

"This food isn't bad," Cheryl said, as we began to eat.

"Do you eat here often?" Will asked.

"No," I said, "hardly ever, but I come down occasionally for a cup of coffee in the evening." The waitress came back and refilled our cups. The café had begun to empty and it was growing dark outside. Cheryl and Will were planning to leave in the morning.

We were sitting silently, each of us thinking our own thoughts, when Will suddenly glanced up and I realized someone was standing beside me, leaning against the low partition that separated our booth from the aisle and the row of stools on the other side. It was Benjamin.

"Hello, George," he said. "You got visitors."

"Yes," I said, and introduced Cheryl and Will to him. His companion passed him, paid the bill, and went outside.

"You're in town late," I said.

"We ... " he began, and was cut off abruptly, pushing almost over the partition into our booth. His hat fell off and tumbled up against Will's coffee cup. Somebody passing by had bumped into him so hard that he had been knocked almost off his feet. I could see by his expression and the way he was holding his upper arm that the collision had hurt him. We all realized at the same time that it had been deliberate. In the confusion, heads turning, voices raised, I looked from Benjamin to the young farmer who was walking fast toward the door. I saw him look back over his shoulder at Ben; I saw he was grinning, and there was a light shining in his pale eyes that was ugly to see.

"He did that on purpose!" Cheryl said, and then to Benjamin, "Are you hurt?"

"No, no," Benjamin said, reaching out to take his hat back from Will. He looked toward the door, but the farmer was gone. Suddenly Harry was there.

"He's drunk again," he said to us. He turned to Benjamin. "You know what Ernie's like when he's drinking. Don't pay any attention to him." Benjamin shakily set his hat back on his head, but didn't answer Harry.

"To do that to an old man!" Will said, his voice filled with disgust, and there were murmurs from people sitting near us.

"That Ernie, he goes too far," Harry said. "He'll wind up in jail yet." The shocked voices around the café were dying down now as people turned back to their meals.

"I ... I go find Joseph," Benjamin mumbled, ignoring our questions, and walked away, a slow, shuffling walk, not at all the way he usually moved.

"Somebody should call the police!" Cheryl said in a loud, indignant voice.

"Shsh," Will hushed her.

"Do you think there's anything we should do?" I asked Harry.

The way Benjamin had walked away, the look on his face, as though he was lost or in shock. But, I thought, probably Benjamin and Joseph are in the van by now, pulling out of town, on their way back to the colony. Harry shrugged and turned to watch the closed door as if it might have the answer written on it.

"Do you know that Ernie?" Will asked me.

"He's in here a lot or in the bar," I said. "I don't know him."

"Let's go," Cheryl said, in a low, choked voice, pushing her half-full cup away. Her cheeks were flushed and she wasn't looking at Will or me. We rose hastily, following her, paid the bill, and went outside into the summer night.

Benjamin was standing alone in the middle of the sidewalk, peering down the street, first one way and then the other. A couple of men stood in the shadows along the wall of the café.

"Are you okay, Benjamin?" I asked.

"I don't know where van is," he said, in a frightened voice. Will was the first to take in the situation.

"I'll run and get my car," he offered in a firm voice. "It won't take me five minutes, and if we can't find your friend, I'll drive you home." He started to sprint away in the direction of my house. I turned to the men standing by the wall.

"Do you know why Joseph left without Ben?" I asked. "Did he say anything?"

One of the men came forward into the light thrown through the door of the café and I saw that it was Martin Gutwin, a family man not often in the café.

"He got in the van and drove away," Martin said. His lined, suntanned face was concerned, and he thrust his hands into the pockets of his pants. "It was the damndest thing! Ernie came barrelling out of the café and Joe was standing right there on the sidewalk by the van, waiting for Ben, I guess. And Ernie shoved him up against the van and swung on him."

Cheryl gasped, and Benjamin took a step toward Martin as if to ask more.

"Then, before we could do anything, Ernie jumped in his truck and peeled rubber outta here. We helped Joe up," he nodded toward the other man still standing back in the shadows, "and Joe got in the van and pulled out. I thought he was going after Ernie, but ... "

"No, no, he never do that," Ben interrupted, shaking his head.

"He went that way," Martin said, pointing down the street. He laughed, turning to Benjamin, a strained sound. "Went off and left you, eh?"

"What's the matter with him, anyway?" Cheryl asked. "Doesn't he understand that these men are pacifists? That they won't defend themselves?"

"I guess he understands that pretty well," Martin said.

"This is incomprehensible!" Cheryl said. "This is terrible." At that moment Will arrived in their old Ford, the brakes squealing. Cheryl got in beside him and Benjamin beside her. I sat in the back, behind Benjamin.

"Are you sure you're not hurt?" Will asked him.

"No, no, no," Benjamin said, "but Joseph?" Cheryl told Will what had happened to Joseph. "I got to find him," Benjamin said.

Will began driving up and down the few streets, all of us peering out the open windows.

"There!" Cheryl cried. The van was parked by the sidewalk in front of the Mountie's office. Will parked behind it under the old cottonwoods, their branches trailing over the car. The light from the streetlight was muted and erratic as it shone through the limbs of the big trees. We saw Joseph coming down the steps from the office where he had been pounding on the locked door. The old man was out of the car almost before we came to a full stop, surprising us with his agility, which had returned when he saw the van.

"They aren't here after five o'clock," I said to Cheryl and Will.

Joseph was striding down the walk with short, jerky steps and as Benjamin reached him, the top of his head coming just up to Joseph's shoulder, he touched Joseph's arm, but Joseph pulled angrily away from him. We couldn't make out Benjamin's words, but he seemed to be pleading with Joseph. The van's motor was still running and Joseph went to it, his long legs scissoring in an awkward, staccato way that expressed his agitation. He began suddenly to shout at Benjamin. The old man followed him, pulling at Joseph's too-short jacket.

Suddenly Joseph turned hard and began to stride down the sidewalk toward us where we sat in the car, Benjamin still hurrying beside him, his head raised to look up at Joseph, still pulling at the boy's sleeve. As they came closer we could hear Joseph cursing. He paced wildly, up and down, cursing at the farmer who had assaulted him, raging, using language that must have horrified old Benjamin.

"Joseph, Joseph, nein, nein, remember ... " and Joseph would jerk away, pace in the other direction, still cursing. His voice disturbed the calm of the peaceful little street. The old man began to cry.

He let go of Joseph's sleeve and came to us, standing on the sidewalk close to the open doors of the car.

"I don't know," he said, spreading out his hands helplessly. "I can't ... He is ... " We could see his tears glistening on his beard.

"I'm sorry this happened," I said. "I'm so sorry."

Joseph had stopped cursing and was standing half-way between the truck and our car in a patch of shadow. We could see his chest and hands, but not his face. He said something in German to Benjamin that sounded harsh and angry, a command. Benjamin went to him at once, remonstrating softly with him in German. Joseph turned away again, went back to the van and climbed in, slamming the door. Benjamin stood watching him for a minute, then came back to us.

"We go home now," he said.

Cheryl spoke then, we couldn't see her face in the shadows either, but her voice was softer now, and her question sounded like a child's.

"But ... what happened?" she asked. "Why did Ernie *do* that?"

"He was just drunk," Will said to her.

Benjamin wiped his face with his sleeve, then touched his beard with fingers that still trembled.

"He's neighbour to us," he said. "We help him with his cattle, we help him cut hay ... "

"Well, you certainly shouldn't help him anymore," Cheryl said, angry again.

Ben ignored the interruption.

"At Christmas," Benjamin went on, "we sell him pair of socks. He said they don't match. We tell him, bring them back, we give another pair, but he ... " Ben shrugged. "He still mad."

Will sucked in his breath. Cheryl and I were silent.

"We go to colony," Benjamin said, his voice soft, and he made a gesture toward us with his hands as if to hush us. "Many thanks." He started back to the van, hurrying now, as Joseph roared the motor. We watched him struggle up into it and shut the door. It squealed away from the curb and roared down the silent street. We watched until its tail lights disappeared around the curve that would take it out of town and up into the hills where the colony was.

In the morning Cheryl and Will were up early, packed, and ready to leave for Saskatoon. We were subdued, as though what had happened the night before had affected us out of all proportion to its importance.

"It's a lousy day," I said. A cold wind was blowing and the sky was heavy with deep rain clouds that I knew from experience would hang there all day and yet not shed a drop. Such a hard, dry country, I thought.

"More coffee?" Cheryl asked. Will and I shook our heads, no. "I suppose we should get moving," she said. Will stared moodily out the small kitchen window.

"But the writer wrote about how beautiful it is here in the winter — the hills shining with snow, the sky above them a clear, endless blue ... "

I could hardly speak, such a heaviness had descended on my spirit. I half-wished Palma would burst in with her cheerful scolding. Cheryl had begun to gather the breakfast plates. Now she set them down and spoke directly to me, her blue eyes meeting mine.

"Come with us," she said. "Come with us now. You can come back for your furniture later." We stared at each other. Behind us Will moved.

"No," he said softly.

"Why not?" Cheryl asked him, surprised. But still he didn't speak, gathering his thoughts, or waiting for us to understand something he had already seen.

"You know why," he said to me at last. There was an intensity in his eyes I hadn't seen in years. "He'll stay here," he said to Cheryl.

For no reason that I could name, I had the impression that there was someone else in the room with us. The sensation was so strong that I couldn't stop myself from looking nervously around. Cheryl, seeing this, did too, then looked at me in a puzzled, questioning way.

"What is it?" she asked.

"Someone just walked on my grave," I said. We stood in the kitchen, the three of us, the normally bright room gloomy. "I'm afraid," I said.

"And so you should be," Will said, after a minute, but he was smiling.

I rode with them to the service station a block away and waited while they gassed up.

"I hate to see you go," I said, when the tank was full and Will had paid. Cheryl put both her arms around me and hugged me hard, pulling me tight against her.

"You come and see us whenever you can," she said. When she stepped back to get in the car there were tears in her eyes. Will and I hugged, then stood back.

"Write to me more often," he said, putting one arm around my shoulders.

"Come more often," I said.

Cheryl called through the open window.

"Next time we'll bring Louise with us. You can show her that dinosaur bone." Will went around the car and got in the driver's seat.

"I mean it," Cheryl said.

I watched them drive away as we had watched the Hutterite's van disappear the night before. Then I walked slowly back to the house where my manuscript waited on the table beneath the window that had the view of the hills and the mouth of the coulee where the dinosaurs had walked.

Mermaid in the Watery Deep

When Steven told Joan he was leaving her, he had been very reasonable about it and had spoken to her in a kind way, as if he knew she would be badly hurt and would need all the support he could give her. She felt that after months of coldness or blatant hostility, this new attitude of his wronged her in a way she couldn't put her finger on and that she didn't know how to counteract. She began to react to it with rage, saying every cruel thing she could think of to him, whether true or not, but no matter what she said or how loudly she said it, he maintained his gentle, loving manner and wouldn't respond to her attacks. Then, whenever he tried to talk to her, she would break down in fits of uncontrollable, body-wracking sobbing, and if Steven tried to comfort her, she would pull away, wouldn't let him touch her.

He had moved out by then and after she began to have the attacks of sobbing, he stopped coming around except to pick up their son, Simon. Joan had been at the same time very glad and very hurt by this, but knew she had only herself to blame, because she couldn't seem to be reasonable, as he could, about the separation and the divorce.

Even though she had been dreading the moment when Steven would finally say he was going — she had been expecting it for some time and hoping against all reason that it wouldn't happen — the finality of his decision and his quick departure had lifted a heavy burden from her shoulders that she hadn't been willing to allow she was carrying. She was left off-balance, unaccountably light-feeling and giddy, gay even, since gaiety seemed the only possible translation of this new sensation of weightlessness.

"Free at last," she said to her friends, and hired sitters to look after Simon so she could go out to bars and nightclubs with girl-friends from work who were, one way or another, single too. She met a lot of men this way, some were clearly unsuitable as potential husbands and fathers, having a dark, dangerous side she could readily see hints of in the way they held their mouths, or grasped her wrist too tightly when they asked her to dance so that it hurt, just a little. Some were too young, fun to dance with, but she didn't feel herself connect to them at all, and some, like herself, had been deserted by their spouses and were bitter, careless about details, and given to moments when they stared off into space and lost all interest in the goings-on around them.

As long as all of them, men and women, stayed clustered together around crowded tables in the clubs and drank and danced with each other and laughed together, things worked out fine. But whenever, rarely, Joan went home with one of them, usually a deserted husband, for a couple of hours, their engagement was without tenderness, or had only a peremptory, false and short-lived tenderness. During the act they would be demanding of each other, silent, sometimes cruel, locked stubbornly each in his own struggle in which the other was only an incidental combatant, a stand-in for something or someone who was never present. Yet each of them knew these forays after the clubs had closed, unpleasant as they tended to be, were necessary. It was not just that their bodies required a sex life, as Joan and her girlfriends liked to tell each other during the long Sunday afternoons they spent drinking wine and lazing together while their kids were at their fathers' and new stepmothers'. It wasn't just the physical drive, they said, and then paused and fell silent, looking away from each other with pained, uncertain expressions. But it seemed that each of them, men and women, craved that moment of facing the other sex undisguised, as if there were still something to be learned, the heart of the secret between the sexes not having been plumbed yet.

One day at work as Joan was walking from the lunch room back to her desk in the office she shared with three other secretary-typists, she felt faint. It was as though the air in the large room, ten stories above the sidewalks, had suddenly thickened, as if all the oxygen had been exhausted and she was suffocating.

Dizzy, she put her hand on the wall to steady herself, but the sensation of weakness and an invading blackness like a flood of dark water that she couldn't beat back no matter how hard she tried, began to engulf her. Candy, Charlene and Shirley coming behind her caught her as she tottered and began to fall. They encouraged her with murmurs, and bird-like coos, glancing worriedly at her as they helped her back to her desk.

"You're white as a sheet," Charlene said, peering anxiously into Joan's face. Candy had run to the water cooler as soon as Joan was safely deposited in her chair and now she handed Joan a plastic cup filled with water.

"Here, drink this," she said, first dipping the tips of her fingers into the water and sprinkling it onto Joan's forehead. Joan was still breathing shallowly, trying to get some air, but she managed to sip a little of the water. Its coolness on her tongue and the roof of her mouth shocked and then calmed her, but as soon as the water reached her stomach, a wave of nausea swept through her, making sweat burst out on her forehead. Candy, seeing this, hurriedly kicked the metal wastepaper basket around the corner of Joan's desk, stopping it at Joan's ankles.

"I'm okay now," Joan said, trying not to look in the basket which was full of crumpled paper, pencil shavings and a mushy brown apple core, but her voice was so weak that they could tell she was not okay. Shirley, who was in charge of them, said authoritatively, "You'd better take the rest of the day off."

"I was just like that when I was pregnant," Charlene said, studying Joan's face, then blushed because all of them knew Joan's situation and that a pregnancy would be a disaster too horrible to contemplate.

"No," Joan said, her voice still weak. "I'm having my period," although what was happening was not exactly a period, but only something like one and had come at the wrong time.

"It's probably just the flu," Shirley told her briskly. "I really think you'd better go home and lie down."

"She's still white as a ghost," Candy said. "Maybe one of us should drive you home."

"No, no," Joan said hastily. "I'll just rest a minute and then I'll be able to drive myself."

Slowly the others drifted back to their own desks and in a minute the muted clatter of typewriters rose and Shirley's phone began to ring. Joan rose slowly, covered her typewriter and put her papers away in her desk while the weakness lapped gently at her, threatening to overtake her again. She held it back while she got her coat and left the building.

Steven had moved from their small suburban house straight into a new house in a more prosperous suburb than the one he had lived in with Joan. His new house was nicer too. It belonged to the woman he had left Joan for, Jill Abbott, a childless divor-cée who had received it in her divorce settlement. Joan had never met Jill, had only caught glimpses of her red-gold hair and the blur of her white face as she waited in the car while Steven picked up Simon from what was now Joan's house.

When Steven had suggested, in his new gentle manner, that the three of them meet to talk things over, "Since there is Simon to consider," Joan had been filled with such disgust and shame at the very idea that she had turned away from him and had refused to reply. When Steven saw finally that Joan wouldn't speak at all, would not even look at him, he had gone quietly away. Joan had stood in the living room, back from the window so she couldn't be seen from outside, and had watched Steven walk down the front steps, cross the sidewalk and get into his car where Jill waited in the passenger seat, the place that for eight years had been Joan's, with Simon next to her, between her and Steven.

The long drive into the city from the suburb had grown increasingly irksome. The house no longer felt like home and the disapproving or curious glances of her neighbours upset Joan, she felt her right to be there in that neighbourhood made up of families had vanished with Steven's departure and she had begun to think of moving, although she had no idea where she would go. Then Charlene decided to move in with her boyfriend and suggested Joan should take her place in the house she was moving from.

Charlene lived in a big, old house in the centre of the city with a half-dozen other unmarried people. The four women and two men lived together, to some degree communally, sharing the rent, the housekeeping chores, and the grocery bills. The house was old and nothing worked very well in it, but unless there was a major breakdown such as a blown fuse or a stopped-up toilet, nobody bothered much about its shortcomings. And the household itself was lackadaisical and haphazard, the singleness of the inhabitants and their offhand attitude toward life the only things that held it together. Everybody who lived there was younger than Joan, but Joan found this didn't matter.

Since she had moved to the big house downtown, Steven had kept Simon with him most of the time, disapproving of her living arrangement as suitable for Simon. Joan hadn't argued with Steven about this, had accepted it as something else she deserved because she couldn't get her life together. Secretly she was grateful not to have to cope with Simon when she knew herself to be in transit, although she had no idea to where, if anywhere. And she was deeply ashamed of being glad not to have Simon with her.

Although she felt weak and ill, Joan managed to drive the short distance home by herself. She went inside and downstairs to her room where she lay down on her bed. Mercifully, the house was empty. It would be several hours before anybody else would be home from work.

After a while she stood up carefully and began to undress. At once the dizziness returned, the weakness invaded her body so that lifting her arms was almost more than she could manage and she knew she would pass out if she didn't sit down at once. She finished taking off her sweater and skirt and her pantyhose seated on the side of her bed, standing only long enough to get her jeans and T-shirt from the chair near her bed. When she had put them on, she lay down and closed her eyes.

She could see the weakness behind her eyelids. It was a pale lemon with faint streaks of white in it like cirrus clouds and a hint of rosy pink behind the yellow. She had given up fighting it and now her joints felt as if they had been melted by it, her abdomen was light and empty, she felt unable to find the strength even to lift her hands and the pad between her legs felt rough and hard against the unbearable, new tenderness of her flesh. She lay and thought about the seeping of her blood between her legs and was comforted a little by its presence, even though it was thin and pale with a mauve tinge, and bore no resemblance to the rich, burning blood of menstruation. She had been flowing lightly for several days now and showed no sign of stopping.

When the other residents of the house came home one by one, they drifted down to the kitchen, which was in the basement down the hall from Joan's room.

"I've got the flu," Joan said to Sukie, then Angie, then Sylvie, as each of them passed on by to the kitchen. Rudy stopped a little longer. By dint of his strong personality and his level head, he was the acknowledged leader of the household and whenever there were disputes to be settled or decisions to be made, Rudy's opinion carried the day.

"I never get the flu," he said, and came in to sit down in the chair opposite her bed, stretching out his long legs and crossing them comfortably. Joan pushed her pillows up and moved to a half-reclining position. She experienced a second's dizziness, and saw clearly the edges of a sea of black water licking at her. She held herself very still and it passed. "You're sweating," Rudy remarked, concern in his voice. "Are you nauseous?"

"Oh, no," Joan said, "but I think I'll skip supper." She laughed, a little embarrassed.

"It sure is too bad to get sick right now," he said. "It's spring out there." He twisted his head and looked up at the small window above him where a bluish, late afternoon light entered the room.

"Yeah," she said, although she hadn't even noticed that the long winter was over and that spring had finally come. Now she saw in her mind's eye that the sidewalks were bare of snow and that even the snowbanks on the boulevards had melted down to the last residue of gritty, dirt-encrusted ice. It gave her a shock to think this. Where has my mind been? she wondered. Out loud, she said, "I'll be okay tomorrow."

"Good," Rudy said, as cheerful as if he were a doctor finishing a house call. He stood up and stretched lazily, then went out of the room toward the laughter and good smells that were drifting down the hall from the kitchen.

After supper Yvan stopped in.

"I hear you've got the flu," he said.

"Yeah," she said. "Don't come in or you'll catch it too."

"I was going to ask you to go to a movie with me tonight," he said. "I don't feel like going alone, and nobody else wants to see it."

"Maybe tomorrow night," she said, wishing he would go away so she could sink back into that cloud of weakness that was at once so frightening and so comfortable. He stood watching her for a long moment.

"You don't look too good," he said, his voice soft, an unexpected hint of tenderness in it.

"I bet I'm a mess," she said cheerfully.

The days began to pass and Joan did not get well. Every morning at her usual time for rising she would get up and go to the bathroom, testing herself every step of the way to see if this was the day the weakness wouldn't come and she would be able to go back to her job. Yet every morning she barely made it back to her bed, the weakness sweeping through her, feeling herself being pulled backward or downward toward that black and liquid pool, so that she fell onto the bed on her side, her face half-buried in the sheet, and didn't move until the coolness of the bedclothes revived her somewhat and the imminence of the fainting retreated.

The bleeding continued too, never increasing, never diminishing, its character remaining the same, pale and watery, the thin blood seeping out of her steadily, effortlessly, without even a warning cramp.

Rudy stopped by every day.

"Did I wake you?" he would ask.

"No," Joan always said, and frowned, because time passed and she never knew if she had been awake or asleep, although she suspected that sometimes she slept even if she had no memory of doing so.

"I brought you a radio," Rudy said. "I don't know why I didn't think of it before." She recognized the small black radio that was kept on a shelf above the stove in the kitchen. He set it down on her night table and bent to plug it in.

"Thanks," she said, knowing she would never even turn it on. He straightened and looked down at her.

"Are you still bleeding?" He asked her this without any embarrassment and she was not embarrassed by his question. When he had asked her to describe her symptoms, she had told him all of them. Rudy had that effect on her. Or perhaps it was the illness itself which sapped her energy so that she found it impossible to muster the strength for subtlety. She lifted her hand and gave a small, noncommittal wave, dismissing his question.

"I don't know why you won't go to the doctor," he said. "It must be ten days now."

Joan had once had a friend who, when her husband was caught stealing from the till at work, had started to bleed and didn't stop for six weeks. Finally the friend had gone to an emergency ward and the doctor there had told her, "There's nothing wrong with you that I can see, and you can bleed just as well at home as here," and had sent her away.

"It'll stop," Joan said, not looking at him. "I just have to lie here till it decides to stop."

Rudy continued to stand close to her bed looking down on her. He was a man, she thought, who sought simple solutions. She could see he was baffled by her refusal to take action.

"Call the doctor today," he said. "You can't go on like this forever. Do you still faint when you stand up?"

"I don't faint," she corrected him. "I almost faint. I've never fainted in my entire life." He looked down at her for a few seconds longer, smiling a puzzled smile, then went slowly out of the room. Joan could imagine the contingency plans involving ambulances and emergency wards, going through his head.

None of the women who lived in the house came into her room. They were all younger than she was and none of them had been married yet. They rushed in and out, disappeared for days at a time, called into her from the doorway as they passed by, as if her disease were catching and they were afraid of getting too close. Joan didn't blame them. She felt humble in their presence, believing herself in their certainty that they would never screw things up as badly as Joan had, and understanding that they were afraid to get too close to her for fear her failure would rub off on them.

"Still living," she would reply gaily to their quick inquiries called in through the open door. "I'm getting up tomorrow."

Most nights she had nightmares that woke her and that frightened her so badly she would turn on the overhead light, the bedside lamp was not bright enough to erase the dream, and would lie the rest of the night with it glaring down on her. In her dreams over and over again she was in a white hospital bed and Steven, who in real life had never laid a finger on her, had never even threatened to, was banging on her door, coming in to kill her, and the dream was such that his breaking it down and her death at his hands were inevitable, and only seconds away. Every time, just before the door burst open she would wake, find herself sitting up in bed, her nightgown wet, gasping for air as if she were drowning, her heart pounding so hard in her chest that it prevented her from swallowing.

Then she would stagger out of bed, fumble in the dark for the wall switch and flood the room with light. Blinded and beginning to faint again, she would fall back on her damp bed before the swirling, dark water that was always there sucking at the edges of her consciousness, dragged her under.

Every afternoon in the silence of the big house, when everyone was gone and a few stunted rays of afternoon sun shone through her high basement window, Joan got up, washed, dressed, and walked around the house. Sometimes she went outside and sat on the steps or walked a few feet down the sidewalk and back again. Once she felt so well that she walked all the way to a nearby shopping mall, going slowly, enjoying the sunshine and rejoicing in the feeling that her weakness and fainting had gone away for good. But by the time she arrived at the mall it had returned and she had been lucky to find a taxi waiting at the entrance to the grocery store, its driver only too glad to find a customer not laden with groceries he would have to help carry. It whisked her back to the big house in minutes, and she stumbled down the stairs and fell onto her bed just before the water closed over her head.

Then she wondered if she would ever go back to her job, ever see Simon again, ever do any of the ordinary, simple things that people did. Every day she imagined herself going to the nearest emergency ward, as in Rudy's plans, and saying, "I'm done for, I can't go on anymore, please take care of me," but her humiliation at what she had come to was too great even to phone a doctor.

Yvan said to her, "You can't keep on bleeding forever, you know. You should go to the hospital." Joan thought it interesting how her steady bleeding worried the men of the house so much. "How long are you planning to go on in this way?" he asked, sitting on the side of her bed, holding her hand and stroking it gently.

"It'll stop," she said, bored with the repeated question.

"Do you need anything?" She shook her head. "I brought you a glass of water." She glanced at it standing on her bedside table next to her bottle of tranquilizers and her bottle of sleeping pills that she had gotten prescriptions for before Steven left, when things had been so bad.

"Thanks."

"Let me get you some aspirins," he said, standing up. She shook her head, made an effort to speak to him feeling his kindness and sympathy made her owe him an explanation.

"It isn't ... real, you know." She was looking at the ceiling when she said this and not at him. He said nothing, but his silences were so full of acceptance of what she might say that she felt free to try to put into words the vague ideas that were floating around in her brain. "It's like this thing that's happening to me, the bleeding, like it isn't ... " She hesitated, searching for the word she meant. "Real," she repeated lamely.

Yvan cleared his throat gently.

"What do you mean?" he asked tentatively, softly inviting her to try again. Tears had begun to run out of her eyes and to slide down the sides of her face.

"I don't know," she said. "Lying here sometimes I start to get a different feeling. It's like ... " She lifted her hand aimlessly, then wiped one side of her face. "I get to feeling so light. It's like I don't really have a body anymore. And then I can sort of see that ... this isn't real blood." The last came out plaintively and she put her hand over her eyes, then took it away again.

Yvan was looking downward at the rug. He had his hands in the pockets of his jacket and she saw for the first time the lines in his forehead showing that he had suffered too and making him look much older than she knew he was. She found herself wanting to tell him about the black ocean that threatened her, but looking closely at him, she thought she saw a hint of it lurking in his eyes. After a pause he drew in an audible breath, then slowly turned and went out of the room without looking at her again.

Years and years later when she had come to a time in her life when she fully expected another period and one didn't come, never came again, she would look back on this terrible time, remembering it almost fondly. And she would remember how she had not been frightened because the blood, which eventually stopped as she had known it would, had been so thin and pale and had seeped out of her slowly, as blood seeps out of a wound.

That night she dreamed she was murdering Steven, hitting and hitting him with a rock until he turned into a huge crab-like creature and scuttled away from her. She woke frightened and filled with self-loathing and horror that she might, even if only in her dreams, be a murderer.

Yvan stopped in each morning and every evening.

One night she said to him, "I'm afraid it may be real blood after all." It was evening and the small piece of sky she could see through her window was a soft, dusky blue. She could hear children's voices on the sidewalk in front of the house and upstairs in the living room above her head two of the women were dancing together to a song she had often danced to in the nightclubs. They shouted and banged into furniture and stamped their feet.

Yvan sat in the chair next to her bed and watched her with his brown eyes. Under his gaze she felt thinner and paler and the black water drew closer. She was afraid that the sea of blackness lapping at her would engulf her if she let go for only an instant. Already she felt it sucking at her limbs, kept turning her face away from it to breathe better. She closed her eyes, then opened them in time to see Yvan disappearing out her door. She closed her eyes again and for some reason, a picture of her first serious boyfriend from almost ten years before popped up behind her eyelids.

He had been everything she had ever hoped to find in a man. He was very handsome with curly black hair and green eyes and wide shoulders of an athlete, and he was well-educated and filled with ambition too. He asked her out, she went with him, and the first time she kissed him she knew she was in love with him. She knew too, from the first moment he kissed her, that he would leave her. She never wavered in this surprising conviction, she never expected the outcome to change, she even asked him on their second or third date if he would tell her when he was finished with her so that she wouldn't go through the agony of waiting week after week for him to call.

One night, after about a year of dating, he came to her and told her that he had accepted a job in another city, that he would be leaving soon, and that he would not be taking her with him. Sadly, she accepted this, neither arguing nor complaining. After he had said good-bye to her, she went home and didn't even cry.

About ten o'clock Joan was lying in her bed in the darkness, the light from the hall reaching only halfway into the room, falling short of the foot of her bed, when Yvan returned. He was carrying something bulky in his arms. He threw it on the floor a few feet away from her bed and she realized it was a sleeping bag. He took off his shirt and pulled off his jeans. Then he crossed the room in his underwear and socks and shut the door, blocking out the light. See heard him pad softly back to his sleeping bag and get into it.

The rest of the house had grown silent, its inhabitants either out somewhere, or sleeping, or too far away for their voices to be heard in this basement room. For a long time now Joan had been able to smell everything. Odours came to her like the blossoming of a flower, with a distinct shape, the petals of scent thinning out if they were further away. If she had chosen, she knew, she could follow scents like a dog. She heard Yvan strike a match on his sleeping bag's zipper and smelled the sulphur and then the smoke. She could smell Yvan's distinct scent too, beyond the odour of cigarettes, she could even smell a hint of pine coming from his sleeping bag.

After a while she heard him fumbling for an ashtray, then crushing out his cigarette in it. He settled back into his sleeping bag.

"Good-night," he said softly to her.

"Good-night."

The room was very dark, there was no light at all coming from the window and someone must have turned off the hall light for the yellow spears around her door had disappeared, leaving only a smooth wall of black. She forgot about Yvan's presence in the room, or rather, his presence grew large, an amorphous blackness that swelled and blended with the blackness of the room.

After a while she saw a shape forming in front of her eyes, appearing so bright against the black that its outline seemed to sizzle. The image was vivid pink, it was her bottle of sleeping pills enlarged and hovering in the air before her. She stared at it, noticing the disordered way the capsules fell, this way and that, inside the bottle. Then a purple line, perfectly straight and horizontal, appeared across the full bottle, two-thirds of the way down. In an instant the image vanished, leaving an after-image which melted slowly away.

This was not the first vision Joan had ever had. She had never told anyone about the others and in fact, was never sure herself that 'vision' was the right word to describe them, but there were moments when she saw things that weren't there, clearly, before her, things that told her in one precise picture, something she hadn't known before.

"Yvan?" she said.

"Yes?" he answered at once so she knew he hadn't been

asleep. She told him what had just happened.

"Yes," he said again, more slowly this time, with a hesitant air, but no surprise.

"I'm not going to take them," she said.

"Good," he said, and she knew then that his presence this night was not a whim of his, and never an accident, that he had indeed come to be with her, knowing she needed him.

Now she wondered if it was true that we choose our own lives, that we ourselves make them what they are. She wondered why it was that she had been so inarguably convinced from the moment she kissed her first boyfriend that he would leave her. She wondered too, if she had expected instead that she would have him forever, if that is what would have happened. Then she would never have married Steven, who had left her and nearly killed her. Or was it that the various things that happened in her life in what seemed a helter skelter, random way, were really part of a plan, designed to bring her to the breaking point? But what the ultimate reason for this might be, the changing of her, Joan, into a different person than the one she had started out as, she couldn't fathom.

One night, she was never able to remember if it had been the same night or a night or even two nights later, she woke and recalled that she had just had an ordinary dream, a dream about nothing in particular, a silly dream. She thought idly, as she prepared to throw back the covers, last night I had an ordinary dream. I must be getting better. The thought arrested any movement. What? she thought. What was that? I had an ordinary dream, I must be getting better. And she had laughed a startled laugh and, carried on it, got out of bed. The next day she went back to work.

Years later when she remembered this time in her life she knew that it had been a pivotal time. She remembered the vision which had told her clearly and finally how many pills she would take and that they wouldn't be enough to kill her, and she remembered how Yvan had come and slept in her room that night. She wondered how he knew that that was the night she would need him, and if his act of kindness had made any difference or not. She thought it must have, though she didn't see how, and she supposed she owed Yvan, who had somehow slipped out of her reach, her life.

The weakness, the sensation of struggling not to be drawn down into the blackness, into the bottomless depths of that dark, watery sea, she remembered only in dreams now and then. The weakness never returned, and the water in her dreams grew less black, eventually took on a greenish hue, there were even times when it was aquamarine and perfectly clear. But she sometimes saw in her dreams as she swam — yes, miracle of miracles, she swam, a mermaid now in this endlessly deep water — she sometimes saw far below her a shadow, the monstrous dark bulk of a huge sea creature, gliding effortlessly in the deep below her body.

The Metric System

At night the birds kept up a steady barrage of sound, a blending of all their whistles, chirps, cheeps, and trills, the volume of which swelled or diminished according to how many sparrows, wrens or swallows joined in or paused. Charlotte had never paid much attention to them before, but this summer she found herself lying in bed listening to them as the long northern twilight dragged on into the early northern dawn. She slept lightly, only now and then, and it seemed to her that it was never wholly dark and they were never wholly silent.

She lay and listened, naming each bird to herself as she picked out its sound: red-winged blackbird, magpie, robin, sometimes even the cry of a high-flying hawk or a night owl. With their house on the edge of the village, they heard many of the sounds people on farms in the country heard. The naming of the birds that sang soothed her: the pair of swallows swooping to their mud nest in the eaves above the kitchen window, the robin on the night-blue back lawn, the red-winged blackbird on the back fence, the hawk over Dave Traub's wheatfield that began a few feet past the fence. As long as they sang their voices gave shape to the night.

Cindy had moved out. She had stuffed her jeans, a few shirts and a dozen of her favourite tapes into her backpack one night when Charlotte and Jerry, Lyle and Dougie were eating supper in the kitchen and she had walked out.

"Bye," she had said, as if she were going to the schoolyard for softball practice. Jerry's shout just before she shut the door, "If you go, don't come back!" had had no effect on her. It was as if she hadn't heard him, or he had said merely, "Take the garbage on your way out," as he usually did to any of their three children as they went out the back door.

Stricken as Charlotte was, as new and unaccountable as all this was to her in what she knew to be her simple and ordinary life, although of course, it had never felt simple and ordinary to her, but satisfying and right, magical even, in what had seemed increasingly to be its pre-ordination, she suddenly knew that what Jerry had said was a cliché, it was banal, and even more dumfounding, she had found herself wanting to laugh.

She had stopped herself only by clapping her hand over her mouth in what she knew too was a reasonable gesture under the circumstances; the circumstances being that Cindy was fifteen and had gone across town to live with her seventeen-year-old boyfriend, Rick, in the old shack he was squatting in next to the railroad tracks that no trains ever rolled down anymore. And neither of them had jobs or went to school. Charlotte didn't know how they would survive.

After Cindy left, Jerry began to watch the Iran-Contra hearings on television. Because of his business, he was the local insurance agent, he felt he couldn't afford to be political, so he had always been involved with politics as he had once remarked to her, on an informal level, behind the scenes, which meant he would talk politics only on weekend evenings when they had a few friends in for drinks downstairs in their family room. And then only in careful, mild generalities.

But now he was watching the hearings as if they were profoundly important to their lives in this prairie village far from that city in the United States that they had never seen. When finally Oliver North had come to the witness table, Jerry had stayed home from his office to watch, leaving the business to his assistant for what Charlotte had at first assumed would be only a half-day or so. But his presence at home on weekdays was so unusual, so inexplicable, that it was as it might have been if he had suddenly been taken seriously ill, and to Charlotte, the house felt weighted with danger.

The first morning he had stayed home Charlotte had followed him as he wandered, carrying his coffee cup, into the dim living room where she had pulled the curtains to keep out the heat. He bent and turned on the TV set.

"Aren't you going to work?" she had asked, surprised. He was wearing a short-sleeved summer shirt, a tie, dress slacks, the clothes he always wore to his office in the summer. Jerry sat, balancing his coffee mug on the palm of one hand, the finger of the other hooked through the handle, not taking his eyes off the screen where Lieutenant-Colonel North's pleasant face sprang from dot to screensize.

"They're trying to find out if President Reagan knew about what they were up to with the Contras. If he was the one who ordered it," he said.

"The who?" Charlotte asked, still disapproving, not quite believing he really would stay home. "Ordered what?" Jerry used the remote control to increase the volume. Colonel North was leaning forward staring at his questioner. Were there tears in his eyes?

"I hate lying, Counsel," he said.

"But," Charlotte said, raising her voice to be heard over North's earnest, steady one, "we're Canadians. What's it got to do with us?" Jerry still hadn't looked at her. He set his coffee cup on the arm of his chair and with a gesture so familiar to her she hardly saw it, or rather, saw it for the first time in years, he used both hands to gently and carefully resettle his glasses over his ears.

Into the silence where Jerry's explanation should have been, North said, "That's why the government of the U.S. gave me a shredder." Jerry laughed.

"I can't figure this guy out. Either he's completely crazy or he's exactly what he says he is." But he was sipping his coffee, his eyes still on the screen, and slowly his face was settling into that expression of silent and pained bewilderment he had been wearing lately. She couldn't remember when she had first noticed it, but uncertainty on Jerry's face disturbed Charlotte so deeply that she had gone back to the kitchen so she wouldn't have to look at it.

Every day now the murmur of the TV set provided unwelcome background as she put the dishes in the dishwasher, a casserole in the oven for lunch, tidied the kitchen, and swept the floor. She took a cup of coffee outside into the back yard as soon as she could, so she wouldn't have to listen to the faint voices coming from the living room. This morning, as she unfolded a lawn chair and set it in the shade, she realized she had gone out forgetting to first pour herself a cup of coffee, but she couldn't be bothered to go back in. She could see Doug, her youngest child, and a couple of his friends with their bikes in the back lane two doors down. Their piping boy's voices blended peacefully with the chatter of the birds in the trees in the back yards.

Ten o'clock and sweltering already. It must be ninety, she thought. Charlotte had paid no attention when the country had converted to metric and now her children spoke a different language than she did when it came to degrees and weight, volume and distance. Rather than trying to convert the children, a hopeless job, she felt, with the school and the government against her, and unable to feel the new system had anything to do with her, she had not learned it, she had instead fallen silent when it came to the measurement of things.

On the other side of the white picket fence, Dave Traub's field of spring wheat was soughing gently in the light breeze, a mottled green and gold as it slowly ripened in the dazzling light. A pair of robins were hopping through the spray from the sprinkler Lyle had set up for her on his way to his summer job at the grocery store. Noisy birds, robins, Charlotte thought. Their rusty breasts were puffed out and shiny and it seemed to her that their hops were heavy with a bright-eyed, knowing smugness. The swallows that were nesting under the eaves swooped away in unison like a pair of stunt flyers and perched on the back fence above the peonies to scold her for disturbing them.

Gradually, over the other chirps, warbles and trills coming from the maples and poplars that lined the back yard, she heard a bird song she didn't recognize. It was a penetrating call, something like the coo of a dove, but harsher, and the coo was interspersed with a couple of quick, rhythmic chirps. It can't be a pigeon, she thought. Pigeons don't chirp. I'll have to ask Jerry. Jerry was the village's scoutmaster, he knew quite a lot about birds and their calls. She stared upward trying to find the bird that was making the strange call, but no matter how she craned her neck and turned her head this way and that, she couldn't see which bird it was, through the clusters of big, shiny leaves. After a while it fell silent and she gave up trying to see it. She wished again that she had brought out a cup of coffee, but still didn't move to go and get one.

Cindy had been gone since the day after Jerry had locked her in her room. Before that she had been gone for two days and had only come home, (Charlotte actually had no idea why she had come home, maybe to have a bath), and Jerry had shouted at her, had almost struck her in the face, but had restrained himself at the last second, contenting himself with catching her pink cotton blouse in each hand. Charlotte could see his hands in perfect, microscopic detail still, she could see Cindy turning away from him, indifferent to his suddenly exploding rage, he had run at her and caught her shirt, bunching it over her shoulders in each fist and had half-dragged, half-pushed her up the stairs to her room and shoved her in. It was a wonder, Charlotte thought now, looking up again into the tree, that the blouse hadn't torn or all the buttons popped off. Or did that blouse have buttons?

Cindy hadn't screamed. She hadn't made any noise. The only sounds in the house were the scuffling on the stairs, Jerry's panting, Dougie's sobbing downstairs in the doorway between the kitchen and the living room. Lyle and Charlotte had stood side by side and Charlotte knew, when she saw how white Lyle's face was, that her face was too. It was a characteristic of her family, the Pratt's, to go white-faced when ill or frightened or even angry, and Lyle was the child most like her.

Charlotte had stood at the bottom watching her husband wrestle her unresisting daughter up the stairs. She had found herself wanting to run up the stairs and kick Cindy, she had wanted to slap her till she cried and begged for mercy. She had wanted to cut off all Cindy's perfect blonde hair. It seemed to her now that she ought to feel terrible for thinking such things about her only daughter, no matter what and even if it was only for an instant, but she didn't. Or at least, she didn't think she did. Cindy hadn't even looked at Charlotte, hadn't called to her for help.

When Charlotte lowered her eyes from the trees she was startled to see Jerry standing beside her looking out to the wheat field, still wearing that expression of pained bewilderment that she disliked so much

"They had no authorization from Congress and they didn't report to Congress," he said. "They even planned to set up a secret government." After a moment he pulled up another lawn chair and sat beside her. "They're taking a recess right now," he said. "I didn't know it was so hot outside."

"I don't know how you can stand the heat in the living room," she replied. "If you must watch, you should watch on the set in the basement."

"They thought they had no accountability to anybody but themselves," he went on. "How could they have thought that. The United States is supposed to be a democracy."

"Listen!" Charlotte said. The strange bird had begun to sing again, a double coo, a couple of chirps, then the coo again. "What is that?"

"He keeps calling himself Ollie North," Jerry said. "Not 'I' or 'me,' just 'Ollie North.' There's something wrong with that, don't you think?"

"Can you hear it? It's not a pigeon, and we don't get doves here — does that sound like a dove to you? I've never heard one."

"He's drinking something that looks like a coke. Beside him, at his witness table. Everybody else has water, but he's got a coke. Or maybe it's iced tea. I never thought of that. I bet it's iced tea."

The high-pitched, cheerful voices of Doug and his friends were coming closer down the lane.

"I'm going to get a drink of water," Doug called. The other boys rode on by without stopping while Doug dropped his bike against the fence with a thump and came through the gate, leaving it open. Charlotte waited for Jerry to tell him to close it, but Jerry said nothing. Doug approached them, then stopped a couple of feet away.

"You should have on a cap," Charlotte said to him. "It must be close to ninety."

"You mean about thirty-five, Mom," he said. "You always get it wrong." Charlotte lifted her head again to look up through the branches of the tree behind her. Perhaps she would catch the bird unaware and would see it then. "I saw Cindy this morning," Doug said. Jerry swung his head to Doug from where he had been staring at Dave's wheat across the fence and Charlotte brought her eyes down from the leafy branches above her. "We were playing on the school grounds and she walked by with Rick." He waited, looking only at Charlotte.

"Oh," she said.

"She asked us what we were playing." He studied Charlotte, his small forehead creased in a frown. He looks like a little old man, she thought and she reached for him, but he stepped back, away from her arms. "I asked her when she was coming home," he said. He sounded angry. Perhaps he was about to cry, but no, he smoothed his forehead instead and lifted his chin. Beside her, Jerry hadn't moved. "I hate that Rick," Doug said.

"Did she say anything?" Charlotte asked.

"She just laughed." He scratched a mosquito bite on his arm. His hair above his ears was damp with sweat and plastered to his skin in little curls. "I want her to come home," he said, and swung his leg to kick at the grass.

"Don't," Charlotte said.

After he had thrust the chair he took from the bathroom under Cindy's doorknob, the room had no lock, Jerry had come downstairs, his face grim, but taking the steps evenly, the way he always did. He had come into the kitchen, but instead of sitting in his chair, he had stood facing the fridge, leaning on it so that his forehead touched the fridge door, high up, near the top.

"My own daughter," he said. "A whore." Frightened, Charlotte had said quickly, "Not in front of the boys, Jerry." She wanted him to sit down, she couldn't stand the way he was leaning against the fridge, but he had ignored her. He had stood like that for a long time while Charlotte, Doug and Lyle sat at the supper table beside him, and Charlotte could feel the cool metal of the fridge door against her own forehead and it had begun to ache. Lyle stood finally and plucked his cap from where he had hung it on the back of his chair.

"I'm going to ball practice," he had said, mumbling, so that it took Charlotte a moment to understand. Then Jerry had taken down his arm and sat at the table across from Charlotte with Doug, who had stopped crying, at his usual place between them.

"McFarlane is coming back to the stand later," Jerry said, rising and folding his lawn chair. "I don't want to miss it." He set the lawn chair against the house, then went back inside. Doug said, "Can I have some Kool-Aid?"

"In the fridge," Charlotte said. "Don't make a mess." But he was gone, running across the lawn and up the steps into the house. The screen door slammed shut behind him.

Then Jerry had called the Mountie. Art was his name and he was a friend of theirs, at least he and his wife had drinks with them and their other friends on weekend evenings in one basement or another while the kids of the house giggled and thumped around on the main floor until their hostess ran up the stairs with an exasperated expression and overhead there was an abrupt silence. Art had come over without his wife and he and Jerry had sat in the basement family room each with a glass of beer while Charlotte had sat outside in the cool shadows under the trees, looking out over the back fence and Dave's wheat field to the birds silhouetted against the luminescent evening sky, and listening to their calls. Vaguely she had heard the front door shut and knew Art had gone home. In a minute Jerry had come to sit beside her. Had she heard the strange bird that night for the first time? She couldn't remember anymore.

"What did he say?" she asked finally when Jerry didn't speak. He sighed. "He said he could go and get her, bring her home, if we tell him to. He said he could evict the kid from that shack. It doesn't belong to him. It belongs to the town, it went back for taxes." The birds had set up that steady, rolling chirp that they always did just before they settled down for the night, when all their songs evened out and you could no longer tell one from the other. Otherwise, the evening was as still as it would have been if they were the only family in the village.

"What did you tell him?"

"I told him no." Even though the sky still glowed with light out over the field, resonant blue over shadowed gold, it was quite dark under the trees and Charlotte could make out Jerry only as an indistinct shadow where he sat a couple of feet away. She was comforted by the darkness under the trees.

"Why?" she asked, surprised. She had been prepared for more shouting, or for more silent violence.

"What's the use? Art's had experience with this kind of thing. He said, 'You bring 'em home and they just run away again.' He said we'd just drive her farther away. At least if she stays in town we can keep an eye on her. Know if she gets into serious trouble."

Charlotte had tried to imagine what serious trouble might be. Drugs, she thought. Or maybe Rick would be cruel to her, beat her up. After all, Rick was a stranger to them, had come from another town. Or she might get pregnant. She would be sixteen in the fall, if she got pregnant maybe they would get married. Married and pregnant. One child after another, no education, a useless husband. She tried to picture Cindy gone fat and slovenly. I must have done something wrong, she pointed out to herself. Somehow or other this has to be my fault.

"What about school?" she asked. "Legally, she has to be in school."

"It's no use," Jerry said. "She's almost sixteen. No social worker is going to waste energy on her. She's too old, there's too many of them. There's thousands of incorrigible teens out there that nobody can do anything about."

Dougie came past her again. He hurried the length of the yard to the open gate and jumped on his bike.

"I'm going to the playground," he called and was gone, his bike tires grating on the gravelled lane.

The next morning Jerry was up earlier than usual.

"Poindexter takes the stand today," he told her. "This is critical." He dressed neatly in his good grey slacks, his grey and blue-striped shirt and his blue tie. She lay in their bed and watched him as he set his glasses carefully on his nose, arranging the arms along his temples and hooking them over his ears. He looks like *he's* going to court, she thought, and laughed to herself. "Aren't you getting up?" he asked, turning to frown at her.

She almost said, if you don't go to work, why should I get up? but the implications of this frightened her, she had a glimpse of their neatly arranged world sliding that easily into chaos, so she pushed back the covers and was on her feet reaching for her dressing gown.

Later in the morning, although she didn't want to, Charlotte felt herself reluctantly drawn into the living room. The sun had moved around to face the front of the house so that its light shining through the gold-coloured curtains had a warm yellow glow that was faintly eerie. Jerry was leaning forward in his arm-chair, his eyes on the TV set where a roomful of people, mostly men, were listening in silence to a droning male voice. She thought of going back out again without speaking, but it seemed that to do this would be to lend the whole business — Jerry's not going to work, the steady, unending murmur of the tv set, the new heaviness in the house — a seriousness she was struggling not to allow it.

"What's going on?" she asked finally, casually.

Jerry didn't answer. After a moment, while she still stood beside him staring at the top of his faintly greying head, a pair of commentators appeared on the screen where the hearing room had been. Jerry leaned back, not so much sighing as exhaling pent-up air. Then he rose slowly, stiffly, and stretched.

"You know," he said, tucking his shirt more carefully into his slacks, "North says there was a fall guy plan — that North would be the scapegoat to save whoever higher up was giving the orders, but Poindexter says there was no such thing, that he would tell the truth and accept the responsibility for whatever he did." He peered into her face and she looked back at him, non-plussed by the intensity of his gaze.

"Oh," she said.

"What I can't figure out is how we're supposed to tell now if this is the fall guy plan in action — to deny there was a fall guy plan — or if there really wasn't a fall guy plan at all, like

Poindexter says." Charlotte hesitated a second.

"I see," she said.

"The point is," Jerry went on, "he seems so honest, but he's lied to everybody: to General Secord, to the Iranians, to Congress. How do you tell if he's telling the truth now or lying again?" Charlotte screwed up her face, just a little, and looked into the distance over his shoulder.

"I don't know," she said finally. She turned quickly and went out of the living room into the kitchen, conscious that Jerry had followed her, but pretending she didn't know he was there. She poured herself a cup of coffee and went outside into the back yard where she sat down on the lawn chair. Jerry came behind her and sat down too. To her relief, he didn't speak, but sat staring out across the sun-and-shadow dappled yard to where the robins were searching for insects in the flowerbed under the back fence. Faintly, through the steady chatter of the birds in the trees, Charlotte thought she heard the strange bird's call again.

"Listen," she said, her voice hushed. "There it is again. What is it?"

"What?" Jerry asked.

"Shhh," Charlotte said, leaning forward in her chair. "Hear that? That *coo-coo chirpety-chirp*." She tried to imitate the bird's call.

"I don't hear it," Jerry said.

"You're not listening!" Charlotte said, angry suddenly. "There!" The call was picking up volume, it rose clearly above the cascade of sound from the trees, a harsher noise. It must be a big bird, Charlotte thought, bigger than a starling or a robin. She wondered why she couldn't see it.

"Oh, that," Jerry said. "I don't know."

"You're supposed to know!" Charlotte said, outraged. "You're the scout-master here! You're the one with the bird books!" Jerry turned to her, his eyes furious behind his glasses.

"Well, I don't know! Why are you bugging me? You're always bugging me about something!" He stood abruptly, anger in every line of his body, and strode away so quickly that his chair toppled over, back into the house, letting the door slam behind him.

Charlotte didn't move, but her hands had begun to tremble

so violently that she spilled her coffee. Carefully she set her dripping cup on the damp grass beside her chair. She clenched her hands into fists, rested them on her lap and forced herself to take slow, deep breaths, the way she had been taught to do when she was in labour. The robins had flown away into the safety of the tops of the Manitoba maples. She closed her eyes and kept taking slow, deep breaths and exhaling gently.

Cindy hadn't explained. She hadn't said anything. She had simply done what she had wanted to do, and ignored everything Charlotte and Jerry had said or done to stop her.

"But why?" Charlotte had pleaded. "Haven't we been good to you? I never took a job, I was always at home looking after you. Your dad never hit you, not once, none of you. You had everything you wanted, that you needed, that we could afford ... "

Cindy had smiled faintly at her, a knowing smile, her small mouth barely curving, her blue eyes deep with knowledge Charlotte didn't have.

"You're fifteen years old," Charlotte said, suddenly conscious that she had said this before and before that, and that now she no longer knew if it was relevant or not. Other sentences rolled around in her head — *how could you do this to us, I guess you'll have to learn the hard way* — but, familiar and natural as they were on her tongue, she didn't say them again. There was a new language to be spoken here, but she didn't know it, the sounds moved around inside her, would not form themselves into words no matter how she strained.

Slowly, as the deep breathing began to take effect and her heart stopped its flutter in her throat, Charlotte became aware that the bird was no longer singing, that it must have flown away. She was torn between wanting to know what it was, where it had come from, what it looked like, and being glad that it had gone. Good riddance, she thought to herself, and then said it out loud, "Good riddance."

Dougie was late for lunch. Lyle had come hurrying in from the grocery store, had washed his hands quickly and then sat down and reached for the casserole in one movement. At seventeen he was always hungry. Jerry sat across from Charlotte eating methodically, neatly, and in silence. When Lyle had finished serving himself, Jerry said, "What I can't understand is how President Reagan could go on making speeches and Nancy wearing those fancy dresses to dinner with famous people and behind it all, this guy North and Poindexter were running their own show and changing the way things happened in the world."

They heard Doug's bike hit the cement patch at the back door with the crash that no amount of scolding seemed to cure him of and then his sneakers on the steps. He rushed into the kitchen, letting the door slam. Jerry looked up, but before he could speak, if he had been going to, Doug said, panting, to Charlotte, "we're having a 20 K bike-a-thon at the playground tomorrow. Will you guys sponsor me?"

"What's 20 K?" Charlotte asked, smiling at him. Doug took a step closer to her, as though proximity might help her to understand

"Kilometres," Lyle said, his mouth full, lifting his glass of milk.

"Isn't that an awfully long bike ride for somebody only ten?" Charlotte said dubiously, "and in this heat."

"Oh, Mom!" Doug said, angry. "It is not!" He was close to tears. "Please?"

"Well, how far is it then?" Charlotte asked. She reached for the salad.

She wanted to tell him to wash his hands and sit down, but he came even closer to her, so that his small, tense face was looking directly into hers and she had to look back at him. The muscles around his mouth and in his neck were taut with the effort to persuade her.

"Why don't you ever know when I say things like that! It's metric! Everybody knows what 20 K is but you guys!" Even his fists were clenched. Startled, Charlotte looked to Jerry to scold him for raising his voice to his mother.

But Jerry was watching Doug intently, seriously, with the same expression on his face he wore when he was watching the Iran-Contra hearings. It was as if he believed if he listened and watched carefully enough, he might finally come to understand something important, something that troubled him deeply, some puzzle that Charlotte had not stumbled on. Carefully, not seeming to notice he was doing it, he readjusted his glasses delicately, using both clean, white-fingered hands.

Lyle said, giving her that same faintly amused, knowing smile Cindy had given her, "Twenty kilometres is about twelve miles, Mom. It's not too much for him. He can make it." He turned to his little brother. "Can't you, buddy." Doug, seeming to know he had won, broke into a smile, then, without being told, hurried away to wash his hands.

Lyle set down his empty glass.

"If I hurry I can get in a swim at the pool before I have to go back to work." He was already pushing back his chair.

"You haven't had dessert," Charlotte remarked, from habit.

"Save it for me," Lyle said. He hurried out of the kitchen. Charlotte and Jerry could hear him thumping up the stairs and almost immediately back down again. He came into the kitchen zipping up his gym bag, went to the back door and paused, his hand holding it open a fraction. He turned back to Charlotte. "The metric system's easy, Mom," he said. "I could teach it to you in a minute." Charlotte moved her eyes from Lyle's across the table to Jerry whose head was lowered silently over his plate as if he were praying. She wished he would speak, or at least look up, let his eyes meet hers, but he remained like that, contemplating something she couldn't see.

Lyle waited a few seconds longer, then, when Charlotte still didn't reply, he went out, shutting the door gently behind him.

Gabriel

All day the smoke had billowed upward into the even blue of the sky to the north. Flare-off from an oil well, Gabe had told his wife, but secretly doubted it. The smoke was not black enough, and lacked the purposeful skyward lunge. It must have been buildings burning, but he didn't tell Frannie this, who wasn't well, hadn't been ever since the miscarriage in the early spring. Now she was lying down in the living room with the curtains pulled shut to keep out the light and the TV set turned on, but without sound. The bright pictures themselves reminded him of fire, the way they flickered, vanishing to reappear in a different form.

He squatted on his heels on the bare ground in front of his machinery shed and squinted through the heat waves toward the house where there was no sign of life. He could summerfallow, he supposed, and gave a wry laugh at his own folly. It was too dry, and if there was no crop to speak of, there sure as hell weren't any weeds either. Besides, the way things were going even if there were weeds, he couldn't afford the fuel for his tractor to go over them. He rose reluctantly, stiffly, and trying to avoid stepping on the few patches of grass left, he went through the powdery dust of the yard to the house.

Just as he opened the screen door he heard a loud hammering

on the roof. It seemed to come from above the bedrooms at the opposite end of the house.

"What was that?" Frannie said. She stood stock still in the centre of the kitchen holding a steaming cup. The kettle on the stove behind her was still hissing. He thought, *tea in this heat?* but said as casually as he could manage, "Oh, God knows. Probably the wind ripping off a few more shingles." She stared at him, her eyes big and dark in the white oval of her face, then went on to the table where she set down her cup, pulled out a chair, and sat down.

"I thought you said it isn't windy today," she said in a low voice.

"A little gusty," he said, although it was the only quiet day in weeks, at first a blessed relief from the incessant wind and then disconcerting, eerie.

"Want some tea?" she asked, her voice changing, softer now, the tension going out of it.

"Don't get up," he said quickly. "I can make it myself. The kettle's still boiling." As he dipped her discarded teabag, which he took from the sink, in his cup of boiling water, he asked over his shoulder, "I thought I might drive into town, see if anything's going on. Want to come?" He heard her sigh, knew she didn't want him to go, and yet would refuse again to come herself. But dammit, a man couldn't hang around all day with nothing to do but watch his farm dry up. A man ... "Come on," he said, "it'll do you good. I could drop you off at Shelley's, pick you up in an hour or so." He had set his cup on the table near hers and stood behind her, his hands on her thin, tight shoulders. He bent forward, lifting his hands to stroke her neck, his nose buried in her thick, dark hair. "Come on," he whispered again, beseeching.

In the evening when the sun had cooled, he asked Frannie to go for a walk with him. She was a city girl when he'd married her, she was the one who'd taught him to go for walks, he'd thought walking over the farm he'd grown up on was only for children, hunting gophers, shooting magpies, stalking deer in the thin brush of the coulees, or climbing up to an eagles' nest high on a clay hillside.

But he went with Frannie and found delight in showing her

things her untrained eyes had missed; the rabbit trails narrow as ribbons lacing over the hillsides, or how to distinguish the droppings of the various animals. Her awe at seeing her first medicine wheels on the dry hilltops to the north had brought back his boyhood excitement at the mystery inherent in them.

"I'm a little tired today dear," she had said, almost timidly, so that he felt like a brute for asking her. He thought of saying again, it'll do you good, but the doctor had said he mustn't pressure her, so he said, okay, and went out by himself. Just as the screen door was closing behind him she called, a note of panic in her voice, "Don't stay out after dark!" Still holding the door open, he had called back almost simultaneously, "I'll be in before dark."

The wind had still not started blowing, it had been more than twelve hours of this startling quiet and he still couldn't get used to it. He felt as though the wind, a malevolent force if ever there was one, was only holding its breath, waiting to catch him when he least expected it, and then it would blow so hard it would blow them all — buildings, cars, animals, people — right off the face of the earth. It would blow them all to kingdom come and there'd be nothing left, not even trees or soil, nothing but bare, wind-scarred rocks and black chasms through which the wind would swoop and howl, screeching like the devil himself.

Gabe shuddered, surprised and frightened by the picture he himself had drawn and abruptly struck out for the hills three-quarters of a mile away. It would stay light till almost ten. He had plenty of time to get there, walk a little and get back before Frannie started to get frightened. And before the noises started again, the thought coming so quickly that it was whole before he could censor it.

He speeded up, striding down the once grassy road allowance next to a bare summerfallow field. At the opposite end of the field he paused for an instant, looking at the fine, dark soil that had drifted off the field and filled up the ditch. As always, he pondered how he could collect it and put it back on the field, then gave the idea up, making a disgusted sound. His own fault that his best soil lay useless in a drift in the ditch. Not enough trash cover, the soil worked too fine, though it wasn't his fault, he didn't think, that it refused to rain. He noticed that the smoke to the north beyond the hills had died away and wondered whose place had gone up this time.

It was a relief finally to be walking in the prairie grass in the steep, rocky hills, too rocky, too steep to cultivate, and he was secretly glad, though he'd never say so out loud, that he had an excuse to leave this last little bit of real prairie. Since Frannie's illness he had come to use it as his thinking place, coming here when he needed to get away from her and her refusal to get well, from the lack of rain, and the worries about bills. Here he tried to solve problems, or sometimes simply tried to clear his mind of everything, to stop thinking, to listen only to the wind whistling across the slopes, to the distant screech of high flying hawks, or to the tiny sounds of the insects, although he'd noticed lately that there were hardly any insects left crawling over the pale, yellowish clay or hanging from the sage and greasewood. What did that mean? he wondered. Probably just another effect of the lack of moisture.

He climbed a low hill and sat on a bare spot. At his feet there were only a few clumps of grass, short and dry, cured already by the heat. He hadn't realized how little grass there was left even here, and now he saw that as the grass died, the hills had begun to erode in the wind. He lifted his eyes to the distance and saw his house, small, the paint too bright under the dead and dying trees, the empty pens where he no longer kept livestock, since the bank had made him sell it all.

He would lose the farm this year. It was no good trying to hide it from himself anymore. It had become inevitable, because there was nothing left that might save it. Drought relief programs weren't nearly big enough, he had no crop to sell, he still had land payments to make, was three years behind in fact, hadn't a cent of equity left in the place so he couldn't even sell and come out ahead. He supposed Frannie knew it too, and that was why she wouldn't get well. Sometimes he could hardly contain his rage at her, as if he didn't have troubles enough without the worry of a wife who thought she was sick when there was nothing wrong with her.

Abruptly, following some urge he didn't even try to explain, he rose, turned his back on the farm and strode up and over the small hill and up the next, higher one. At the top he went straight to the medicine wheel that crowned it and stopped in its centre. Wordlessly, he stretched both arms high and wide, sucking in his belly with the stretch, throwing back his head, his eyes opened to the radiant sky. Now, he implored silently. Now you bitch, stop this, give us some rain. Give us some water, goddamn you, save us.

In the stillness, standing like that, extended and helpless, he waited. The earth dragged him down, he could feel it tugging at his heels, inexorably drawing him downward till he fell to his knees in the centre of the medicine wheel and fell further, dropping his forehead into the dust where grass no longer grew. He listened, but all he could hear was the pounding of his heart and the dry groan wrenched from his own throat. He thought he could feel the sky on his back, felt it drop down his sides, surrounding him. Give us some rain, he whispered into the earth, the sky cradling him, give us some goddamned rain.

Frannie's pale, mute face rose up in the darkness behind his closed eyes and he stood quickly, dusting off his knees, feeling absurd, glancing around as if by some miracle a neighbour might be standing there watching him make a fool of himself. He rushed down the hill and over the next one, striding through the stillness, making his own wind as he passed. As he hurried down the road allowance the coyotes began their twilight singing, pulling on the descending night.

And Frannie was waiting at the kitchen door for him, clutching her arms across her chest, peering out, waiting for his form to emerge out of the dusk.

"I was so scared," she cried.

"For God sake, Frannie," he began, then caught himself. "Why? Was there ... "

"Yes," she whispered, "creaks and more banging on the roof."

It had begun, he thought, after the miscarriage when Frannie had almost bled to death, or had it been before? He no longer knew for sure, had been able for a long time to ignore it, to pretend something else was causing the noises: the frost coming out of the wood, the wind which never let up, birds, until they had all disappeared when the nearby dugout had dried up. Now he knew it was ghosts. Hadn't the slightest doubt, had decided to wait it out. What else could they do, having nowhere else to go and no money to go there with?

Frannie lay in the crook of his arm, her head on his chest, her hair tucked under his chin.

"I heard today the rattlesnakes are moving in," he said.

"Oh, no," she whispered. They had lived in a pocket free of rattlesnakes with rattlesnakes both east and west of them. "How do people know? Did they see them?"

"Somebody lost a horse," he said. "You know how horses are. Curious. Must have seen one in a field, put his nose down and the rattler got him on it. Poison went straight to his brain and he died. Richard Blakely says he's got a gelding with a leg that's swole right up, you can see the two bloody holes where the fangs went in." Frannie turned her face into his flesh and a shiver ran through him. "So don't go walking in any tall grass," he whispered, his voice tender, and they both laughed, for there was no tall grass from where they were all the way south to the Missouri far below the border.

He was wakened around two by the sound of footfalls coming down the hall toward the bedroom. Not again, he thought, his fright mixed with irritation. He lay rigid and listened. The footsteps were muffled, but sounded like those of a large, heavy man. The first time this had happened he had felt huge goosebumps rise on his arms and legs and he had broken out in a cold sweat, but despite his fear he had managed to reach for the bedside lamp and turn it on. There was no one there. Now, as frightened as he was, he didn't bother to reach for the light. When the footsteps reached the bathroom next to their bedroom, they halted. He waited for them to start up again, but they were gone.

He found himself wanting to wake Frannie and shake her, and realized for the first time that he blamed her for the ghosts, felt somehow that she, with her love of death, was bringing them around to plague them. He'd had enough of the blankets being pulled off them in the night, of being wakened by the sound of coins being jingled at the foot of the bed, or of someone standing by the windows breathing deeply and sighing. He wanted to shake her and tell her to stop.

But it wasn't her fault she'd lost the baby. God knew, she wasn't the only one. There'd been a regular epidemic of miscarriages that people were blaming on the grasshopper spray, potent stuff that killed birds, other insects, and sometimes even the family dog, everything but the goddamn grasshoppers. Frannie had been further along and sicker than most afterward, and who knew, maybe the stuff had gotten into her system and that was why she was still sick. Her friend Shelley had been sick for a year from something the doctors couldn't give a name to. And there she was, as thin as Frannie, with a pinched look to her mouth, and the last time he had seen her she had that same look in her eyes as Frannie had, like she was bothered by ghosts too.

He got out of bed and felt his way into the living room. Without putting on the light he went to the big window and stood looking out into the night. His mind went as always to what would happen when the foreclosure came. Where would they go? What would he do to support Frannie and the baby he hoped to persuade her to have, maybe next year, when she was stronger?

He would have to get a job, but where? And doing what? He had no education, he didn't know how to do anything except fix a little machinery, farm a little. And jobs were scarce, everybody said so, and he wasn't any eighteen year old anymore.

He hit his fist on the window frame, then held himself still, listening, afraid he'd wakened his wife. But there was no frightened, "Gabe?" from the bedroom. He dropped his arm, the knuckles aching in a way that almost pleased him, and watched the stars. The truth was, he couldn't imagine life without the farm, or maybe he still wasn't ready to try. Every time he started to get a picture, anger and revulsion rose up in him so hard that he hit something, or cursed with such viciousness that he disgusted himself. Once he had even caught himself crying and that had scared him more than anything. So if he could help it, he didn't think about what it would be like.

He began to make out the constellations that he had been looking at from this window ever since he was a child. He traced their shapes and grew calmer. Behind him, the house was silent, no knocking, no unexplained creaks, no glasses tinkling in the cupboards. A blurred star hung so low on the horizon that it might have been resting on the hilltops. He watched it, thinking, is that a star or a light? But no, it was late, and the constellations wheeling through the sky were circling lower, beginning to set. He wondered why its light wasn't diamond-hard and clear like the other stars, but instead, had a smeared look. Mist rising off the hills, he supposed, then snorted. It takes moisture to make mist, he reminded himself, and there sure as hell wasn't any moisture out there. Or maybe there was a smear on the window that he couldn't see in the dark.

In the morning the wind had resumed howling around the house, scudding small clouds of dust across the yard or whipping up whirlwinds that raced down the road and played themselves out in the fields. And yet the heat was incredible, had been record-breaking for days

"Sleep well?" he asked Frannie who was at the stove cooking him eggs.

"Mmm hmmm," she said. "I didn't hear anything, did you?"

"Not a sound," he said. "House was quiet last night."

Gabe turned on the radio. It was getting so he could hardly stand the lack of voices in the house. All the time he'd been growing up there'd been his mother and father and his two sisters to make a racket. He and Frannie couldn't make enough noise to fill one room. He wondered suddenly if the house had always had strange noises in it and they'd never heard them because they were making so much noise themselves. Could be, he thought, and there wasn't even a drought then.

Abruptly the wind rose with a screech, batting against the walls and the roof.

"Wow, look at that!" he said, and jumped up to look out the window above the sink. A huge dust devil, a whirling cone of dirt, grass, weeds and small stones was bearing down on the house from the field to the west. "Quick, shut the door." Frannie did so quickly, then came to stand beside him to see what it was he'd seen. "It must be a hundred feet high," he said. It was on them that quickly, a roar of sound, the view from the window blanked out by a wall of beige dust and then it was gone, one Russian thistle hitting the window, then falling away. It roared across the yard. "That was goddamn near a twister!" he said.

As if from a great distance he heard the radio announcer say, "Damage was severe in towns for fifty miles along the river." He held himself still, not even breathing as the announcer went on to describe a tornado that had torn the roofs off barns, flattened steel bins and destroyed houses in a swath a mile wide fifty miles to the north of them.

It seemed to him for an instant that the world must be coming to an end: the terrifying heat that wouldn't let anything live, the insane winds, the lack of rain that went on for longer than anybody could remember. He tried to picture what the people in the cities were doing this morning — going to work, drinking coffee, riding bicycles, making deals.

Frannie threw her arms around him and looked up into his face. "Oh, Gabe, don't," she begged, and he wondered what he had been doing.

"Come to town with me today," he said.

"Yes," she said at once, frightened.

He took her into the cafe, making an occasion of it, insisting they each have a hamburger though they could ill afford it. He was cheerful, making her laugh, inviting people they knew who passed their booth to sit for a minute, encouraging her to chat. Afterward he went with her to the grocery store while she bought a few things and then insisted she come with him to the hardware store where he intended to pick up some shingle nails so he could fix the roof.

"What is that?" Frannie said.

"What?" he asked, stopping in the middle of the sidewalk, knowing even as he said it what she was referring to. In the distance they could hear the low roll and boom of what sounded like thunder. "Maybe it's going to rain," he suggested, half-kidding.

"Rain!" she said. "There isn't even a cloud in the sky." They looked up as though they had never seen the sky before. From horizon to horizon it was perfectly clear. Further down the street a cluster of men had come out of the cafe and were peering up too, their hands in their pockets. At the beauty parlour across the street the two hairdressers in their sundresses gazed up at the sky, shading their eyes with their hands, while the hot wind whipped their skirts. The sound faded out, then rose again above the steady whistle of the wind.

"Sounds like thunder," a man they hadn't even noticed standing beside them, said, his voice incredulous.

"Can't be," Gabe said. Nobody spoke, and slowly the sound died away. One by one the people who had gathered outside went back to what they had been doing. Gabe held the door of the hardware store open for Frannie and then followed her in.

"Maybe I could use a new mixing bowl," Frannie said absently, as if she were thinking about something else.

"Hi, Gabe, how you doing, Fran," Arvid, the owner of the store said. He was sitting in front of his new computerized cash register working the keys and occasionally stopping to thumb through a pile of bills beside him on the counter. He paused and rested his hands on the keyboard. Gabe said, "Hot day."

"Sure is," Arvid said. "What was that noise I heard out there?" Frannie wandered over to the side of the store that displayed kitchenware.

"Don't know what it was," Gabe said. Another man, someone Gabe knew to see but whose name he couldn't recall, came in and leaned on the counter beside Gabe. While they chatted, Gabe watched Frannie out of the corner of his eye. She lifted a plate from a rack and turned it over to read the writing on the underside. He turned his attention back to the men.

"Business must be good," the newcomer was saying, "if you can afford one of them things." Arvid snorted.

"I'm part of a chain," he said, "and if the head office says I gotta have one of these, then I gotta have one." He swivelled back to the cash register and began to press the buttons again. Suddenly there was a tremendous boom, Gabe felt the floor heave under his feet, the cash register made a poof sound followed by a rapid sizzle and Arvid slumped forward onto it. Gabe grabbed the counter to steady himself and only then noticed that the other man was on his knees on the floor, already beginning to get up.

Gabe rushed to Frannie who had dropped and broken the

plate. As soon as he touched her tears began to ooze from her eyes as she stared up at him, eyes wide and mouth trembling. He turned and saw through the window that people were clustering in front of the store and that Arvid had recovered, was standing, holding his head.

"Sit down, sit down," he shouted to Frannie, although there was nowhere for her to sit, and rushed outside.

The people who had appeared out of nowhere to gather in front of the hardware store were staring downward this time, at the sidewalk. Gabe stared down too. There was a jagged, circular hole a couple of inches in diameter in the cement sidewalk in just about the place he and Frannie had been standing a moment or two before. Deep cracks ran out in several directions from it.

There were confused exclamations and a babble of voices. The word, 'lightning,' emerged and was repeated and people began to look upward again. But again there was nothing to be seen except a few wispy white clouds floating harmlessly in the distance.

Still Frannie did not say, I want out of here, get me out of here, and Gabe was grateful to her for that. Soon enough, he replied grimly to himself, when he could tell what she was thinking. Soon enough.

But still he couldn't bring himself to make specific plans for what they would do when the final foreclosure notice came. Exactly how much money would he have in his pocket the day they would have to pack their suitcases, get in the truck and drive away for good? And to where would they drive? He knew he should be driving into town everyday, buying the city newspapers and studying the want ads. He should have made a trip to the city already to size up the job situation first hand and to check into places to live. He knew he should have everything set up and ready to go for Frannie's sake and for the sake of the child she wasn't even carrying yet. He supposed that deep inside he was still hoping for a reprieve even though he knew perfectly well that none would come. And lightning out of a clear sky now.

It was three or four in the morning and he was standing at the window in the front room again, looking out at the stars. He thought of the blurred star he had seen hanging over the hills, but tonight it wasn't there. But of course, it was later now than when he had seen it before and it might have set.

It was still out and very dark. The stars kept their clarity even in the drought and shone, if anything, more fiercely than usual. He became aware of a moving point of light and thought, a plane, a satellite, a shooting star.

He watched. The light grew brighter as if it were coming nearer. It dipped, then rose again and its hard white light changed to a greenish shade. He stared hard, not taking his eyes off it. It lowered itself into the hills where he liked to walk, almost as if it were resting on top of one of them, but it was too dark for him to make out the horizon so he couldn't tell if it was in the sky or on a hilltop. It grew brighter, raised, lowered a little, and remained still. It occurred to Gabe that nobody could drive a vehicle up there, and that no star behaved in such a way. Gradually he realized that there was a good chance he was seeing a UFO. This didn't alarm him, since peculiar lights in the sky were not unknown in the region, and besides, he felt safe here in his own house. He watched.

After a while he heard in his head, or somehow knew, since there was no voice and no sound, 'we're leaving now.' So he watched with renewed concentration. Soon the lights around the object, he could tell now it was an object, burned red and for an instant he thought he saw them as several evenly spaced red lights around a circular rim. Then it rose a short distance, hovered, in a split second grew smaller, and disappeared.

He searched the sky, but all he could see were the constellations shining immovably in the blackness. He couldn't hear a sound.

The next evening he walked up to the place in the hills where he judged the light must have been. He only half-believed in what he'd seen and he walked thoughtfully, no longer able to screen out the ache in his gut where the impending loss of his farm sat now all the time. What will we do? Where will we go? It seemed to him that he loved even the Russian thistle blown several feet thick up against his fence line, threatening to topple it, that he loved even the stone piles gathered with such pain into the corners of his fields, even the dirt so dry that it no longer held together when he took up a handful of it, even the great cracks in the prairie that he had to step over. Every step of the way was pain and sorrow-filled, his own, private *via dolorosa*.

When he reached the hill where he thought the UFO had landed, he stood on its crown and tried to line up the right section of the far off front room window with the right spot on the hill. When he was satisfied, he began to walk, carefully studying the ground. In just about the right place he found two rocks — he couldn't think what they were called, sandstone or shale, but they looked as though they had been formed by the compression of soil from the hill. They had each been about the size of a breadbox and both of them had been shattered, the small broken chips were scattered down the hillside for a couple of feet below each rock. He squatted and lifted a couple of the broken pieces. Each of them left a slight imprint in the soil where it had lain. He studied them. They looked as though they'd been rained on and something in them had leached out and stained the ground a rusty colour.

But he had seen shattered rocks before, he thought, although not in this particular stretch of hills. It was said that the frost shattered them. Perhaps it had and what he thought he'd seen the night before was only an illusion he'd thrown up himself.

Ah, Gabriel, he said, you're losing your mind.

Suddenly it occurred to him to wonder who the ghosts were that bothered them. He'd never thought of that before, had thought of them only as disembodied things that made noises in the night, that tried to wake them, that seemed intent on scaring them. And he had blamed Frannie for them. Now he wondered if they had anything to do with Frannie, if maybe the ghosts were trying to tell them something that they couldn't understand, or were trying to alert them. His mother and father maybe, or his grandparents who couldn't sleep either because the world they'd left behind was no longer recognizable.

He rose slowly, painfully, and began to walk again. He went toward the highest hill, for some reason craving height and more height, wanting a clear view of his place nearly a mile away, sitting so small in the big landscape. To the west the sun was dropping lower, had almost disappeared behind the rim of the earth. It was a blazing, fiery red with a golden edge to it where it touched the hills and now it seemed the margin would ignite, the fire would burst out and consume the earth.

He found a large rock, one that came to mid-thigh with a depression in the bare soil all around it where cattle had once stood to use it for a rubbing stone, and before his cattle and his father's and his grandfather's, buffalo had used it. He leaned his buttocks against it, half-sitting, and was surprised to find it was warm, still radiating heat from the sun. He wondered how far inside it the heat had penetrated.

The rock was granite and that peculiar shade of pink with minute points of light in it and other, equally small points of black. He swivelled and ran his hand over its hard, rough surface and noticed for the first time how it was almost covered with patches of ivory-coloured lichen and patches of the palest green.

It struck him then that the rock was a beautiful thing, miraculous, and that it had sat in this spot for a very long time, so long that he couldn't imagine all the years it must have been there. He stood, then squatted on the ground beside it, put his arm around it, and lay his head against the bulge of its side.

And then he saw how it would be.

The hills would turn to hoodoos, were half-way there already. His land would lie fallow, he couldn't tell for how long, but a very long time. He and Frannie would move to the city. Frannie would recover, she would get a job sooner than he would; she was younger than he was, smarter than he was in a quick way, she would regain her old determination, and a woman, she would not mind taking orders. They would have children and the children would be fine. By then he would have a job as a mechanic or a construction worker or a maintenance man in some high-rise building. They would live both better and worse than they lived now. Evenings, he would sit in front of the television with his feet in their grey workman's socks up on a footstool, his muscles aching pleasurably from his day's labour. He would grow sleepy, he would doze, and from then on, for all the rest of his long workingman's life, his dreams would be of the farm.

What the Voices Say

When I was young, the only family I knew aside from my parents, I was an only child too, were three cousins, two girls and a boy, my father's half-brother's children. I say 'knew' because they are all three dead now, Antonio committed suicide at seventeen, and I think now there must have been a curse on that family, though it didn't seem so to me at the time. Then I thought their lives thrilling beyond words, and even though I was often frightened by the things they did, or had apparently done, or that happened to them, I could never understand why it was that none of them happened to me or to my family, but only to theirs. It made me feel I wasn't quite real, a shadow, destined always to live only on the fringes of the lives of others. And since Morgan, the oldest, was a world-traveller from her first backpacking trip around Europe at eighteen till she disappeared in the Orient years later, and Rhonda, the youngest, changed her name to Pamela Sue, ran away to become a starlet in Hollywood, I even saw her in a picture once, and died from a drug overdose at twenty-four, while I have done what I said I would do, become a writer, and an unwilling recluse, it turns out that my childhood perception, which I spent years trying to shake, was true.

Still, when I was young I was glad to claim them as relatives.

My tales of their exploits gave me an importance among my friends at school that I could never have earned myself. I shared my stories in the girls' washroom at recess and on our walks to and from school, and it was gratifying when every once in a while, a girl I hardly knew would sidle up to me and ask, bright-eyed, what the latest news of my cousins was, and then listen intently while I told her

Rhonda was closest to me in age, only a year older, Antonio was five years older and Morgan six, but ages didn't really matter since their's wasn't an ordinary family where the kids played together and went places together. When I visited them it wasn't to do things with my cousins. Mostly I just skulked about the house and watched and listened and went on my own private and blissfully unsupervised forays here and there on the acreage where they lived a few miles from a city. Every summer for at least a month I visited them and it was when I was there that I experienced the only freedom I knew as a child, for their house was an escape from the cold rigidity and painful, pathological cleanliness of my home, that seemed to me constructed to hide only emptiness, a terrible, emotionless void.

At my cousins' I slept in an extra room where my cousins had their rooms, in the basement, which had never been properly finished. The rooms were all framed, but they had no doors and the interior walls were closed in only half or three-quarters of the way up, so that the basement was more like one giant room with a lot of unmade beds shoved into it and piles of dirty clothes on the floor or clean ones hanging in closets that were framed and had doors, but no walls. The basement was always gloomy too, since the only windows were small rectangles high in the walls which opened up and out onto the backyard.

I had adventures in my cousins' household, things were always happening, secret, nocturnal things mostly, things you couldn't talk about. I didn't do them myself, but I was allowed to be present when they were happening. I remember waking to find Morgan sitting on the floor on her side of the half-wall that separated our rooms, a boy beside her, drinking whiskey from a bottle and smoking and giggling in the dark, then, after a lot of panting and moaning, the boy climbing out the window by standing on Morgan's dresser, and the soft click of the window as it fell in place behind his legs and feet; Morgan offering me a drink from the bottle and my startled, confused refusal.

"It changes everything," she told me. "It makes everything different," her voice trailing away in the darkness. By the summer of my story, when I was twelve and Morgan eighteen, she had already come and gone from her home quite a few times, sometimes for a weekend, sometimes for as long as two months according to Rhonda; where, nobody seemed to know or to care. Yet, when she came back, nobody remarked on it either.

The fiction behind my visits was that I would be a companion for Rhonda, but Rhonda was a secretive girl who had little tolerance for my timidity; a wildly imaginative one, who acted parts by herself, made costumes out of rugs or bedspreads or even curtains which never got hung back up again, and danced in the backyard in the moonlight when everybody else was asleep.

Even though I knew my aunt didn't really like me much and probably would have preferred not to have me around, I kept coming. She would greet me cordially enough, but there would be a wry twist to her mouth, she would inspect me in an amused, scornful way that, for the few seconds it lasted, made my hands sweat. But I was stubborn, I didn't expect love, my own mother was severe with me, acted often without even fondness, and as long as my aunt didn't tell me to stay away or blatantly mistreat me, I would overlook her lack of warmth in order to escape from my mother and to be where I felt I could at last see what I thought must be real life.

My own home was a model of regularity and, as most households were in the early fifties, geared to my father's schedule and wishes. We ate breakfast together, my father as silent as my uncle was, (except that, rarely, my uncle told stories), my mother speaking only to instruct or criticize me. But my aunt never got up before ten and when she did get up she did nothing I could see in the way of housework, so that the house was in a state of chaos all the time and, while my family ate dinner at precisely seven every evening, at my cousins' meals were eaten when somebody got hungry enough to make them.

If my aunt didn't like me, she didn't appear to like her own children any better, and snapped and snarled at them and gave exaggerated sighs or bored, monosyllabic replies when they, very seldom, asked for something. But she didn't stop them either, from doing anything they wanted to do, so that they grew up restless and daring and filled with arrogance and scorn for the rest of the world.

My aunt had been born in England, the daughter of an actress who, I found out when I was grown, had never been married and who had never given her daughter any kind of family life. Aunt Jacqueline must have had ambitions at one time, although I've no idea what they might have been. She spent a lot of time reading magazines, and in the afternoons she liked to drive into the city, never taking anyone with her or telling us where she went or what she did, and though my cousins might have known, I never heard them ask. She didn't even say good-bye when she left, simply went out the front door, got into her Audi and drove away, returning hours later, not one whit changed that I could see, and usually not even carrying a parcel.

As I have said, she read only magazines, while my uncle was always reading books, strange, heavy volumes, often of poetry, sometimes in other languages. And my cousins were always angry and shouted at each other, except for Antonio, and sometimes even pushed or hit one another. But alone with me, one by one, they revealed an intense interest in everything, they had a dynamic way of viewing the world that was new to me, as if they conceived of themselves as a part of everything, a brilliance would appear in their eyes when they were thinking about things; their fearlessness and the weirdness of their fantasies enraptured me and kept me coming summer after summer.

There were a lot of visitors to the house, people like my aunt and uncle who didn't fit into the mold of what I thought was normalcy. At our house people came only if they were invited, and not too many of them at once, and they all dressed properly and behaved with restraint. My aunt and uncle's visitors came at strange hours, they either didn't speak at all or they talked too much.

One evening we were eating supper in the kitchen when the front door opened and a dishevelled young man in a stained and wrinkled raincoat, though it wasn't raining, hadn't rained all summer, came striding through the front room into the kitchen where half of us were eating gummy macaroni and cheese and the rest of us were eating chunks of garlic sausage washed down with water. My aunt was a terrible cook, bored and perfunctory, and made meals only with things that came in cans or were frozen or instant.

He rushed through the doorway, came to a dead stop as if he'd expected to find the room empty, his dark eyes were wild and he stared at all of us as if he were about to speak. We all stared back at him, me, no doubt, with my mouth hanging open. He turned to my uncle, then thinking better of this, to my aunt, threw his hands up, then turned and rushed out again without having uttered a word. When he was gone, my aunt began to laugh, she laughed so hard we had to slap her on the back and offer her water, and my cousins laughed too, but my uncle only fixed a mild, level gaze on her and finally got up and left the table, though he hadn't finished eating.

Another time, about eleven o'clock at night, an hour when I would have been long since asleep if I'd been at home, the door-bell rang. What was astonishing about this was that the doorbell had actually worked. Another of the peculiarities about the house, one which I found especially satisfying, was that nothing worked, everything was broken or taken apart by Tonio and left that way in pieces. So when the doorbell actually rang, we all turned toward the door in surprise. It opened before anybody made a move to go to it, and a young woman, maybe nineteen or twenty years old, with long, straight, light-brown hair and the smoothest, finest skin I'd ever seen stepped inside. She was very pale and dressed in a peculiar, dark red, shabby cotton dress that ended above her knees showing the baggy cotton slacks she was wearing under it. She had on her feet moccasins with bright beading on the instep. I remember I was fascinated by how small her feet were and how, once she was seated, she couldn't keep them still.

"Oh, good," she said. "You're still up." She came in and sat down, though nobody had asked her to, on a stool beside the chair where my uncle was sitting. He didn't appear to look at her, but held his face stiffly, his eyes lowered as though he didn't wish to give anything away, but if he spoke to her, I don't remember. I remember mostly how very pretty she was, despite her paleness, her full pink lower lip, how large and bright yet glazed her blue eyes were. My aunt at first sat up straight when the girl came in, but as she began to talk, my aunt relaxed back in her chair and ignored her.

The girl's conversation, if you could call it that, seemed directed at my uncle, although she didn't always look at him, but stared into space and chattered away as brightly as a little bird, and with as little sense. She didn't wait for anyone to reply, nobody was paying any attention to her anyway, and as time passed, it seemed to me that she began to talk faster and faster, although I'm pretty sure I've imagined this part, but she was like a talking doll that had been wound as tightly as the spring would go; she was working at full pitch and would until either the spring broke or the works ran down.

After a while Rhonda said she was going to bed. Reluctantly I got up from the floor where I'd been lying on my stomach pretending to watch television. There was something in my uncle's posture, attentive, but pretending not to be, that made me want to stay even though I was becoming frightened for the girl, afraid for what would surely happen to her soon: nothing good.

I don't know whether my aunt went to bed or stayed, but later I was wakened from a deep sleep by what I thought had been a scream, not one of Tonio's, and by muffled, hysterical weeping. Then a door shut, a car started and drove away and there was silence.

And in the morning things were as they always were: my uncle reading a book while he drank his first cup of coffee at the kitchen table before he went upstairs to his study where he and my aunt had their bedroom too and which was off-limits to the rest of us; my cousins straggling in one by one, grouchy and quarrelsome, Antonio staring around the room with a stunned expression as though he had never seen it before, and my aunt not putting in an appearance till after my uncle had gone upstairs, and then not dressed, but wearing her embroidered, blue Japanese robe.

There was an atmosphere of strain in that household, of tension, that was separate from the sense of mystery I found there, of unplumbed, dark, subterranean currents. It was perhaps hysteria, or a sense of approaching crisis, as if at any second all the lies might surface and be shown for what they were, all the deceptions, the secrets, the corruption that lay beneath the surface of that family's life. I articulated none of this as a child, but as an adult, having followed my uncle's calling, and having developed the writer's habits of introspection and reflection. I thought a lot about them, and as an adult I realized that what had fascinated me about that family was not the things that happened, but the current of hidden, seething emotion, of passion, that lay below the surface, and the constant possibility of revelation.

Sometimes I have even wondered if Antonio was really a schizophrenic as we were told later, or if that was a fiction the family put out to explain, in a way that would relieve them of blame, his suicide. But then, remembering him, I have to admit he was strange, that he took pills every day, and heard voices, and that if he was absent when I arrived for my summer visit, I was told he was on the psychiatric ward of a hospital in the nearby city, the hazy, blue silhouette which we could see from the front steps, though I was never taken there to visit him, and I never knew of anyone else going either.

He was younger seeming than his years, a loner in a family of loners, secretive like Rhonda, silent like my uncle, and he seemed not to live in the house so much as to haunt it. You were always coming on him when you least expected to: sitting outside on the front steps when you came back to the house at night and the outside light burnt out so that you stumbled over him in the darkness; getting up in the middle of the night to go to the toilet and finding him sitting on the bathroom floor with the light on, not doing anything, but just sitting there, and if you asked him what he was doing he'd say, "I'm watching the bugs," although I could never see any bugs or mice or anything else he claimed was there.

Every night Tonio woke us with his moans and cries, and more than once I woke to find him standing in my room, sometimes at the foot of my bed, sometimes beside me or again, facing one of the half-walls. I learned to say, "Tonio, you're in my room, go to bed," and he would obey, although at first I was terribly frightened and shrieked and woke my cousins who were angry with me, saying things like, "Oh, it's only Tonio for god sake, what's the matter with you," so that I learned to suppress my fear and to respond to him as they did, matter-of-factly.

Sometimes Antonio had fits. Or what my cousins called fits, although he didn't roll up his eyes, foam at the mouth and thrash about on the floor as I'd been told epileptics did. We would be sitting at the table eating or lying on our stomachs watching television and suddenly Tonio's eyes would widen, his mouth would fall open and then stretch into a terrible, mirthless grin and he would scramble backwards making gasping noises and my uncle would have to catch him and hold him before he ran away or started to scream and break things. Sometimes he would be alone in another part of the house when it would start and we would all run to him and block his path so that my uncle could catch him. Then he would take Tonio away into his bedroom and what he did after that I never knew, but it always quieted Tonio and we wouldn't hear anymore from him for hours.

When this happened, my aunt was the only one who didn't help. She never rushed to him or tried to hold him or spoke to him. She watched him, her body rigid and her hands clenched, her dark eyes brilliant with light, but hard somehow, and if it got really bad, she would close her eyes and put her fists over her ears, her face contorted, as if she couldn't bear it, simply couldn't bear it.

Tonio never talked much to anybody. His sisters would speak to him in a gentle, jocular way: "Move over, old Tonio," they'd say if he was in their way, or, "Hey, old Tonio, that was some dream you had last night," or, "Tonio, Tonio," half-sung, "How's your eyes and earlobes today," which made no sense to me, but apparently alluded to something that he had said when he was a child. He was the only one in the family who was treated with tenderness. I even saw my aunt sitting in her chair in the living room once with Tonio seated on the floor in front of her and she was brushing his hair back with the palms of her hands, gently, absent-mindedly, while he sat before her, his eyes closed, mute, as content as an animal being stroked.

My uncle was a writer. He wrote long magazine articles about politics, or history, or discussions about society and culture, and he was always working on a book. He was away a lot too, gone for months at a time during the winter, my cousins said, researching articles, doing interviews, studying cultures. He had light brown hair which Tonio had inherited, that he brushed straight back from his high forehead, and he wore neat, gold-framed glasses. Unlike my father, who was tall and spare, he was a stocky man, and his skin was scarred and pebbled, probably by adolescent acne, although I never guessed that when I was young. I thought his scarred skin beautiful. It too, spoke to me of mystery and of probable suffering, the existence of which was confirmed for me by his silence and his way of looking, with an expression filled with pain, right through you.

I was in love with him. I'm not talking about the kind of love a child feels for an adult who treats her well. My uncle didn't pay any attention to me, he rarely even spoke to me. But I loved him, I saw him and my little girl's legs went soft with love. It was perhaps bizarre, but it was real, it was the same feeling I have had since for men who became my lovers after I was grown, and it was at its worst when I was ten and eleven, though I never really stopped loving him.

The summer I was ten I kissed him. He was sitting across the room from me reading a book, there was no one else about, and I stood in the doorway for a moment watching him, then walked quietly across the room and kissed him gently on his forehead.

He didn't move, only blinked twice, didn't raise his eyes from his book. I turned and went out of the room as quietly as I had entered it. I don't know what I expected from him; I wasn't disappointed in his lack of reaction and I knew nothing conscious about adult love and what it led to, why I kissed him I don't know, other than that I loved him so much I couldn't stop myself.

In that household I survived by keeping quiet. If the adults were around, and sometimes this applied to Morgan too, I spoke only when spoken to, and I was careful to keep out of my aunt's way, to set the table if there was to be a meal and when we finally did eat, to stay after and clear the table, and if somebody was doing the dishes, to help. I had been trained to silence by my mother, who liked to say that children should be seen and not heard, but at home it wasn't hard to be quiet because there was never much I wanted to know about. At my aunt and uncle's it was a harder task, I was full of questions yet when I walked in their door, I buttoned my lip, as my mother said I should. I was always taking deep breaths and letting them out slowly till my aunt once snapped at me, "For god sake, Charlotte, have you got asthma?" But it was only that I wanted to speak, had opened my mouth and taken a breath and then, remembering the precariousness of my position in her house, had shut it quickly, then let the air out slowly to cover up that I had been going to speak.

My aunt had to be avoided, but at least she allowed you to avoid her, not like my mother who hung just a step behind me always, keeping a constant watch on me, making sure I lived exactly as she wanted me to. Yet, strangely, in the summer she would wash her hands of me, I was sent off to do whatever I would.

One day my aunt arrived home from one of her long afternoons in the city and said, to nobody in particular, but as it happened we were all there, "Dorcas is coming to visit." To be told in advance that someone was coming to visit was in itself so unusual that I had no trouble recognizing this as important. My cousins were silent; there were none of their usual groans or screams of laughter or immediate, violent quarrels. Antonio spoke finally.

"I'm afraid," he said. "Tell her not to come."

"Why, Tonio," my uncle said mildly to him, "she wants to see you." But Tonio only shook his head violently and then covered his face with his hands. He did look frightened, haunted even, or perhaps it was only that he had one of his terrible headaches. My aunt was smiling to herself and sat down on the sofa, kicking off her high-heeled shoes that she only put on to go into the city.

"She's my cousin," she said. "My only cousin." I realized she was speaking to me. "I was raised with her," she said, and there was in her tone a brooding resonance.

"You have lots of cousins," my uncle said, but he didn't even look at her, "and you were hardly raised with her." Morgan said to me, loudly, "Spirits talk to Dorcas." I stared at her, unable to tell if this was a joke or not, and wondering why people were suddenly speaking to me.

"Where's she coming from?" Rhonda asked.

"She's been working in Italy," my aunt said. "How the hell do I know where she's coming from?" I was dying to ask what Dorcas did, why she was coming to visit, how she was going to get here, but managed, with one gulp of air, to suppress my questions. "You'll have to sleep on the couch in the sitting room," my aunt said to me.

"Sure," I said, quickly, brightly.

It was a tiny room on the main floor overlooking the back-yard where a garden would have been if there had been anybody to look after one. The room was never used, when we were in we spent our evenings sprawled in the living room where the television set was. The yard the sitting room overlooked was overgrown with wild grasses which had invaded even what must once have been elaborate flowerbeds. There was shrubbery too, lilacs, honeysuckles, spirea, rosebushes and neglected plum and apple trees. With all the shrubbery and the fact that nobody ever picked the fruit from the fruit trees, the backyard was always full of birds which, in the early mornings were so noisy that sleep in that room would have been near to impossible. We didn't hear their racket in the basement, but my aunt was always complaining about it.

I suppose that back sitting room with the big window in it had been placed there by the builder of the house so he could sit and enjoy his garden. There was once a view too, of the land sloping away to the river a mile or so back from the edge of the property, but the shrubbery had grown up so tall and bushy that now the view was hidden.

At supper that night Aunt Jacqueline remarked that Dorcas had never married, looking at my uncle as she said it. "She has all kinds of lovers, though," directed at nobody in particular. "She even had a child by one of them. I forget which one."

"Dick, the farmer," Morgan said grumpily and threw down her fork. "The poor kid." I never saw anybody as angry as Morgan. It was a surprise to me to hear her say she felt sorry for the child, since Morgan never felt sorry for anybody, except maybe Tonio.

"She raised her," Aunt Jacqueline said. "What was her name?"

"Sybil," Morgan said, slamming down her water glass so that some of the water sloshed out onto the table. "Sybil. And she didn't raise her. Dick did."

"Once Dorcas knew Sybil was going on a boating trip with Dick," Rhonda said, her voice light and excited, "and Dorcas dreamt there was a storm and the boat tipped over and Sybil and a bunch of people fell out and drowned." She paused for effect. "Dorcas is an actress," she said, looking at me with such intensity that I lowered my eyes. "So she was in a play in London, but when she woke up and remembered her dream, she jumped on a train, just like that, and went up to where Dick and Sybil lived and stopped them from going. And you know what?" I said nothing. "The boat they were supposed to be on did tip in a big storm and a bunch of people on it did drown." I stared at her. "Close your mouth," she said.

My aunt made a few concessions for her cousin's visit. She tidied the living room and brought home a bouquet of late summer flowers, daisies, zinnias, tiger lilies, from a florist in the city the afternoon the cousin was to arrive. And that evening when Dorcas was due in from town, my uncle having gone to get her, my aunt went upstairs and came down wearing a long purple robe, a sort of caftan, though I didn't know the word then, made of rough cotton with designs around the hem. It emphasized her height and the wide silver bracelets and heavy silver earrings she wore I had not seen before. She was dark-haired, with dark, almost black eyes, and an olive complexion. I had heard her claim in an amused way more than once, as if she were testing to see if you would believe her, that she had gypsy blood. My cousins said she was half-French and half-Italian, and my father, that his half-brother had met her in Paris where he had gone to spend a year after he finished university. She had run away from the house her mother had put her in in England and would have starved in Paris if he hadn't found her, fed her, and eventually married her.

Though she was not beautiful, tonight she looked regal and so striking I found I couldn't take my eyes off her, yet somehow at the same time, she looked older, almost haggard. It might have been that the heavy purple colour didn't suit her, but I don't think so. Looking back, I remember that she moved more quickly than I had seen her move before and that she seemed tightly strung and yet quite sad. Thinking back, I'm tempted to say that the gown was funereal, but I might be investing the memory with something that wasn't there when all this actually happened.

It was growing dark outside, it was late August, I would leave in ten days to return to school and to my home two hundred miles away. The evening was cool with crickets chirping outside the open windows. Rhonda had fallen asleep on the floor beside me. I had wakened the night before when a window had creaked, meaning that one of my cousins was coming in from or going out to some nocturnal adventure. I usually roused myself enough to find out who it was and if I could, what it was about. Last night it had been Rhonda crawling out her window, pulling her bedspread behind her. I had crawled up onto the chest of drawers in my room to watch and to see what she would do with the bedspread, which had come from Italy and was a lovely blue-green colour with a pattern woven into it of flowers, criss-crossed with shiny threads that caught the light and glittered.

When she was outside, standing in the shin-deep wild grass under the moon, she swathed herself in it, twisting it around and around herself till she was wrapped like a mummy in it. She began to turn, slowly at first, unwinding the cloth until she could move her feet and legs freely, then she began to spin and to leap and when she fell, she rolled on the grass till the bedspread caught on a low branch and pulled away from her. When that happened, she scrunched herself up into a little ball and stayed that way, as if she were waiting for her dizziness to pass before she rose again and stretched as high as she could on her tiptoes, reaching with fingertips for the moon.

I had seen it all before, or versions of it, but I still couldn't stop myself from watching her, it was all so frightening and bizarre and beautiful and forbidden.

I realize now, when I think about it, that my mother must have known how it was in my cousins' house, and my father too. Why did they never stop me from coming? I always had the feeling that my mother wanted to punish me for some crime I had unwittingly committed, an awful crime, but one that I knew nothing about, and that maybe her letting me come summer after summer to my cousins was supposed to be some kind of punishment for whatever it was I had done.

And it *was* a punishment, you know. In a way it was, for it was a frightening household and my aunt was a wild and cruel woman, quite crazy, as my mother said she was, and all my mother's drastic predictions about my cousins' fate came true. When I came home from there each fall I had nightmares, I had a hard time adjusting to our scheduled, colourless lives, my appetite was poor, and I would catch my mother looking at me when she thought I hadn't seen her, with her lips pressed together tightly as if to say, that will teach her. Though what it was supposed to teach, I never knew, just as I never knew what my crime was, and each summer I asked, I begged to be allowed to go back again, and even worse, she always let me.

The crickets chirped, Rhonda stirred and brushed her tangled hair from her face. My aunt was leaning back in her chair in her dramatic gown, her eyes closed, although I could tell she wasn't sleeping. Tonio was in the big chair in the corner where my uncle usually sat, sitting very straight, his hands clasped between his knees, his pale skin paler even than usual. He kept moistening his lips, staring ahead at nothing, and once or twice he rocked his body back and forth and then stopped. He was in a state of extreme tension, though that was not unusual for him.

Tonio saw things that weren't there and voices that none of the rest of us could hear sometimes spoke to him. Still, occasionally, he would seem perfectly normal. He would make his own toast in the morning, he even made toast for me when he was having a good day. He asked me if I'd slept well, and once he asked me what grade I was in, and what I was going to be when I grew up. A writer, I think, I had replied, and he had stopped what he was doing and given me such a strange look that I wished I hadn't told him.

"Really?" he said finally, then cocked his head as if he were listening. "Maybe," he said, his voice rising at the end of the word as if he had just heard that it would be so. And he smiled at me, a real smile, as if he were seeing me as I was, and not as if I had sprouted horns or fangs or like Alice, had grown so large I was in danger of not fitting into the kitchen. It was the only moment of meeting I ever had with Tonio, and that strange, tentative, then accepting, 'maybe' of his stayed with me whenever I faltered in my resolve to be a writer, a resolve I had never dared to tell my parents about, and it gave me the determination so that I didn't give up.

"Dorcas is in movies," Rhonda said to me, suddenly opening her eyes and bouncing to her knees. I thought she was asleep and was startled. "And I'm going to be in movies too."

Morgan strode into the room again and then out. She was built like my aunt, tall, with olive skin and a lot of thick, curly hair that she made no attempt to tame so that it hung down her back in a tangled, thick mass and frizzed around her face like a halo. She seemed angry, her strides made the living room floor shake so that Rhonda and I could feel the vibrations in our stomachs. Her anger seemed so real and threatening to me that night that I drew in my feet and sat up, a little afraid she might kick me on one of her passes down the room.

Just then there were a couple of thumps at the front door and then it opened. We jumped up, my aunt's eyes suddenly opened wide as if she had been dreaming and was startled to find herself here in her own house. Tonio turned his head to the door as if he were underwater, a slow-motion movement, and I thought, at some level below the conscious, that his movement was filled with dread. Morgan stomped back into the front room and went toward the door.

My uncle entered first carrying two heavy-looking, shabby canvas suitcases. He was concentrating on the suitcases and didn't look up at us. When he was safely inside and had set the cases down, there was a dramatic pause, the door open to the cool, late summer night, dark because the moon had not yet risen, and Dorcas appeared in the doorway.

She was a small, slender, fair woman, seeming too tiny for the space in which she stood with all the night behind her, and not nearly big enough for my imaginings. Her blondeness was another surprise, I had pictured someone dark and glamorous-looking like my aunt with a lot of blusher on her cheeks and much dark lipstick. But Dorcas was fair-skinned and had short, pale blonde hair and grey eyes. She paused, evidently waiting for her eyes to adjust to the light. Nobody spoke, she began to smile and took a few steps toward us all standing in the centre of the room to receive her. She looked around at everyone, seemed about to move toward my aunt, she had already begun to lift her arms, when she stopped, a shiver ran through her, we could actually see her body contract, and the look on her face was as though someone had just given her news that was so horrible it appalled her.

I thought we all felt it; the sudden, soul-shaking horror that struck her. It was to me as though the lights had failed and the room momentarily darkened, or the house had been set spinning through space, and outside that open door was only endless darkness. I swear the room turned cold.

For an instant, perhaps it was longer, nobody moved; then my aunt gave a little jerk and went to Dorcas and, in one of the few gestures of tenderness I ever saw her make, she took her cousin in her arms and kissed her gently on each cheek. She released her and, still trembling faintly, Dorcas went to each of my cousins, took their hands, looked into their eyes, it was a marvel how each of them acquiesced to this, and finally reached Tonio.

Tonio had risen to his feet, but he wouldn't look at her and she had to reach for his hands that hung in fists by his sides. She took them in hers, pressed them to her cheeks and they opened slowly, like flowers, while Tonio looked at the floor, then she let them go and he sat down again, pressing them once more between his thighs.

Then voices broke out, two or three at once, and there were

shrieks and laughter, and everybody was moving around, finding places to sit, settling in.

"You've forgotten to introduce someone," Dorcas said. Her voice was light and high-pitched, childish-sounding. My aunt said carelessly, not looking at me, "That's Charlotte, Richard's daughter."

"She comes every single summer," Rhonda said, and everybody looked at me. I could feel myself blushing.

"It's lovely to meet you, Charlotte," she said, giving my name the French pronunciation, so that it sounded beautiful and strange.

"How do you do," I stammered, and everybody laughed and then ignored me. They began to pepper Dorcas with questions about her life, about what she had been doing and where and if it had been exciting or not, and if peculiar things had happened and what they were like. After a while Morgan got up and went into the kitchen and came back with a tray that held many different kinds of fruit all peeled and sliced and arranged so beautifully it was breathtaking. Then we drank tea and after that, brandy, even me, and more brandy, while the long evening turned hazy and warm and the corners of the room filled up with velvety shadows. Then I was being wakened by my uncle and led stumbling to my bed in the sitting room. He left me there and I did not even undress, but fell asleep with my head on the folded sheets I had been meant to put on the couch.

When I woke it was just beginning to be light and the birds were singing madly in the lilac and honeysuckle bushes right outside the open sitting room window. My head was throbbing and my mouth parched. I sat up trying to remember where I was and why. Gradually it all came back to me and in that grim awakening, the first of my life like that, an adult awakening, I remembered not the gaiety of the night before, but the strange thing that had happened when Dorcas had walked into the house.

I got up, still in my clothes from the day before, and went toward the kitchen to get a drink of water. The house was shrouded in silence and shadows and the noise of the birds faded as I moved into the kitchen.

Someone was sitting at the table against the far wall, the face a pale oval floating in the grey light. I stopped, frightened at this apparition, not even surprising in this house of mute voices, of veiled forces. The house was foreign this morning, it was as if my visits to this place had changed irrevocably, as if I had been on my last visit and had not even known it; perhaps it was over already. I paused, frightened, and rubbed at my eyes.

"Charlotte," the apparition said, and I recognized Dorcas. I wanted to speak but my throat and mouth were so dry I could only make a croaking sound. "Come and sit here," she said. Obediently I crossed the room and sat beside her. I shivered a little, perhaps I was still afraid, and she took my aunt's shawl that was hanging over the back of a chair and put it around my shoulders. It was a delicate grey, fringed, and made of wonderfully soft wool.

"I sent her this from Peru," she said, her voice distant, yet fond.

"Peru?" I croaked, hardly knowing what I was saying. She lifted a teapot and then I noticed that she had been drinking tea. She poured me a cup, it was pale and hot, and I took a slow sip, barely lifting the cup from the saucer.

"I thought I might have company," she said.

"Is it time to get up?" I asked, the tea having loosened my throat. I squinted, trying to read the clock on the stove across the room.

"No," she said. "I haven't been to bed," and she gave a little, conspiratorial laugh.

"Why not?" I asked, astonished.

"I had things to work out," Dorcas said, "and I knew I wouldn't sleep."

"I always think that," I told her, "but the next thing I know, I'm asleep." I was rueful, remembering the times I had tried to stay up with my cousins, who thought nothing of staying up all night and sleeping all day. I noticed that when I tried to lift the cup my hands were trembling. I looked at them, puzzled.

"It's the brandy," Dorcas explained. "It'll pass when you sleep some more." Even though the light coming through the window was turning golden as the sun rose, it seemed to me that everything was grey. There was a heaviness in the air, it was as though if I tried to rise from my chair I would not be able to, and I could not shake the feeling that something was over, that something had ended, although I didn't know what.

After a while Dorcas asked me in a gentle voice, "Do you like coming here?"

"Yes!" I said at once, with a passion that surprised even me, and then, softly, shaking my head, near tears, "no." Dorcas smiled.

"I know," she said.

We sat without speaking for a minute while I gratefully sipped the hot tea and tried to shake my feeling of the inexorable sadness of things.

Gradually I began to feel calmer, my hands stopped shaking and my thirst was quenched. But the strong emotion that had me in its grip remained. When I think about it now, I realize that something emanated from Dorcas. It was that she was more of a person than her small body had room for and so the force of her character, or its aura or something, existed for a radius of several feet around her, and if you sat near her as I was, you found yourself inside her. That's how it was that morning, I think. It was though I was inside Dorcas, and everything I saw or felt was coloured by what she was seeing and feeling.

"You are much like I was when I was twelve years old," she said to me. I turned to her, doubting what I had heard.

"What?" I asked, faltering.

"I too, had a childhood without delight," she said, and smiled at me. I wanted to ask her what she meant, but I was confused and dizzy from being told that I was like her, which I wanted to believe, but could not.

"Do spirits really talk to you?" I asked, then ducked my head, embarrassed.

"Yes, they do," she said, gravely. "Ever since I was a child."

"Like Tonio's voices?" I asked, gaining courage.

"No," she said, "at least I don't think so. Tonio's voices are cruel." She hesitated, turning her head away, blinking, then steadily, back to me. "But they tell me things, and I have dreams, too. I dream things."

"What things?" I asked, breathless with apprehension. I had dreams too, many of them, that I told no one about. I didn't like them, they were too frightening.

"Oh," she said, careless now, "you probably don't remember this, but not long ago a plane crashed with an important British diplomat on board. And as it was happening in Japan, I was at home dreaming about it." She paused, then went on, her voice livelier, as if this interested her. "Or I find lost things in my dreams. This ring." She lifted her hand, the one on the side away from me, and I saw again the elaborate silver ring with the large, lustreless green stone in it that I had seen the night before. "I lost this once during a trip I took with a friend. I wrote letters to the hotels where I had stayed, I searched my friend's car, but it was nowhere to be found. Then in a dream I saw it in the tall grass against the old stone wall in a churchyard we had walked through looking at the graves. I went back, and there it was, exactly as I'd dreamt."

A moaning cry came floating up the stairs from the basement, followed by another, fainter.

"It's only Tonio," I said, anxious to reassure her. "He doesn't sleep very well. He has dreams too."

"Yes, Tonio," she said softly, but the feeling I was getting from her, that feeling of something being very wrong and changed forever grew so strong that I almost cried out to her to stop. She looked at the tabletop still dusted with crumbs from our evening meal the day before, and said, "Charlotte," again the French pronunciation that sounded so beautiful to me, "Charlotte, what you feel in this house is really there. You must go home, and don't come here anymore." I thought about this for a moment, but I was not surprised. I had known she would say that, sometimes I think I had wakened that morning, lying on that hard couch, knowing this very thing, and that she would say it.

She put her hand on mine, the one that had trembled when I lifted the teacup. Her hand wasn't much bigger than my child's hand, but more delicate than mine and fine-boned, and I felt now an overwhelming warmth coming from her that comforted and soothed me, from the pain that I suddenly understood I had always been in, because of the mystery of the world and all the things I didn't know or understand.

"Go back to bed and sleep," she said, and she leaned toward me and kissed me with formality on each cheek. I can still feel the kisses, it seems to me that the love they expressed lingers, cannot be erased.

I was about to tell her that I couldn't move, when I found myself rising, as if on the air, moving away from the table, across the room, going into the sitting room where I pulled the blanket someone had tossed onto the couch up over me and went at once to sleep.

I have said that my uncle spoke very little, except occasionally to correct my aunt who was given to lying, in a mild, passionless, yet incontrovertible manner. Yet sometimes, very rarely, he would begin to speak, and when he did, everyone would stop whatever they were doing — Morgan's sulk would melt, Rhonda's inattentiveness and nervousness would dissolve, Tonio would close his eyes and slowly relax, and even Aunt Jacqueline would look right at him as if she couldn't have looked away if she tried — and everyone would listen.

Then Uncle Hector would tell stories that didn't really seem like stories but were, that were very long, with many ins and outs so that you would forget that he had started out talking about something which he had dropped, when he would go back and effortlessly pick up that thread and carry on with it as neatly as a woman knitting a complex pattern, yet never dropping a stitch.

In his stories he would explain things about the world: how coffee was made and how people got started drinking it and why; how a northern forest grew and died and renewed itself and died again, bit by bit, in the midst of life; how the people in a certain far-away, forgotten place lived; all about times lost long ago to history and times yet to come, and interwoven with these explanations about the world were bits of poetry, sometimes snatches of songs, and whole paragraphs in other languages, that sounded so beautiful you felt you understood their meaning. And there were parts about people he knew or had heard of, about the strange things they had done or that had happened to them, what they said, how they looked when they said it, what they wore, and how they knew what they knew. And when he was finished two or more hours later, the room would be so silent you could hear your own thoughts, you felt dizzy with the fall from the places he had taken you.

Then, slowly, each of us would get up from where we were and wander quietly away, and when we met again, hours later, we would blink and be embarrassed, we would take a while to be ourselves.

When Dorcas came everything was different. Everyone wanted to be where she was, even my uncle, so that the house felt congested with everybody always crowding into the same room. It was different too, because somehow she made me feel that I was part of things, that I could talk to her too, if I wanted to, and not be afraid that she would send me back home if she noticed me, even though she had said I should go home. No matter what I had told Dorcas there was still a part of me that wished to be a member of my cousin's family, another neglected, ungovernable, and stormy child of my aunt and uncle's. Part of me wished to dance in the moonlight alone, to see things that weren't there, to wear ragbag costumes, to stomp about violently and make the floor shake.

Although we all hung about Dorcas, there were times when she went off alone with each member of the household, one by one. I wanted Dorcas to have a private little talk with me too, but mulling it over, I realized that she had talked to me, that morning after she had arrived, when I had wakened feeling an adult, feeling the world had changed and not for the better, that my time in this household was over, that the world was about to fly apart, that morning when she had been invaded by knowledge so immeasurably terrible that her mourning had communicated itself to me. We had had our téte-a-tète.

One morning Dorcas left. She had told us that her visit would be a short one because she had to get back to England to begin shooting a film she had a small part in. She left very early, but my aunt actually dragged herself out of bed in order to go with Dorcas and my uncle to the airport on the other side of the city. Morgan, Rhonda, Tonio and I didn't know exactly when she was leaving, only that it would be soon, and so none of us got to say good-bye to her.

But she had sat up with us all the night before while Uncle Hector launched into one of his stories, the only one that summer, that had gone on into the late hours of the night, and when my uncle had finished, the pits in his skin looking deeper by lamplight, almost grotesque, so that my heart ached with love for him, she kissed each one of us, Tonio three times, and then she went to her room. I never saw her again. And even though I know the names of a few of the films she had small parts in, I never seem to be where they are showing, I've never seen her on the screen.

Sometimes I wonder if I imagined her, but then I remember that moment when she entered my aunt and uncle's house and stopped, stricken with horror by something she knew was present in the room, that none of the rest of us, except possibly Tonio, knew.

That night Tonio killed himself. He hung himself from the open studding above the doorframe of his room, using a new brown hemp rope he must have bought especially for the purpose.

Rhonda found him. She had staggered out of bed at five in the morning to go to the bathroom and groggy, half-asleep, she had walked into his dangling body. She told us that she said to him, "Tonio, you're in my room, go to bed," and when he didn't move, she had opened her eyes and found him hanging there, dead.

She didn't faint or scream, but instead backed away and started up the stairs with some vague idea of telling someone to make him get down, and she met me at the top of the stairs coming back from the same errand she had been on originally. Her face was white, her blue eyes wide and dark, and unable to speak, she pointed down the stairs, only pointed, and I went down and saw Tonio hanging from the doorframe, dead.

I was the one who screamed. I was the one who went racing up the stairs and on, all the way up the second flight into my aunt and uncle's bedroom where I had never been, screaming and screaming, and they leaped up, I pointed down the stairs as Rhonda had done before she fainted to lie in a crumpled, little-girl heap at the top of the basement stairs, they went on past her, knowing somehow that Rhonda was not what I meant them to see, down to where they found poor dead Tonio, and Morgan kneeling at his feet, clutching him to her, her face pressed against his legs, her jaw set, her eyes wild.

Then my uncle took charge. The details are lost to me, or rather, even now, years later, waking from a sound sleep a detail will pop into my head, something I had forgotten, what my uncle said to me, what Morgan was wearing, or where my aunt stood at the service for Tonio. I remember that since my parents were there that same day, someone must have called them, and they took me away to a hotel where we must have stayed, since I also remember being at Tonio's service, and my aunt and uncle scattering his ashes on their land in defiance of the law, out toward the river, into that view that you couldn't see anymore from the house. I can't put it together very well, don't actually remember, sometimes even wonder if it wasn't all a story my uncle told and there wasn't, never had been, Tonio or Dorcas, or that gloomy, tumultuous house set in a ruined garden in the country, outside a city I never entered. My memories are confused and incomplete, yet there is a layer as clear and as dark as a forest stream, a layer where I know everything that happened.

Of course, I never went back to my cousin's house and as they never had visited us, I don't think I saw them again, although somehow or other I know what happened to each one of them. I suppose my mother phoned me and told me, in her many unwelcome, late night phone calls she began to make after she started drinking so heavily.

"Why did you go away and leave me alone? Come back, come back, I love you," she would implore me, her mouth too close to the phone so that the words always came out cracked and thick.

After Morgan and Rhonda left, my aunt and uncle went their separate ways, my aunt to Europe, probably to find Dorcas, though I have no way of knowing that. Since Aunt Jacqueline wasn't a relative by blood, only by marriage, I didn't feel an obligation to keep in touch, nor did I want to, nor apparently, did she.

My uncle continued with his writing, but he travelled more

and more, we used to get torn and wrinkled Christmas cards from him, the ink blotted and smeared, in February or March, mailed from Lusaka or Kuala Lumpur or Reykjavik. 'Merry Christmas,' that was all they said. I saw him once on television, giving an interview about another book he'd just published, and though he looked much the same as when he took all that long summer night to tell us, in a voice both quiet and compelling, one of his long runes about something which I've never been able to remember, I found, when I saw his square, pocked face, his tormented, distant eyes, that I didn't love him anymore.

Dinner on the Edge of the City

When I first thought about it I was driving down Twentieth to visit Donna and Doug. Since I had last been in the city they had moved from a downtown apartment to a house in a suburb on the far west side of the city, a place that had been a wheat field when we were kids. I was thinking about the ways in which Twentieth Street had changed since I had last driven down it, very few actually, and at the corner of Avenue B, while I waited for the light, I found myself peering down the Avenue to see if a certain house was still there, the one we used to watch the prostitutes going in and coming out of. Prostitutes?

The word caught me by surprise, the picture it evoked rising up suddenly, vivid and richly-coloured. The aging, black-haired woman with the painted face punching the side of the bus under the window where I sat. Perhaps I had dreamt it?

The light changed, I edged forward into the traffic which was as heavy now as it had ever been. The street was still only two lanes wide with cars parked bumper to bumper down each side. Why had I chosen to drive down it when I knew Twenty-Second was wider and designed for cross-town traffic?

My mind would not let that flash of memory alone. The high heels, their staccato drumming on the cement getting louder, drawing closer through the darkness. I could feel a prickling on the back of my neck. If I could remember so much and so clearly, it must surely have happened.

The traffic suddenly halted for an old lady crossing the street at an angle, oblivious to the line of cars backed up in each direction waiting for her. She was short and stout and wore a brightly coloured flowered and fringed shawl over a shapeless black dress. She carried a bulging shopping bag hanging from each hand. I had to slam on my brakes to keep from hitting the car in front of me and I knew by the screech behind me that someone had almost run into me. I thought all such old women had long since died. I watched her cross and, without willing it, without being able to prevent it if I had wanted to, the whole thing ballooned up at once from whatever darkness it had been hiding in all these years.

I was thirteen. I was with Erin. It was Saturday night and we were on our way home from a movie. The bus had stopped at that corner to let somebody on or off. It was dark, it was summer. The bus windows were open, it must have been hot and I could feel the warm night air on my face and bare arms.

When suddenly we heard the sound of high heels clattering up that dark side street toward where we waited, the bus door open, in front of the beer parlour that used to be on that corner. A woman burst out of the shadows into the light, leaped onto the steps close to where we sat near the front, the bus scooped her up, the doors shutting behind her, when two more women pounded into the light, their faces contorted, shouting curses, and just as we pulled away, one of them hit the bus just below my window with all her strength. I had looked full into her black eyes, I saw her sagging, rouged cheeks, her shiny, purple mouth; I saw the wrinkles in her neck, and that her long, black-as-coal hair was dyed. I saw where the dye had stained her scalp.

I gave my full attention to my driving and found I was climbing Pleasant Hill now, the traffic was lighter and I was passing my old school where I had gone for a year, passing the church hall where we used to go every night, passing — but I didn't recognize anything else. From there on everything seemed different.

Even though they had given me good directions, it took me

some time to find Donna and Doug's house. It was because I was disoriented by this maze of crescents and bays that had sprung up in what had always been the mysterious, shimmering blue edge of the city.

I came upon the house suddenly, accidentally. It was handsome, a two-story white stucco with dark brown trim and a deck all around the back which I could see as I approached it. There were at least two other identical houses on the crescent. I was nervous, I hadn't seen them in four or five years, but I rang the bell without hesitating and Donna answered it at once.

"You haven't changed a bit," she said to me, as we embraced.

"If only it were true," I said. Doug was standing in the living room at a teak bar across from a white brick fireplace. There was no fire in the fireplace, it was summer after all, and the bricks were pristine.

"Marion," he said. "It's good to see you." He made us drinks and Donna and I sat on the sofa while Doug sat across from us in an armchair.

"The strangest thing happened to me on my way here," I began to fill the sudden silence. Doug laughed.

"A funny thing happened to me on my way ... " he said. I had to laugh too. Donna, frowning, took a sip of her drink, then quickly a couple more.

"I suddenly remembered something that happened when I was thirteen," I said. "Something I had utterly and completely forgotten." I told them about the prostitutes, and although they listened intently, when I was done, I was left with a curious, unfinished feeling.

"What were you doing on Twentieth Street at night when you were so young?" Donna asked, half-disapproving, half-amused. We hadn't met till we were in university when my father owned three not very profitable florist shops which had made our family name a familiar one in the city. Her father had been a gynecologist.

"When we first moved here," I explained, "my father was just starting his own business. It was quite a gamble and for a year or so there, we could only afford to rent an old house on

Twenty-First Street, off Avenue H or J. I forget which."

"Really," Donna said. "I never knew that. That must have been ... an adventure." I looked at her but she was smiling so falsely at me that I hardly recognized her. I couldn't remember why I had liked her well enough to ask her to be my bridesmaid. Eddie had been Doug's closest friend so naturally he had asked Doug to stand up for him, and since I had no sisters and we double-dated all the time — that must have been how it had happened.

"How is your mother?" Doug asked. "How's dinner coming, Donna?" he said to her before I could answer. He had gone back to the bar to refill our glasses. Without answering, Donna went into the kitchen.

"She's recovering, but it's slow," I said. "She's in her seventies, after all. Anyway, I'll be able to go back to Winnipeg in a few days."

"That's good," he said. "I don't remember her, you know. When you called Donna, I was trying to remember all about that time. I know the four of us spent a lot of time at your parents' house, but I can't remember what your mother looked like."

"Tall," Donna called from the kitchen, "with dark brown hair and glasses." Doug's face went blank, as though he had heard nothing.

"I look like her," I said. He handed me my drink. He wasn't listening. "Lately I've been thinking that a person should try to remember everything. To go over his whole life, I mean, and try to fill in everything."

"Why?" I asked. He shrugged his shoulders.

"Because ... " he said calmly, and wouldn't say anymore. Donna returned from the kitchen and took her second drink from the bar.

"Not me," she said triumphantly. "The less I remember, the better. It's all water under the bridge anyway." She drank half her drink at once. Doug watched her. I looked away. At home Eddie would be drawing the drapes, switching on the television.

"On my way here I saw an old Ukrainian lady crossing the street, you remember, the kind we used to see? All dressed in black with a babushka over her head and shoulders, carrying a couple of full shopping bags. She was like an apparition out of the past. I thought that generation had all died."

"I can't remember ever being on Twentieth Street when I was a kid," Donna said. "It was the wrong side of town." She sighed, and looked around the big room disapprovingly.

"We got this place for a song," Doug said to me. "The contractor went broke."

"It's a beautiful house," I said.

"When the market improves, we'll sell it," Donna said. "And move across town to something a little more ... "

"Fashionable," Doug said, straight-faced. "To a smarter address."

"It's funny how Twentieth Street has changed and yet not changed," I said. I couldn't seem to let the subject go. "There used to be a big department store on the corner ... "

"Out of business years ago," Doug said. He's a salesman of some kind and always knows about things like that.

"I remember little shop after little shop. They sold all kinds of strange things: peasant shawls and scarves and handiwork, all sorts of religious things, and embroidery thread, musical instruments, and fresh vegetables. And there used to be an old-fashioned soda shop, when I first came here." I could see it, the oily wooden floor, the old man who ran it leaning on the counter, smiling at Erin and me as we drank our cherry cokes. "It had those old-fashioned, round-bottomed chairs with the heart-shaped wire backs ... "

"Really?" Donna said. "I thought those only existed in movies." She got up to go back to the dinner, but I couldn't stop.

"I went to school on Pleasant Hill," I said. "What a year that was! And I'd forgotten all about it. Can you imagine that?"

"Sure," Doug said. "People forget important things all the time. I'm trying to remember them. Every one of them."

"I had a best friend named Erin. I wonder whatever happened to her. We used to go skating together on the outdoor rink at Avenue L every night in the winter and on Saturdays we went to movies. And we looked for boys."

"Sounds pretty harmless to me," Doug said.

"I suppose so," I said, bewildered, "but when I remember

those women and the bus, there was so much more there. I could feel it." It was strange, like I had had a dream and could remember only snatches of it, impressions, but I thought if I struggled with it, it might all come back. "Erin was a funny girl, now that I think of it. Wild for excitement. Nothing scared her. But then, the kids were tough, the school was tough, there were gangs ... "

"Gangs!" Donna said. "Open the wine, will you, Doug?" She handed him the bottle and a corkscrew. "My, you do have a shady past." Whoever Donna had been was retreating farther with every sip of alcohol and this brittle mask was sliding into place. What had she been like when we were young women? I couldn't remember.

"Yes," I said, doggedly. "There was a gang of girls, older than we were. Some of them, now that I think of it, might already have been prostitutes. I'm not sure about that. They used to get into fights all the time, with other girls. They wanted us to fight them."

We went into the dining room and sat down to dinner. The meal was simple, but excellent: wild rice, shrimp, mushrooms, salad. The dining room seemed very big for the two of them and empty. Donna's first baby had died. Her second had grown up and gone to university, married, and gone away somewhere to live. I wasn't sure if it was a boy or a girl.

"My father died five years ago," she said. "Did you know that?"

"Yes," I said. "I was so sorry. He was a fine man."

"He was," she said. "He was a wonderful father."

"This is a marvellous dinner," I said. "I didn't know you were such a good cook."

"Mother hated my father," she said. "Can you imagine that? And last year when she was so sick and we all thought she was dying, I asked her why? Why did you hate daddy so much? And do you know what she said?" She raised her head and looked into my eyes. Doug had set his fork down with a patient air. I shook my head, no.

"She said, 'I don't remember. Oh, Donna,' she said. 'I can't remember anymore. He was only a man.' " Doug picked up his fork again.

"Maybe she just didn't want to tell you," I offered, "to spare you something." Donna shrugged as though she had lost interest in the matter.

Doug said, "I've been over my whole childhood, every second of it. I had a happy childhood. My father was a farmer."

"I remember that," I said, although why I should remember such an unimportant detail, I don't know. Doug must have lived in the city for thirty years.

"I remembered my first experience with a girl," he said. "I was twelve."

"Really, Doug." Donna lifted her head and stared at him as she had done to me a moment before. "I'd be more interested in your more recent experiences," she said slowly. He ignored her. I rushed on.

"I think that was the year I discovered sex too. When I was thirteen, although I didn't know that was what I was doing," I said.

"How could you not know?" Donna asked. "And anyway, what is there to discover? Sex is sex. You have it, you've discovered it." She paused, took a sip of wine, set her glass down. "And then you can forget it." Doug moved his glass a little to the right, then put it back where it had been. But by now nothing she said would have made a difference. I was in the sway of a compulsion and had to go on.

"Our teacher was a man, principal of the school, and he was big and violent, always hitting the boys and pushing them around. And he was never in the classroom, always busy somewhere else and they used to do anything they wanted when he wasn't around. Grab at us in the classroom, say dirty things to us and about us," I said. "We got to like it," I said. Doug laughed. Donna stared at me again. "One time, I remember, during health class, we were taking artificial respiration. They call it something else now."

"Resuscitation," Doug said. "C.P.R. Whatever that stands for."

"He was teaching us how to do it so he had us all standing around him in a circle at the front of the room, and he looked around for somebody to be ... "

"The drownee ... " Doug offered.

"And naturally, we all thought — well, I guess we didn't think about it, we just took it for granted that he'd pick one of the boys. But he didn't. He looked around at all of us and he said, 'Erin.'" Donna and Doug were both listening to me now, not eating. "I can still remember the looks on the boys faces. They looked sort of uneasy, and right away they hid their looks, smoothed their faces out, but I can't remember how the girls looked. We were just scared, I guess, and embarrassed."

"Why?" Donna asked. I went on as if she hadn't spoken.

"We were only kids but some of us were grown up physically. Erin was the most grown up girl in the class. And we were all wearing skirts. It was a Catholic school, we weren't allowed to wear slacks. He made her lie down on the floor in the middle of the circle, on her stomach, and he knelt over her, straddled her with his knees just at her hips and every time he lifted her elbows, that was how they did it then, his tie brushed her back." I can still see that tie. It was navy blue with diagonal red stripes. It had moved down her back, lifted, moved down her back. His face had been closed, like the boys', his eyes half-shut.

"The old bastard!" Doug said. He seemed more surprised than upset. "So that was how you discovered sex." I could hear Doug's voice, deep and masculine, carrying across the table to me. It echoed faintly in the big, empty room. Donna's fork clinked against her plate with a precise, musical sound. The air in the room seemed heavy to me, and much too warm. Donna was standing again, reaching for our empty plates to take them to the kitchen.

"My discovery of sex was so long ago, and since I was raised on a farm," Doug said, "I suppose it had to do with calves and foals or dogs and cats. It seemed to be something I've always known. No trauma here," he said, and raised his glass, tilted back his head, and drained it. I could hear Donna moving dishes around in the kitchen. Her breasts on the dirty, wooden floor, his big hands flat on her shoulder blades, visible through her white nylon blouse. The room was so stuffy, I was having trouble catching my breath.

Once he stood in front of my desk and read a story to us

about one of the saints, and all the time he was reading he was rocking back and forth against my desk, the top of it meeting the top of his thighs; then he'd push away, a slight movement, barely noticeable to anybody else, lean toward me, push away, lean toward me — and all the time he read I watched, fascinated, the bulge in his grey flannel pants directly in front of my eyes, that grew more distinct as he leaned toward me and diminished as he pulled away.

"More wine?" Doug asked.

"No, thanks," I said.

"Just a drop," he said and filled my glass again. "We'll finish it off." The wine was a dark red and it glowed as if the light from the chandelier above the table was inside the goblet.

I tried to think of something that would bring me back to the dining room, to Doug sitting across from me. Donna came in carrying the dessert, a pale meringue filled with glistening, multi-coloured fruit that shone like a jewel. I could see that even Doug was moved by its beauty.

After dinner we went back into the living room. Donna wouldn't let me help her with the clearing away or the dishes so Doug and I were left alone sitting across from each other with a glass coffee table between us.

"Do you remember when we were all best friends?" he asked me. I nodded, although I did not and the longer I stayed, the less I could remember. "Your being here has brought it all back to me," he went on. "The June-in-January dance, the wiener roasts, the weekend in Edmonton when none of us were married."

"Doug, why do you think I blotted out that whole year?" I asked. "A whole year! And it was filled with such significance." I was still remembering things: the winos on the hotel corner who used to try to touch our breasts when we passed by, roughhousing on the grass long after dark, boys and girls together, till the police came and chased us home.

"You should know," he said mildly. "I don't." He was staring into his coffee cup, his hands lying loose on his lap. Was he trying to remember some faraway, lost moment? I wanted to ask him, are you happy?

"Why do you want to remember everything?" I asked, softly,

so as not to disturb him. He didn't lift his head, but I could see the movement of his lips.

"How else to forget?" he asked.

I drove home to my parents' house through streets nearly deserted and black with rain. I longed for Ed and the comfort of his arms.

We had moved away. I had changed schools. I remember that for a long time afterward whenever we drove downtown and I saw the smokestacks of the power plant that marked the eastern boundary of that neighbourhood, I would think about my life there.

But time passed, things happened. I thought of the old lady with the shawl and the shopping bags. I began to doubt I had really seen her. My car hissed down the silent, wet streets, passing through pools of water and I could imagine behind me a long trail of bright reflections, shimmering and broken.

Babette

"I had the most wonderful dream last night," Emmaline said, "and now, I am no longer afraid to die."

Babette observed her warily. Emmaline lay propped up against her fat white pillows, her even whiter hair fluffed out like cotton wool around her face, her thin, crooked-fingered hands still wearing the worn wedding ring, holding the upper edge of the quilt. She was not looking at Babette. Babette swung her foot once or twice in an annoyed way, then stopped because it hurt, and because it tired her. She had so little energy.

"Oh?" she said, smiling. "What did you dream about?"

Emmaline raised one trembling hand and made a gesture which, had she been well, would have been sweeping. As it was, her hand moved an inch or two in each direction, then dropped back to hold the edge of the quilt again, as if a stranger who couldn't quite be trusted not to try to touch her, were in the room.

"I was in a beautiful house, a most beautiful house which was filled with people. All kinds of people, fine people, good people, and the son of the owner came up to me and welcomed me. Then he took me all through the house and introduced to me the other guests one by one. All of them gracious, all of them friendly, pleased to see me and to talk with me. It was a most lovely time." She smiled, a little colour appearing in each cheek.

Babette thought, those drugs, oh, those drugs, and she shook her head, just a little, barely perceptibly. Her thigh had begun to ache, and she waited, testing, to see if the pain would leave or if she would have to rise and drag herself downstairs, she thought of it as dragging herself, to the kitchen where her Brompton's Cocktail, a combination of morphine and cocaine and god knew what else, waited in the fridge.

They could hear someone mounting the stairs slowly, and Babette turned her head and Emmaline her eyes, to watch the open door. Ginny entered carrying a tray with a teapot, two teacups and saucers, a cream pitcher and a sugar bowl resting on it. She set it down carefully, without speaking, on the table between the two old ladies.

"There," she said. "I hope it's not too strong."

Emmaline observed her daughter thoughtfully.

"They served us ... champagne, I think. Yes, champagne, in crystal glasses that threw rainbows of light." She seemed no longer to see her daughter, nor her daughter's mother-in-law, so pale and fragile, sitting across from her. She paid no attention to the tea.

Ginny began to pour the tea. The amber fluid streamed soundlessly, steaming, into the blue-shadowed cups. His hands on my waist, she could feel the smallness of her waist under his hands, could feel him drawing back to thrust gently again into her, as she lay, face down, crosswise on the bed, her arms stretched out on each side of her head, feeling the cool sheet under her palms.

"Such a pleasant temperament your daughter has, Emmaline," Babette said softly. Ginny couldn't tell if she was being serious or merely malicious. "Always with a little smile, a softness in her eyes."

Emmaline said, "And the rugs, so soft and thick, so very blue they were."

"What is that, Mother?" Ginny asked, turning to help her mother raise herself against her pillows so that she could hold her teacup herself.

"My dream," Emmaline said. "I was telling Babette about my

dream." She looked hopefully at her daughter who was folding back six inches of quilt and sheet and smoothing them down neatly, just below Emmaline's flat breasts. Ginny didn't meet her mother's eyes. The skin of his back as smooth as any woman's, like satin to touch, but firm underneath, and low, where his buttocks began there was the hardness of his spine.

She handed her mother her filled teacup which Emmaline rested on the folded bedclothes. Ginny turned to Babette then, but Babette was already reaching to lift her cup and saucer carefully and bring it toward herself, her rings glinting.

"Such a dream," she remarked. "I could use a dream like that," and she sighed, half-smiling, half-wry. She dreamt of dark places, of black-bottomed wells, of empty spaces. When she was bad and had to take a lot of Brompton's, she sometimes hallucinated her dead husband and mother.

"I'm glad you feel ... ready," she said to Emmaline. Ginny stood between them, but back a little, closer to the window, so that Babette and Emmaline could see each other. She appeared to be thinking about something, one hand raised to touch her cheek, her dark eyes, so like Emmaline's, gazing at some spot in the air between the table and the doorway. It's hard for her, Babette reminded herself, both of us sick, Emmaline dying, Armand away all day.

Ginny roused herself to ask, "Would you like a biscuit, Babette?"

"No, thank you," Babette said. "A piece of toast was more than enough."

"You don't eat enough," Ginny said mildly. "Half a biscuit? Mother?" She turned to Emmaline and looked down at her reflectively while Emmaline reset her cup in its saucer with a shaky hand, then leaned against her pillow and closed her eyes. The saucer tipped a little and the tea washed slowly up the side of the cup. Ginny reached down and took the cup and saucer from her mother and set them back on the tray. Emmaline's mouth slowly opened.

She set them down as if she were thinking about something else and Babette thought with irritation how she had never liked that dreamy quality her daughter-in-law had. Armand so quick and brusque, as she had once been herself, before the tumours had begun to strike.

Tumours! she thought, although she had thought of all the things she might call them and had decided to call them tumours. She would have kicked out her leg fiercely, but refrained because of the pain. There was something new going on in her left arm, it had begun yesterday. She wasn't ready to say anything yet. More radiation. She sighed, but thought, by the time I have it, I am always glad of the relief it brings.

"Did Armand talk to the doctor for me?" she asked Ginny without bothering to lower her voice. When Emmaline slept, nothing could wake her. It was the drugs, they were all sure.

"Armand?" Ginny asked, looking at her mother-in-law. "Oh." She caught her breath guiltily.

"Your husband," Babette said, wry again. Ginny laughed, colouring.

"I remember," she said, lifting the tray and sliding it off the table. Babette set her teacup onto the tray and waited.

"He said he'd call from the office, and then he'd phone here if he could catch the doctor in." And his mouth on her breasts. My god, his mouth. She caught her breath, then tried to turn it into a sigh. Beside her, as she passed her going out of the room, Babette was rising slowly, reaching for her cane.

"Just wait," Ginny said. "I'll run this tray down to the kitchen, then come back and give you a hand."

"No need," Babette said, her breath growing short already, but Ginny was gone, running lightly down the stairs, her feet making a swishing noise on the thick carpet.

Babette began the painful, slow walk to the doorway using her cane, concentrating on getting her right leg to move forward, so far, not too far, thinking, damn, damn. Why is Ginny the way she is? She thought of turning to Emmaline who might be awake now, behind her, watching her with her big dark eyes and asking her, what is it with your daughter? What is it she is thinking about?

Ginny was hurrying up the stairs now, coming toward her, for Babette had managed to progress out the door and the few steps to the top of the stairs. She waited, panting, while Ginny reached her, turned sideways, and took her arm.

"Lean on me," Ginny said, and although Babette hated the very idea, she found herself leaning slightly against Ginny's warm, plump arm and shoulder. In fact, as they began the slow, halting descent, she felt the heat from Ginny's body beginning to warm her. She concentrated on each step with such intensity that there was only the mechanics of descending the stairs and the animal heat of her daughter-in-law's body melting into hers. Against Ginny she suddenly felt how thin she had become, so that she was all hard bones, yet against Ginny's solidity, how light. My bones have hollowed, she thought, with surprise and certainty. She could sense Ginny's bones, blood-filled and glowing, her curved abdomen full of round hot organs, her thighs, fleshy and plump, her breasts, warm as bread. She could have wept right there, descending the stairs in her daughter-in-law's house, for the way she felt herself dissolving into air.

"Where do you want to go, Babette?" Ginny asked, her breath warm and moist on Babette's cheek. Babette had not yet caught her breath and the tumour in her thigh was screaming. Her arm where Ginny had held it ached with a steady pain that threatened to grow worse.

"Tele ... vision," she said. Ginny waited, and when Babette finally began to turn, she turned too. "You take such good ... care of me," Babette said. "How hard it must be, the two of us."

"It's not hard," Ginny said, but Babette heard how her voice had gone dreamy again. How I opened my legs. Did he open them for me? Yes, with his hands, gently. He put his mouth ... Ginny helped Babette lower herself into the armchair in front of the television set. Without speaking again, she turned it on and tuned it to the late morning soap opera Babette had inexplicably taken to watching. She faced Babette, then quickly turned away again and left the room.

Babette had closed her eyes, but vaguely she could hear the fridge door opening and shutting. She heard Ginny say, "Here," in a gentle voice. She opened her eyes again and saw Ginny's face close to hers, holding in one hand a spoon filled with a clear liquid, and the dark brown bottle in the other. She was about to refuse, not yet, but her hip was swelling with pain, and all at once she relinquished something and opened her mouth as Emmaline had when she fell asleep. The Brompton's tasted hateful. She could hardly bear to swallow it. When she had managed to get it down without gagging or coughing, she leaned back and closed her eyes again.

"Thank you," she said.

In the kitchen Ginny set the spoon in the shiny sink, then stood looking out the small window above it at her neighbours' snow-filled backyards. She remembered her mother, and almost ran upstairs to see how she was, then thought better of it. Later, in a minute. She sighed, thinking how he would stand behind her when she was undressing, bend to put his mouth on her neck and his hands would creep around her to flutter teasingly over her breasts, how ...

She thought, I have to stop thinking about this, I can't — but the thought of treading through these days, up and down the stairs, watching the looks on their faces, giving pills or fluids, emptying basins skimmed with their scanty vomit, and Emmaline's occasional, embarrassing bedpan, washing their frail bodies, without the things she thought about, so appalled her as it sank in, that she spun around and stared at the patterned vinyl floor, one hand up on each side of her face.

She began to plan lunch, checking in the vegetable crisper in the fridge and lifting the quart of milk to see how much was left. She thought about her mother's dream and wondered if it meant anything. She should go upstairs quietly, and sneak a look into her room.

But Emmaline was not asleep.

"He was very slender, the son," she said, "and so beautifully dressed." Ginny, who had paused in the doorway, was a little disconcerted by the look in her mother's eyes, or perhaps by the absence of the look she had come, over more than forty years of daughterhood, to expect. She came all the way into the room and stood by her mother's bed looking down at her.

"Would you like a little mushroom soup for lunch?" she asked. "You always liked mushroom." Unexpectedly, Emmaline laughed, a short, light sound in the still house. Ginny could imagine that the sound would not be heard beyond the doorway, that Babette, sitting exhausted in front of the television set, would not even know Emmaline had laughed. "And some fruit?" Ginny said. "I have some lovely ripe cantaloupe."

"We used to call it muskmelon," Emmaline said, then smiled slightly, looking beyond Ginny. Perhaps she's gone to sleep again, Ginny thought. She went quietly back downstairs to the kitchen. The TV murmured faintly in the next room.

She hesitated, trying to decide whether to put in a little onion or not. Both women's stomachs were so touchy, Ginny had to be careful about spices and flavourings. She found the plastic-wrapped package of fresh mushrooms and lifted them out from behind the left-over casserole she had served Armand for dinner the night before. She frowned when she saw it, but when the mushrooms bounced out of the package onto the counter beside the cutting board, she could feel herself smiling again. Buying them in the supermarket on the other side of town where she knew no one and no one knew her, alone, her flesh still hot from his touch, she felt as if she carried him invisibly surrounding her body, she had not felt alone at all.

Remembering Babette now, she set down her paring knife and went to the door of the family room. Babette, her long, elegant bones pronounced through her thin flesh, her rings gleaming, loose now on her long fingers, sat with her head back, her hands spread flat on her lap, watching the television set.

"Can I get you anything?" Ginny asked. Babette's pale blue eyes shifted to her, held, then shifted back to the television. Her lipsticked mouth, its outline as austerely beautiful as ever, worked, as if she were saying something to herself she didn't wish to say out loud.

"Cancer!" Babette said, still not looking at Ginny, taking her cane in her hand and grasping it tightly, angrily. She moved the head of the cane back and forth jerkily, not attempting to rise with it. Ginny watched her for a moment.

"The nurse comes this afternoon," she said uncertainly, then went back to the kitchen.

She began to wash and slice the mushrooms. Their texture reminded her of flesh. He would run his hand up and down her back, over her hips, across her stomach. Such skin, he would say.

Such skin. I've never known a woman with skin like yours. When he was kissing her abdomen, or the inside of her thighs, his face pressed against her, she would think, what else can there be but this? And she would not think about the two dying old women at all, or she would not have to because they were an unspoken presence wherever she was.

But she could not discover the connection. Try as she would, she could not understand. Suddenly she wanted to go to Babette and shout angrily, flesh is flesh! But she did not know even what this meant.

She set the skillet on the stove, turned the burner on, and dropped butter into the pan. Next she took a small, heavy, red-enamelled pot from the cupboard and measured a little flour into it, then searched for the quart of stock she kept in the back of the fridge. The butter had begun to melt and she lifted the cutting board heaped with the sliced mushrooms, smelling of the earth, faintly musky, and pushed them into the butter. She turned them with a wooden spoon, listening to the sizzle, watching them turn golden in the melted butter and the heat.

In the evening Armand came home.

"How did it go today?" he asked from the hallway where he was hanging up his coat. She came and stood in the doorway, wiping her hands on her apron.

"All right," she said. "The nurse came."

"I know, it was her day," he said, moving his briefcase to a corner where no one would trip over it, although it had been four years since the last child had left home and much longer since any of them had raced, giggling and shrieking, through the house. "Did she have anything new to say?" Ginny watched the polished brown leather case gleaming in the corner. She shifted her eyes to her husband, who stood running his hand over his thick, yellow-brown hair.

"You got a haircut," she said, putting up a hand to touch the short hair high on his neck, where it glinted in the artificial light. It felt prickly against her fingertips.

After dinner Armand came upstairs to pay his daily visit to his wife's mother.

"Emmaline," he said, smiling. "How are you this evening?"

Ginny was sipping a cup of coffee and sitting in the chair Babette occupied in the mornings before she made the journey downstairs. Emmaline lifted her hand again, and again moved it back and forth an inch or so in each direction.

"I am well tonight," she said. "I had the most wonderful dream."

"Really," Armand said. He came into the room and sat down beside Ginny in the only other chair in the room, and crossed one leg over the other with a gesture that was polite, not quite weary. In this light Ginny noticed the grey in the hair above his ear and shifted in her chair, resting her head on its back as though she too were weary, although she wasn't.

"I am not afraid to die now," Emmaline said. "Everyone was so kind to me, so gracious and interested." She waved her hand again, the other one still holding onto the top of the quilt. "Such beauty." Armand glanced at Ginny, then looked back to Emmaline.

"That must be a comfort," he offered, finally, again adjusting his position slightly.

"Aha," Emmaline said. "If only Babette could have such a dream." Armand looked back down to his lap and moved his hands. Ginny could always feel how all he wanted to do was rise and go. Just go.

"Perhaps she will," Ginny said, to quiet her mother. It was time for her mother's evening pills. She rose and opened the drawer in the bedtable by Emmaline's head. The drawer opened smoothly, it was amazing how smoothly it always opened, and the round white vials sat smugly at the front of it. Ginny wanted to press her palms against the tops of them, to feel their hard plastic biting into her flesh.

"I'll get some fresh water," Armand said, and was gone before she could turn around.

They settled Emmaline for the night, moving her brass bell that had come from India close to the edge of the bedtable. Even if she were able only to knock it to the floor, Ginny would hear it. Emmaline sighed, almost happily.

"Mother," Ginny said, brushing her cheek and forehead with her lips. Emmaline appeared not to have noticed or heard. She lay there, half-smiling, her eyes open, looking out into the room, even as Ginny turned out the light and moved the door so that it stood slightly ajar.

"I think there may have been dancing," Emmaline said, "and tapestries on the walls were woven with red and blue and gold thread." Ginny hesitated, about to ask her mother a question, then instead, hurried downstairs to the family room where Armand was reading the paper and his mother sat in the armchair watching the television set. Babette's cheeks were flushed a rosy colour, as if she had been out walking in the snow.

"What is this dream?" she asked Ginny abruptly, fiercely. "What is it?" Ginny sat down on the sofa beside Armand, and tried to think of a reply for Babette. "It's ridiculous," Babette said. "She should be in the hospital." Armand crackled his newspaper, lowering it.

"Mother," he said.

"Perhaps you're right," Ginny remarked, after a moment.

"Get me my Brompton's," Babette said, her voice wavering between querulous and outraged. Armand rose quickly and went into the kitchen. Ginny didn't move. She found the room a little chilly, she preferred warm rooms, especially in the winter, but right now Babette suffered terribly from the heat. Funny, Ginny thought, when she's so thin. And me so well-padded, yet loving the heat.

Armand had returned with the bottle of medicine and a teaspoon and stood in front of his mother, filling the spoon with the pain-killer, bending to set it in her mouth.

Ginny was suddenly freezing. She tucked her icy hands under her thighs and rocked back and forth, shivering. Goose bumps stood out on her arms and her toes felt as if the blood had stopped circulating in them. Even the end of her nose felt cold.

Babette swallowed, gagged, choked, suddenly sat forward, coughing. The unexpected thrust of her head knocked the bottle out of Armand's hand. It fell to the floor, the liquid swirling out onto the rug.

Ginny stood up. He puts his mouth on my breasts, she wanted to shout. Yes! She felt as if she were choking herself.

Armand was kneeling, touching his mother's knee with one hand while he righted the bottle with the other, saying, "You're all right?" to Babette, who had stopped coughing. He lifted the bottle to the light. "There's still a couple of doses left."

Ginny almost spoke then, but Babette was looking at her, silencing her with the fierceness in her pale eyes. Ginny hugged herself.

"It's so cold in here," she whispered. "I'm so cold."

Sorrow

I was dreaming and when the phone rang, I woke confused, still back in Saskatchewan on a hot summer afternoon, running down a dusty road toward my father who was walking home, swinging his arms, quickening his pace when he saw me running out to greet him, wearing a smile both gay and tender and the dream was mixed with the shrill ring of the phone — my father coming toward me, swinging his arms and smiling, and me beginning to stumble.

James was turned away from me, his greying hair rumpled, the sleeve of his pyjama jacket twisted oddly around his shoulder as he spoke into the phone.

"Oh no!" he was saying. "Oh, god," then a pause and, "yes, tomorrow, four o'clock." Another pause. "Yes, all right then, Connie. Yes. Till tomorrow."

James' father had died. Another in the series of deaths that dogged our middle age: first my father, then his mother, my mother, and now, his father. And now it would begin again — the travel, the pain and tears, the rituals, and all the same questions rising up to echo, unanswered, once more.

"I'm so sorry, dear," I whispered. James had turned so that he was lying on his back looking up at the ceiling. I lifted myself on my elbow and saw that sorrow and resignation had crept into his eyes and settled in the lines of his face. At first I wasn't sure if I should touch him. I put my hand gently on his shoulder and began to straighten the twisted sleeve of his pyjama jacket. He lifted his shoulder and arm to help me, then turned to me, leaning against me, and began to shake with those silent, agonized tears men have.

Connie met us at the airport in Saskatoon, standing out in the crowd as she always did, thin and smartly dressed in a pale gold linen suit, her dark hair arranged in a chignon, but set apart less by her appearance than by a certain indefinable brilliance that clung to her that was composed partly of tension and partly of a brittleness I always felt but couldn't comprehend. She had recently gone through her third divorce.

James and Connie hugged briefly and brushed each other's cheeks. Grief, for he had loved his father deeply, had made James tentative, blurred him, as if he too might melt away, was only waiting, hovering in a confused way till things came clear to him, while Connie vibrated with some barely controlled, unacknowledged emotion, that was not, couldn't be, sorrow.

"Poor dad," James said to her, blinking, holding her hands and Connie said, "Yes," in a harsh voice and looked away.

Standing in that small, crowded airport as we waited for our luggage, making disjointed small talk about the flight and the heat, I remembered that in the dream and in the actual waking moment too, I also had loved my father. I was about eight years old then and I had loved him unconditionally.

In the end of the dream, as the phone woke me, I had been stumbling. Stumbling? Yes, of course, one day when I was not even out of the yard, I stumbled over a stick and fell head-long on the path. The stick had a rusty nail in one end and it cut my ankle in that soft, fleshy part on the top of my foot, just below the shin and there was blood everywhere, and always on the edge of panic as a child — terrified at the blood, I turned away from my father and ran screaming into the house to my mother.

Then, because the ankle became infected and refused to heal, I had to go to the hospital where I stayed for over a week, running a fever the whole time, in constant pain, while they gave me antibiotics and soaked my foot twice a day in an antiseptic bath that was so hot I could barely stand it.

After a week of lonely misery, lying silent and bundled up in the bed as if it were blizzarding outside, although it was the height of summer, my ankle still not healing, the doctor scooped me up in his arms, carried me to an examining room by the ward office, gave me a whiff of anaesthetic, the memory of which still sends a little shiver of fear down my back, and when I woke I was back in my hospital bed and my mother was sitting beside me smoking. I remember how she made a little drawing on her pale blue Players package of the sliver of wood the doctor had removed from deep inside the cut.

Then I went home to find that I was so weak from lying in bed that I could barely walk. And it seemed to me, although I would never know this for sure, that I never again ran out to greet my father as he came home.

The luggage began to tumble from the opening onto the belt. James moved forward, jostling my arm, to pick up our suitcases.

"This way," Connie said, leading us toward the exit to the parking lot as if she thought we'd never been in the Saskatoon airport before. She had been in the city a week, ever since their father's first heart attack. She could do that because she didn't have a job, her divorce settlements having left her secure. We stepped through the sliding glass doors and were immediately enveloped in the baking prairie heat.

When James saw that Connie was driving their father's car, a fifteen-year-old blue Buick from the era of big cars, still in mint condition, tears came into his eyes. He blinked them back, then set the suitcases in the trunk Connie had opened. But when he had laid them inside, and the trunk was closed and Connie was opening the door on the driver's side, James paused, lifted his eyes from the car, and stared around at the few trees stunted by the jet exhaust and then up at the huge, hot prairie sky.

"I thought we had more time," he said.

"I did too," Connie said briskly, "but more the fools us." She got in the car and slammed the door. James didn't move.

"James," I said softly. He turned his head slowly toward me, smiled vaguely, then got into the front seat beside his sister, while I got in the back.

"It was sudden, James," Connie said, as she put the car in gear and backed it out. "He didn't feel a thing. And the attack that put him in the hospital was a mild one. He didn't suffer much." She said this not in a comforting way, although I believe it was her intention to comfort him, but angrily. Did she not love their father? I wondered. Had there been trouble between them? If it was so, James had never mentioned it. He often talked about his father in a warm, loving way, what a good father he had been, how understanding, how supportive. And how close they had been. I had assumed Connie had been included in this and I had envied both of them.

Connie paid the toll then drove us out of the parking lot and into the light traffic moving away from the airport.

"I waited for you to come to make the arrangements," she said. "Are you up to stopping at the undertaker's right now? He needs to see us, the sooner the better." James gave a little start, he turned to look at Connie, and then the surprise faded and was replaced again by that deep sadness. Connie kept her eyes on the traffic, refusing, I thought, to look at him, and there was such tension in her neck and shoulders that I thought I had better act as go-between.

"What do you think, James?" I asked, leaning forward. The leather of the seat still had a faintly new smell when you came close to it.

"Yes, sure," James said, and I was grateful to hear the steadiness that I loved in him returning even under his shock and sadness. He would suffer, I knew, was suffering, but he would be all right.

Connie changed lanes, moved out into the more congested lane of traffic going downtown, still not even glancing at James. She drove aggressively, angrily even, and looking at their backs, brother and sister, in the seat in front of me, the one tense and dark, the other fairer, relaxed into his sorrow, it seemed to me that a conflict was inevitable, although why or what about I didn't know, and I prayed that when it came — if it came — it wouldn't be too bad.

They talked to each other in low voices about other family members who had still to be called, and about the neighbours and their father's friends, reminding each other of this person or that. My mind drifted and I watched the cars pass us, and the buildings, altered now by time, that had once been so familiar to me.

We drove with the windows down since the car, despite its luxurious interior, didn't appear to have air conditioning. I rested my arm on the open window and as we waited at the stoplights I could feel the reflected heat rising in waves off the asphalt. I was suddenly back a teenager in this city, waiting at bus stops on my way home from the swimming pool, going out on dates summer evenings to movies downtown. I couldn't recall my father ever meeting or talking to one of my boyfriends. I couldn't even recall one of them in the same room with him. And yet, the night before my wedding to James, he flew into one of his rages, starting out in a mildly accusing way because I was marrying out of his church, and when I didn't try to placate him, his voice began to rise, he played off his own outrage, used it to let out all the unexpressed anger he had been hoarding over my neglect of him as my father, and my turning away from him.

I cried, after he had worn himself out as he always did eventually and had gone to bed, standing out on the dew-dampened front lawn in the thick summer darkness. It was late then, after midnight, and I was to be married to James the next morning. I thought how I would be gone the next day, gone for good.

The neighbourhood was very quiet, except for the sound of distant cars that rose to a hollow whine over the treetops and houses. All the time I was crying I could hear the sound of those cars, people going and coming to movies and parties or dances on that Friday night. I was filled with pain, seeing no end and no solution to my unhappiness except through the act of leaving for good. And I was unable to say even then, riding in James' father's beautiful old car down those familiar streets that I now wished not to be on, of what my feelings consisted. I cried over the impossibility of ever turning it all simple again as it must have been when I was eight and loved my father unconditionally.

By ten that evening all the callers — neighbours, friends, a few relatives — had gone home and the three of us were left alone in the comfortable, once elegant living room. We had opened all the windows and doors to the prairie night, hoping to catch any breeze that might come up, and it seemed to me that the warm outside darkness had a gentle hum to it that might slowly seep into the shadowy room where we sat in silence, was held in abeyance only by the fragile skeleton of the house.

"Funny, I feel so little," Connie said. James didn't say anything and I tensed, hoping Connie would not go on in this vein. "I never felt I had a father," she said, holding her glass of whiskey up to the light. "I guess it's no wonder I don't feel much." I could feel James closing himself off from her, turning inward, refusing her invitation to quarrel.

Trying to take the tension out of the moment, I took Connie's remark as a casual one, as if I didn't know how loaded with emotion it was.

"I felt the same way about mine," I said. "But now, years after his death, I find myself thinking about him, missing him, in a way I never do my mother."

"My father didn't love me," Connie said, not looking at either of us, her mouth twisted. She quickly got control of herself. "Don't tell me yours didn't love you either. What is it with these fathers and their daughters?"

James stood slowly, a big, rumpled, tired-looking man, his expression carefully neutral.

"I'm going to bed," he said, in a mild tone, as if he hadn't heard what had been said. "Good night," and he went out of the room. Connie watched him walk away, then kept her eyes on the wall as if she could see through it to where we could hear him moving slowly up the stairs. Her eyes were very bright now and fierce. I yawned and stretched, intending to follow James as soon as I decently could.

"A long day," I said. "I'm tired."

"I'm not," Connie said, abruptly, almost rudely. "I don' t know how the hell I'm going to sleep tonight. I'm wide awake." She stood abruptly and moved into the armchair that James had been sitting in, that had been their father's chair. She leaned back, then put her arms carefully out on each armrest as if she were trying it out to see if she would buy it or not. "Keep me company for awhile."

After a moment I said, "I've been thinking about my father, how I loved him when I was eight and when I was ten I was already turning away from him, till when he died we were barely acquaintances."

"At least you had a father till you were eight," she sad. "I never had my father. He was wrapped up in James. All he needed was a son. He never knew I existed." Her anger was palpable, throbbing around us. At last I knew what that barely contained emotion I had been feeling in her since she met us at the airport was. It was rage.

"And now he's dead," Connie said, her tone fluctuating between bitter and wry. "I'm the one who'll be stuck with going through this house, deciding what to do with everything. James won't be any help."

"I'll help you," I said, "if you'll allow me." She was silent, and I was too, wondering if it was true that her father didn't love her, suspecting that it was since James hadn't even bothered to deny it, wondering if my father had loved me when he died. I had no idea. I doubted it.

"The will will be fair, you know," Connie said. Her voice had deepened and she looked directly at me. I felt it was the first time the real Connie had ever spoken to me. "It will be scrupulously fair, but somehow ... " She looked away, her mouth working, trying not to cry. "Fair hurts even more." Then she shrugged and lifted her eyes to me again, the tears gone. "Silly, isn't it, at my age. But what could he do now anyway, to make up for all those years of benign neglect?"

At least it was benign, I thought, but decided not to say it. The air between my father and I had been so charged that I didn't like being in the same room with him, and he knew it, and was uncomfortable around me, so that we avoided each other. Or was it only that I avoided him?

"I had a bad relationship with my father," I said. "But it was as much my fault as his."

"He was a good father?" she asked quickly, fastening those brilliant eyes on mine.

"I don't think so," I said. "I doubt it." I looked away from her. "But he was only an ordinary man, you know. He wasn't anything special. He did what he knew, that's all. I don't blame him so much anymore. Or at least, I blame myself as much."

"You were only a kid," Connie said indignantly. "Kids aren't supposed to know what to do. Adults are."

I leaned back against the sofa and sighed. I wanted to ask her, you're an adult — do you know? Connie sat in her father's chair with her eyes closed. There was no sound from upstairs. Moths bumped softly against the screens.

"Let me tell you something I did," I said. "It was the first thing that I can remember doing against him. When I was ten I started to get sick. I'd catch a cold, it would get worse and worse, I'd run a fever, I'd develop a pain in my side, and then I'd be sent to the hospital. The doctor could cure me with antibiotics, but he couldn't figure out what was causing the trouble, so that winter I was in the hospital three or four times for a week each time." Across from me Connie sat motionless, pinning me with her large, dark eyes. I shifted my eyes to my knees.

"You know I came from a big family, and my mother was busy and overworked, so when I got sick she would make a bed for me on the couch in the living room where she could keep a close eye on me and so she wouldn't have to keep running upstairs. At night my father would carry me up to bed."

"One night, I think it was my second or third bout with this sickness, and it was just before I went back to the hospital and I was feverish and suffering with a steady, dull ache in my side, my father came and picked me up gently in his arms. We lived in a small, crowded house and when he moved from the living room into the hall he had to change directions with me in his arms to go around the newel post to start upstairs. He had to do this carefully in that cramped space so as not to bang me up against it. This particular night when he rounded the newel post, I cried out, and my mother came from the kitchen angry with him and criticized him for not being careful enough with me. And he said to her, he was hurt and puzzled, that he hadn't even touched the newel post." I lifted my eyes to Connie now. She was still staring at me, frowning now, listening intently. I was a little embarrassed and began to wish I had never started the story.

"Do you know, he hadn't touched the newel post? I faked the whole thing."

"Why did you do that?" Connie asked. I shrugged.

"Looking for attention, I guess," I said, deciding in that instant not to tell her anything about the dynamics of our family. She was silent, thinking.

"But he would never have known that you'd faked it," she said. "It shouldn't have affected his attitude toward you."

"But the point is," I said, "why did I do that to him if I loved him?" Suddenly I knew the answer, something I'd been secretly puzzling over for years. I opened my mouth to say it out loud, then held back. My poor father, eternally caught between my mother and me.

"Oh, who knows!" Connie said, suddenly impatient, her anger returning. "My father used to take James hunting. He wouldn't take me. I asked him if I could go, but he just laughed and said girls didn't hunt. All that stupid stuff that was typical of that time. And he coached James' soccer team for a couple of years too, but he never did anything with me. Christ! I can't remember ever doing something with him, just the two of us. Not ever in my whole life. I can't forgive him for that."

"I don't think I can remember being alone with my father either," I said, a little surprised at this realization. We were silent for a time, listening to the soft hum of the summer night. "I still dream about him," I said.

The funeral was a typical, simple ceremony, so smoothed out by the funeral director's craft that there was no way to tell that it was James' and Connie's father's funeral except when his name was mentioned and the details of his life recited. I liked James' father. He was once a big man with a gentle air and a sort of distance to him that I was beginning to see in James. I thought of the big room below us full of empty coffins, 'caskets' the funeral director had called them, with price tags placed discreetly on the quilted satin interiors. The departed one. It saddened me that his funeral was so smoothed out, so homogenized. I pictured us dancing around a fire, screaming and crying, throwing spears, drawing blood, and for an instant I felt better.

But James' grief got the better of him, and when he broke down and sobbed Connie handed him her hankie without even looking at him. She stared straight ahead, her face a mask, her lips tight, her hands pressed together in her lap. I felt more sorry for her than I did for James, because he was at least able to get some satisfaction out of his grief, knowing as he did that he felt as he was supposed to.

I thought about Connie saying that she hadn't one memory of doing something with her father, and that I had agreed. But I had suddenly remembered that once my father took me fishing.

One summer our parents packed us and half our household goods into our old car and took us for a holiday at a lake not far from the city. We stayed a week, crowded into a rented, one-room cabin with a toilet out back in the bush and every day my father went fishing. One morning, I don't know how it happened, but he took me with him. I remember creeping out of bed very early when everyone else was still asleep, and the two of us going out into the bright morning. He rowed us in a rented rowboat out into the middle of the lake where we stopped and he baited my hook with a minnow. Then I trailed my line in the water while he cast. After a while I felt a tug. I was very excited, and with my father's help, I reeled in a small fish, a perch, I think.

When we got back to shore, my father having failed to catch anything, I raced up to the cabin to show my fish off. Then my father, not my mother, lit a fire in the cookstove and fried my fish. And the two of us alone, ate it for our breakfast.

But even though it was the only fish I ever caught in my life, and my only memory of being alone with my father, no matter how hard I searched, it didn't feel like a special happening. It lacked the feel of intimacy and the tender joy such memories are supposed to have, and I couldn't understand why.

The following morning we began to clean out the house, to ready it to be sold. I was surprised at how well James lent himself to the enterprise, seeming even to enjoy it a little. The three of us traipsed down the stairs to the musty, badly-lit basement.

"You go through that closet, Carol," Connie said to me. "It's only old clothes and I think it can all be thrown out, but if you see anything fit for the Salvation Army, put it in a separate pile. I'm going to go through this junk." She nodded to one corner of the basement that was piled high with rolled up rugs, broken chairs and small tables, floor lamps without shades, neatly closed dusty cardboard boxes and scarred, dust-covered suitcases. James watched her. Connie didn't invite him to help her, and after a second, he went to the opposite corner where the old water heater stood and a set of cobwebbed shelves laden with objects made mysterious by their covering of dust.

Connie began pulling out a broken wooden chair which fell apart in her hands, the pieces rattling against the cement floor. She sneezed when the dust flew out of a couple of faded scatter rugs as she pulled them down and tossed them behind her.

"Well, for heaven's sake," she said. James and I stopped what we were doing to come and see what she had found. She crawled over the suitcases, pushing them out of the way, and threw back the last corner of the sheepskin rug that had been covering the tall cabinet with the murky glass doors standing against the wall.

"It's dad's gun cabinet," James said. Connie rattled the doors, trying to open them.

"Let me," James said, and pushed more boxes and suitcases out of the way till he reached her. She stood aside, he bent, did something with the latch, and the doors opened with a squeak.

It seemed to me there was an unnatural silence in the basement as James reached in and lifted out a long-barrelled gun.

He fingered it for a moment, rubbing his palm along the scarred stock, then said to me without lifting his eyes from the gun, "It's dad's old twelve gauge. I used to hunt ducks with him. He let me use it." He lifted the gun to his shoulder and sighted down its barrel, then swung the barrel in an arc as if he'd sighted birds, one eye screwed shut.

"Oh, for god sake," Connie said. "Here, let me." He looked a little surprised, but took it down from his shoulder and handed it to her. I expected her to sight down its barrel too, but she didn't, she merely held the gun in front of her as if she were weighting it, then abruptly she let go to put one hand to her face. She did it so quickly that the gun over-balanced and would have fallen to the floor if James hadn't caught it. They stood for a second, not quite looking at each other, the gun between them.

"It sure needs cleaning," I said.

"Dad used to keep it clean," James said. "I guess he lost interest in duck hunting after mom died."

"It looks old," I said. The gun had a handmade look about it, compared with the few guns I had seen with their gleaming barrels, sleek, polished wooden stocks and lethal-looking, streamlined breeches.

"It belonged to his father," James said, taking it back from Connie and rubbing at the engraved patch on the breech using his handkerchief. "And now, I guess it's mine." He broke the breech and peered into its workings.

I could feel Connie suddenly become alert at this, as if it hadn't occurred to her that this object wouldn't be given away or thrown out like the others, but she didn't speak, and because James didn't either, I said, "My father never hunted. I can't remember even hearing him talk about hunting." The thought of my gay, sensuous father going out to hunt in the cold fall mornings struck me as incongruous. He liked dances and parties for recreation, he liked to sit in the bar with his friends, he liked talk best. Only fishing sometimes, that was the only thing he did.

"It was his arthritis," James said. "He had to give up most things after his arthritis set in." His voice broke and he cleared his throat.

"He managed pretty well after mother died," Connie said. "Once he got a housekeeper." Their father had always been going to move to an apartment in a month or so, or in the spring, but five years had passed and now he had made his final move.

"He isn't suffering anymore," James said, and I thought he would cry. "I'm glad to have his gun." Again I felt Connie tense, less suddenly this time, but again she didn't say anything.

I felt myself irritated with her, although guiltily so, reminding myself that she had just lost her parent, but when my father died he had nothing; there was nothing to quarrel over. Their tiny house that wasn't even paid for went to our mother, and other

than that, and his old car which went to a teenage nephew for a
jalopy, he had lived his life without acquiring anything of value,
sentimental or otherwise. Is that sad? I found myself wondering.
Did he know that? Did he care? Was it deliberate?

Thinking of his old car reminded me of the time he offered
me a ride to school that I didn't want to take because I wanted to
walk with my friends. But he insisted that I go with him and I
knew if I refused he would have given me one of his accusing
glares, he would complain about me to my mother, and then
he'd stomp out of the house and slam the door. So, to avoid the
fuss, I consented to be driven.

It was early fall, it had rained the night before and then
frozen, so that all the city streets were coated thinly with ice.
My father drove slowly, and it was early enough that there was
hardly anybody out. He stopped at an intersection only a couple
of blocks from home and a woman coming up behind us mis-
judged the slipperiness and ran into us. My father got out, I
thought there would be shouting and swearing, but there was
none, and when he got back into the car, thinking somehow that
this was a reprieve, I said I'd walk the rest of the way. He became
very angry and growled at me and glowered and would have
shouted, but I said, 'okay, okay,' quickly. We drove the rest of the
way in silence and I was half an hour early for school.

It took us three days to finish cleaning the house and to make
the arrangements for the disposal of the furniture which was sold
to an agent, and for the house, which was going to be handled
by a realtor. We had packed the dishes and the bedding and the
personal items and had made arrangements to have them
shipped either to Connie's home in Montreal or to ours. There
was nothing more to be done.

James and I were in the guest bedroom packing. Our suitcases
were open on the double bed and the room had been stripped of
knick-knacks, bedding and curtains. Connie knocked on the
door.

"Are you finished packing?" I asked her.

"Not quite," she said, in a tone that made even James look
up. Now I was the one to tense, seeing the expression on her
face. She was dressed for travel in a white suit, her hair was up,

formally arranged in a chignon again and her makeup was fresh, but mask-like it was so thick. She lifted her hands and placed them together at her waist like a choir girl. Her heavy gold bracelets clinked dully.

"I want dad's gun," she said.

"What?" James said.

"I want his gun." It lay on the bed above our suitcases, its long, heavy double barrels corroded and dirty. The leather padding at the end of the stock was worn through and the stuffing was spilling out onto the mattress. The breech and its workings were black. It was a very old gun.

"You don't hunt," James said.

"Neither do you."

"Yes, but ... " James began, then looked at me. When I said nothing, he went on, "I used to hunt with dad all the time." His hands went to the gun and then he was lifting it, putting it to his shoulder again, sighting along its barrel. "I remember the first time I fired it. I accidentally shot both barrels at once and the recoil knocked me flat on my back. You should have seen the bruise I had on my shoulder. I thought I'd broken it." I realized he was talking to me, but he was looking at Connie, pleading silently with her. She took a couple of steps toward him, her expression not wavering. "I think it rightfully belongs to me," James said stiffly.

Connie said, "I want it." She did not say, both of you owe it to me, although it seemed I could hear the words between them. After a moment James set the gun carefully against the bed, its butt resting on the floor. Connie went out of the room.

When we were finished packing, James took the suitcases and I the smaller bags and we started out of the room. I hesitated a moment, looking at the gun, but James didn't turn or look back.

Connie wasn't in any of the rooms we passed and she wasn't downstairs. We went out to the car and James began to put the cases in the trunk of his father's car which it had been decided we would drive home. When we got it there James would sell it and divide the proceeds with Connie. When he was done, I said, "James, what about the gun?" He slammed down the trunk lid, then stood still, looking down at the pavement.

"Dad always said it would be my gun one day." He turned away from me and leaned, chest first against the car, his arms extended over its roof, and looked down the street of his childhood, squinting as if to see better — a small boy leaving in the early morning with his father, putting guns in the trunk, the neighbourhood still asleep, the birds just beginning to stir, the sun appearing over the horizon.

He turned back to me and took my hand.

"Don't worry," he said. "I always knew something like this would happen." Together we went back into the house. As we entered Connie was coming down the stairs. Behind us, as James shut the door, there was the roar of a big truck pulling up in front of the house. After a second we could hear a truck door slam.

"Good-bye, Connie," James said. He waited for her to reach the bottom of the stairs. Someone began walking up the sidewalk briskly.

"Good-bye James," Connie said evenly. I thought they might embrace again, but although Connie was right in front of him, they merely looked at each other. There was a knock on the door behind us. I opened it to find a husky young man in coveralls standing there.

"Movers, Ma'am," he said. "Could you move those vehicles out of the driveway?"

"Yes, right away," I said, and shut the door. James and Connie were still facing each other.

"Good-bye, Connie," I said. "I hope to see you at Christmas." She put her hand out to me, I took it, we brushed cheeks, and I turned back to open the door. James murmured, "Bye," again, not looking at Connie. The driver of the truck beeped the horn twice, reminders to us. I looked back at Connie as James stepped out onto the sidewalk and saw that her face was still a careful mask. Her eyes flickered to mine, but I could tell she'd barely noticed me. Other things were on her mind. I followed James outside, pulling the door shut behind me.

We got in the car and drove away, leaving Connie, as we had arranged, to supervise the movers. We had gone a hundred miles when James said to me, lifting one hand from the steering wheel in a gesture of relinquishment, "I wonder what she'll do with the gun."

Neither of us could imagine it in her smart Montreal apartment.

"Yes, I wonder," I said. But thinking about it, I imagined that she would not take it with her, that she would leave it behind in one of the empty rooms of the house. I imagined, too, that it would cost her much to do that, but that she would not regret it.

The last time I saw my father alive it was early winter, and though there was no snow on the ground yet, the mornings were cold, the ground frozen hard with a covering of frost on it before the sun rose high enough to melt it. I was walking to my secretarial job on the university campus. To get to my office I had to pass the university hospital and all its satellite buildings and the parking lot for out-patients at the cancer clinic. The chilliness and the layer of morning frost had dulled and softened the outlines of the city that could be seen across the wide river. That is how I remember that morning: softened and faded, still as in a prophetic dream.

As I approached the entrance to the parking lot I saw a man walking slowly toward me. A few more steps and I saw that he was my father. When we met, we both stopped. He was out of breath and I thought, had to stop to rest before he went on to his car. He had been a labourer all his life, but when he was not wearing his workclothes, he always dressed formally, and now he was wearing his good black overcoat, a neat, small black felt hat, and a fringed, white silk scarf tucked around his neck. His colour wasn't good, there were red spots on each cheekbone that had never been there before, but what struck me most was a gentleness that appeared in his face when he saw it was me.

We spoke, but we had so little to say to each other that I have no memory of our words. It was too chilly to stand for long, and he was worn out by whatever they had done to him at the cancer clinic and needed to get to his car so he could sit down and then drive himself home. I watched him walk away slowly in the still, frosty morning, then went on to work.

But, reflecting on that meeting now, long after it took place, I knew he had looked at me in the way he had when I was a child, when we had loved each other without conditions or reflection. The paleness of the morning, the chill, the tender way he held his mouth.

Broadway Shoes

I've been thinking a lot about my mother lately, and I know it is time finally to go to the basement, to search in the closet in the storage room, and to bring out the box that Eric found after she died, thrust far back in a drawer of her dresser, buried under her best nightgowns. When Eric lifted the lid and saw the box contained only photos, he didn't even look at them, but he and his wife, Lise, seemed to feel that I, as the only daughter, had an automatic right to them which they wouldn't even question. I didn't want the box to tell the truth, but I knew that I should, so I took it, though I was rendered mute by the tumult I could feel rising in my chest, and ever since Eric handed it to me, it has been sitting, unopened, in a storage closet in my basement.

What is it I am afraid I might find? Or is it that I have already found it, whatever it is, and don't want to be reminded of it, or to have to look at the evidence? I pour myself another cup of coffee and stare at the small box marked 'Broadway Shoes,' a company long out of business, once situated in the city where my mother was raised, which she left when she married, and where her parents lived, died, and are buried. Or is it only that I don't want the old pain of her irreparable loss to envelope me again, as it is sure to do when I at last open her private treasure?

I lift the lid carefully and set it aside, expecting perhaps that her ghost will waft upwards from it, hovering above my kitchen table, smiling, wearing the pink dress with the pale blue flowers on it that was her favourite when I was about ten, and that had a way, at least in my memory, of transforming her into a younger, prettier woman.

Maybe in here I will at last find a photo of her wedding. The thought jars me, I sit down. It is not that I had forgotten what my uncle told me, but only that I had pushed it away, refused to examine it, held it in abeyance for the time when I might be ready to confront it.

Though a shiver runs down my spine, she isn't here; no ghostly voice whispers her name, her image doesn't appear shimmering in the doorway, I don't smell her perfume.

The secret, told to me a long time ago by my uncle, is only this: that when she married our father, she defied both her parents, especially her beloved father, since they had forbidden her to marry him — he was Italian and Catholic and they were Norwegian gentry and Protestant — and that neither set of parents would come to the wedding; that not only did she break with her family, but she defied those unwritten, unbreakable rules of her class and her society. The mystery is, why?

The photos have been shaken up by my almost dropping the box when I brought it down from the shelf, and some of them are standing on edge. They seem to be nearly all black-and-white snapshots, the kind people take in abundance with cheap cameras at the slightest pretext. I lift about half of them from the box and fan them out on the table in front of me. Not one of the photos is familiar — so we were right: in this box are the ones that, for reasons only she knew, she prized and would not put in the growing collection of family albums which I have placed neatly on the shelf in the rumpus room for anyone to look at.

In front of me is a photo of my mother and some women standing around a piano singing. You can't see who is playing, and my mother, standing at the end, turned toward the piano player, is the only full-length figure. Struck by her expression, I study the picture.

She wasn't a pretty woman, but she always had an appealing liveliness about her. I had seen her use it more than once when I was growing up, though I probably didn't know what it was, only knew I was confident in her ability to make things right with people. Yet that smiling intensity that could sway and then captivate people, served to hide a will as determined as any queen's or general's.

The other three women crowded together behind the upright piano are looking at each other over mouths puckered into 'ohs' as if they are singing the final note of the song and will break into laughter the moment they run out of breath. Mother's left hand rests on the piano top, her right hand hangs by her side, but it is not relaxed, it is clenched into a tight little fist. Her expression is sad, as if the song has made her think of something that opens a hidden well of melancholy deep inside her.

How she wanted that piano. I remember when I was eight how mother insisted to my father that I was old enough to begin piano lessons, that I must have a piano. I remember our father replying it was impossible, a piano was too expensive for a family like ours, so that I forgot about piano lessons, which I hadn't much wanted in the first place. But the next thing I knew, when I came home from school one day that very piano was sitting in our living room. I began lessons the next day, and I guess I took it for granted that our father had relented and bought it.

But now I wonder, did her father buy it? We hardly ever saw our grandparents, and on the few occasions I can remember when either we went to visit them or they came to see us, I can't recall our father being there, only mother, Eric, and me. And it seemed to me even when I was a child that there was a stiffness there, a coldness. I remember once my grandmother bending as if she meant to pick me up in her arms and then drawing back, as if she had seen something on my face or clothes that should have been wiped away before she could hold me, and for years, I wondered what it might have been. Then we didn't see them anymore.

I wonder now why it was that when my uncle told me, I didn't rush to my mother at once and ask her why. Why did you do it? And though I loved my father, even I doubted she had been seized by any burning passion for him. I could see he wasn't especially handsome, that he had only a high school education, that he wasn't and never had been rich. As a teenager, those were the only things I could think of that might explain what my mother had done. But I never went to her and asked her to explain, and she never mentioned it that I can remember, and I am sure I would remember.

Once I asked her why there were no pictures of her wedding and she said, shrugging, not looking at me, "I guess nobody had a camera. It was just a little wedding." And I didn't ask again.

So it doesn't seem likely that her parents paid for the piano. It is more likely that mother went downtown with her chin tilted in that determined way she had and, despite what our father had said, ordered it herself, presenting him with a *fait accompli,* to which he must have felt he could only acquiesce. It makes me wonder, did she blame him somehow for her alienation from her family and from the society in which she had grown up? Had he, falling under the sway of her powerful will, submitted to her point of view, and so gave in about the piano? Why does she look so sad, when everybody else is laughing? Is the song, perhaps, one that reminds her of her youth? Of her family? Of Norwegian traditions she left behind when she married?

And why did this photo belong in her private treasure of photos, the ones the rest of us never saw, discovered only after she was dead? Is it because of the gleaming, rich wood of the piano? The three laughing women? Or is it because she is so slim when in later years she grew stout and breathless? I despair of ever fathoming her secret, of ever finding anything to explain what her parents could only have seen as inexplicable treachery, which even she, at least once in a while in some secret place in her heart, must have regretted.

I reach for an ashtray and light a cigarette. My fingers tap through the snapshots and pull out a picture of two girls on a tennis court. They stand side by side at the net, holding tennis racquets and wearing white, knee-length tennis dresses. One is my mother, she must have been about eighteen, and the other I don't recognize. A tall girl, with dark hair pulled back from her face, and long, thin arms and legs. Mother looks so eager, so daring, as if she is just a little out of breath, she must have just won the match, and doesn't the other girl look a trifle sulky around the mouth, as if she never does win and knows she is expected to be cheerful about it?

I turn the photo over. 'Klara and Mercedes,' someone, not my mother, has written in blue ink in a scrawling, luxurious hand, '1933.' Mercedes is a name I know; mother's best friend from her school days, though none of us ever met her: "She married an engineer and went to South America to live. We lost touch." But there were plenty of Klara and Mercedes stories, pranks mostly, and wonderful good times to be relived in the telling by mother, Eric, and me. They involved campfires and horses, swimming in cold northern lakes, dancing, and tormenting teachers, first in high school and then in business college.

Mother looks fearless in this photo, willing and able to take on any challenge. Perhaps that is why she treasured it, because it reminded her of what she had once been, and of what she might some day dare to be again. Or it might be because it is her only photo of her girlhood friend.

Some of the pictures are so old that they are done in sepia and the people in them are posed formally and wear the clothing of the last century. No mystery as to why she might have kept these; I can even see the family resemblance in some of them. I reach into the box and pull out the last few pictures.

Here is an occasion I recognize — Eric's wedding. Eric is three years older than I am, and despite his name and his lineage on our mother's side, he is no Viking, no Norse god like his grandfather was, but a man of average height with brown eyes and light brown hair. Somebody snapped this picture at the reception and Lise is seated in her wedding finery while Eric bends over her. They might be saying: Are you all right? I'm managing, how are you? Chin up, it'll soon be over.

Mother is standing behind Eric as if she is waiting to speak
to Lise, but she is looking at me, where I stand beside her in
my sleeveless short dress and my veiled, pillbox hat. I am
turned away from her, smiling at someone who isn't in the
picture. It is the look on mother's face that makes me set
down my cigarette and push the ashtray away, then take off
my glasses to peer closer at the photo, trying to fix precisely
what her expression is saying.

It is both questioning and faintly disapproving, although I
don't seem to be doing anything but smiling in a polite, social
way at whoever I am looking at. I would have been twenty-
one, the same age my mother was when she married our
father. Is she afraid I am about to do the same thing she did? I
peer even closer to see if disapproving is the right word, but
the closer I get, the more the image of her face dissolves into
shades of grey, patches which no longer have any meaning,
and if I were to get the magnifying glass and peer even closer,
her face would disappear altogether into the texture of the
paper on which the picture is printed.

I can't see anything remarkable about this photo. It isn't
even a very good one, just an amateur snapshot of some people at a wedding reception, caught unaware, each looking in a
different place, isolated, except for Eric and Lise, in her own
drama. I don't know why she would want to keep it in a secret
cache.

I am nearly at the bottom of the box now and it occurs to
me that I haven't found one photo of our father. The thought
is enough to stop me in the act of lifting out the envelope
that lies at the bottom of the box. Why no pictures of our
father? Not even one? In the box I have found, now that I
think about it, images of every person in her life who meant
something to her: Eric and me, Mercedes, the women who
were her friends when she was a young housewife and mother, her parents, her ancestors, but there is not one picture of
our father, not at any age, not doing anything, not even in the
background. He simply isn't there.

Tentatively now, with a peculiar, breathless sense I can't
quite put my finger on, as if the air in the kitchen has picked

up electricity, or as if someone else is there, waiting with me, I take out the yellowing envelope, spread it open with my fingers, and peer into it. Inside there is only a lock of faded, pale blond hair, pressed flat. I touch it with the tips of my fingers; it is unbelievably soft. I know this: it is a lock taken from mother's hair when she cut it just before she and Mercedes started off to business college. I know because she often mentioned how fair her hair had been until the end of her teens and how it had been so long she could sit on it, how she had kept a lock from that ceremonial bobbing. And when I would ask if I might see it, she would reply, "It must be around here somewhere," but she never seemed to find it.

I lift it from the envelope, lay it on my palm and stroke it. It is so soft, so pale, so lovely; it brings tears to my eyes. The girl my mother was before I knew her lies in the palm of my hand, the sweetness of her youth blossoms around me, and I am overcome with grief for her joyous, evanescent, lost girlhood, that a box of photos cannot ever bring back.

I put the small lock of hair tenderly away in its envelope and set the envelope next to the pile of snapshots I have looked at. Then I notice there is one photo left in the box, a photo in deplorable condition with edges worn away to raggedness, a blotch on the background, and one corner torn away.

It is a picture of a man in an overcoat leaning against a stone wall or fence in front of a large house that I don't recognize. The top of the wall forms a ledge which he rests his elbow on. It is winter and his unbuttoned overcoat has snow on the elbow that rests on the fence, around the skirt and up its front as if he might have just been in a snowball fight. I can tell by the length between his ankle and knee and his long thigh that he was a tall man, and his shoulders seem broad, although that might be an effect of the overcoat.

I study this picture for a long time, longer than I have looked at any of the others, because something tells me that this is it. If I can read this picture accurately, I will find the answer to the question I have for so long refused to ask. Why? Why did she do it?

But I see only a man strikingly handsome in the way of

movie stars, a self-confident man, which shows itself in the easy way he leans against the fence, an arrogant man, spoiled, I'll bet, too. There isn't any writing on the back and the only other clue is that the photo must have been handled a lot to be so damaged. But I don't like this man. Dislike of this man makes me drop the picture carelessly onto the table.

My uncle had been drinking, he always did drink too much, it was at my cousin's wedding and after the reception when the bride and groom had left, he got to reminiscing, and that is when he told me. I was too astonished and too dismayed to even ask him a question. Yet I know what he said was true. I didn't want to know about it, I had enough intuition to know there was something there I didn't want to know, or why did I not at once demand to know all of it, the whole story? Instead, I pretended to myself that I'd forgotten what I'd been told.

It's too melodramatic to be true, I think, it's too obvious. That she loved this man, whoever he was, that her parents disapproved of him and somehow prevented her from marrying him, that she rushed off and married a man who stood for everything they most held in contempt, in order to get even with them, to hurt them as much as they had hurt her.

I would have to dredge up all my memories, though I didn't want to, all the little unexplained moments I had observed between my mother and father, that as a child, confident in their love of me, I had ignored. I would have to think of all the things she had said about our father when he wasn't there, the way she behaved toward him when she was thinking about something else and would have forgotten to disguise her feelings, if that is what she had been doing. I would have to re-examine her life, the one I had seen. I would have to rewrite her past, and mine too.

Slowly I put the lid back on the box and stare at the writing, 'Broadway Shoes,' the name conjuring shiny red tap shoes with sparkles on the toes and diamond buckles, flappers and champagne.

The central act of a parent's life — how mysterious, a thousand times more so because never explained, never even mentioned. It's like the existence of a black hole, I think; it is possible from gravitational effects to guess that it is there, but there is nothing at all to see, no light rays or anything else close to it can escape its pull, and if someone should be so unlucky as to be sucked into it, that someone will vanish forever into darkness.

Domestici

It was a shock when Jim Hearne said to me, grinning and yet with a hint of surprise in his eyes, as if he might not know me as well as he thought he did despite having been my doctor for twenty years, "Jeanne, all that blushing and sweating is the beginning of menopause, you silly girl." But I was genuinely shocked; I truthfully had never thought of such a thing, it had never entered my head, although forty-seven isn't young and I guess a woman should be thinking about menopause.

But driving home from his office in the noon traffic, I had to remember ruefully that I'd been just as surprised by menstruation. I was one of those lucky girls who hardly noticed her menses, never felt a thing, so that when I was young I was forever finding a little patch of blood on my panties in the washroom when I was at a school dance, or playing scrub at a family picnic somewhere out in the country, until finally somebody told me about the twenty-eight day cycle.

Ridiculous, when you think of it, for a mother not to tell her daughter anything about menstruation and then, when it catches her out of the blue one day, to neglect to tell her that there is any kind of sense to it. But she hardly seemed interested, much less helpful, but rather, irritated and even a little disgusted. It's one of the things I have a hard time forgiving her for. But I couldn't blame this new surprise on my mother. I can't imagine why I didn't think of menopause when I started feeling all these strange sensations.

The phone was ringing as I entered the house and I hurried to answer it. Julie picks the most unexpected times to call, usually because she is on the other side of the globe and can't be bothered to check to see what time it is here. I suppose I shouldn't complain. At least she calls now and then, two or three times a year.

But the call was not from my errant daughter, it was my former sister-in-law Rose, from whom I hadn't heard a word in over ten years.

"Hello, Rose," I said, too surprised to be cool to her. "Whatever are you doing in town?" But I was thinking, remembering how she had been, I'm not married to her brother anymore. I don't have to be nice to her.

"I'd like to come and see you, Jeanne," she said, ignoring my question.

"Well, of course," I replied, hoping she hadn't noticed my second's hesitation.

"I have something to tell you," she went on, with a touch of the self-importance in her voice of a person who knows herself to be insignificant generally, but this once is glad to be the bearer of important news. "I'd like to come right away." My heart sank.

"Right away?"

"I'll be there in about an hour," she said firmly, not asking.

"You're not going to give me a hint?" I asked, getting annoyed, but she only said, "See you soon," with that same smugness in her tone, and hung up. Morosely, I hung up too. Now what, I thought. As if menopause weren't enough for one day.

As soon as Jim said the word 'menopause,' I knew at once he was right. I could feel the truth of it all through my body, the way one does sometimes. I didn't for a second question what he had said.

It was the same way when I started to menstruate. I had left my classroom at school, grade seven, I think it was, though I've never been certain about that, to go to the washroom and there, for the first time, I discovered a little spot of blood on my panties. And I had been feeling so strange all afternoon, it's hard to say how, except that I'd had a funny feeling in my abdomen, not exactly a pain, but a sort of interior twisting that was new to me and yet not really frightening, and other things that are now so familiar that I can hardly remember if I really felt them then or not, or if so, to what degree — an unusual perspiring, a clamminess, a special kind of mild tiredness, and the world taking on a different, less vivid colouring.

But when I saw the blood I was very shocked, just as I had been when Jim told me about menopause, and then, at almost the same time, I knew it was all right. I didn't know what the blood or the feelings were, but I knew it was all right. And it puzzles me, how a person knows a thing like that. For no one had ever breathed a word to me about that kind of bleeding, I was taken completely by surprise, my mother wasn't even at home, but off visiting her parents, and when she did come home and I told her, she seemed angry with me, and offered no explanation at all.

I never had any trouble after that, I never had a cramp, not even a twinge, until somewhere in the first year of my marriage when I had a painful period with a much more copious flow than I'd ever had before. The painful downward pulling in my abdomen lasted the better part of a day and ended when I passed a large clot, the first I'd ever known myself to pass, along with one last wrenching cramp that left me gasping and filled with amazement.

Yet this didn't really worry me either. It only made me think of my younger sister who had suffered from painful menstruation from the day she began her periods. It was so bad sometimes that she had to go to bed for a day or so, and I was jealous of the attention it earned her from our mother.

Lying on the couch in the living-bedroom of our dim basement apartment, all my new husband and I could afford since we were both still students, I didn't mind the pain much either — it made me feel womanly, which the ease of my periods had never allowed me — and with my husband sitting in the kitchen talking and drinking coffee with his best friend, a brilliant graduate student who later became famous in his field just as we all expected, I felt peaceful and contented.

I think, even then, that the idea that this might be a miscarriage and not just a painful period hovered somewhere just out of reach in my mind, but it was many years before I fully articulated it, and finally began to believe it actually had been one. There was no other explanation for such pain, and the memory of the clot, once I understood more about such things, convinced me.

But as I lay there all that long afternoon, I wasn't unhappy. I liked the feeling that the two men's voices in the kitchen, easy, friendly, punctuated by quiet laughter, gave me. Having come from a home where our parents were eternally at war, it made me feel I was a success in the world to have my husband at home enjoying the afternoon with a friend, without a quarrel anywhere, or a hint of a quarrel. And I knew I was liked by his friend, who'd been best man at our wedding, and that I was actually loved by my husband, which, given the family I'd come from, seemed no small feat.

So I felt snug and safe as I lay there on the fold-out couch in the living room, looking up out the tiny, ground level window to the dying pink petunias the landlady had planted around the window, and above them, to the sliver of white stucco wall of the house next door, while I had what I think now was almost certainly a miscarriage.

I went back to the hall and gathered the mail from the floor. Nothing from Julie, a letter from an old aunt of mine, some flyers, a couple of magazines. I made tea and took it into the sitting room and sat down with the magazines in the warm, early afternoon sun. I had remembered with some relief that you couldn't depend on Rose. She might come, she might not.

When Victor and I were married maybe three years, she had come to stay with us, Julie was a baby then, and she spent hours following me around the house as I made the beds, did the washing, the cooking and the dishes, talking to me in a low, anguished voice about her relationships with the children she had gone to school with, especially about how it had been in high school, and with her various female relatives. Nobody, it seemed, could get along with Rose. Everyone was insensitive or unkind or downright malicious where Rose was concerned.

Still, there was a shred of truth in all that she said. She lacked a sense of gaiety, she had never been, Victor said, a happy person, and unhappy, sensitive, overwrought people are not much liked by anybody. All the slights Rose recounted were real, and she mulled them over constantly, retold them from room to room in our small suburban house, and asked from me, not help, but intimacy, and a sympathetic ear. Then she had had a major seizure in our bathroom, Victor said because she hadn't been taking her pills, she never would take her pills regularly and was always having seizures they would have controlled, and she had abruptly left, but not before I had seen in her eyes her bottomless self-hatred and shame, that she could do nothing right and was cursed as well.

I flipped through the university alumni magazine. I never knew why I bothered, since I don't remember more than four or five people from the large provincial university I attended, and I wondered where the idea of the coziness of college campuses came from. It seemed American to me, a product of a country with a number of small colleges where everyone knew everyone else, or maybe it was a literary fiction, the result of stories written by people who had all graduated from small private schools. Or more likely, it was just a fantasy from television-land. I always read through the announcements and the obituaries, though, in case I recognized a name.

And there it was, under DECEASED: Homestead, Victor Allan. My former and only husband, father of the prodigal Julie, my only child. It must have happened some time ago; these announcements are always long after the fact. That must be why Rose wanted to see me, to tell me. Does Julie know her father is dead? Does Rose know how to find Julie while I don't? Behind this jumble of thoughts an ache was growing, and a trembling that threatened to become tears.

It had been more than a dozen years since I had last seen Victor, we had parted in rancour, I was not sorry we had divorced, our relationship had become so acrimonious that I had never even considered marrying again. I wanted nothing more to do with marriage, although Victor had been briefly married for a second time.

But still, I felt very sad, and filled with regret. And my menopause seemed linked to his death in a deep and significant way that left me unable to think coherently, to form any clear ideas or words. Except, nothing dies but something goes with it.

"Someone should have told me!" I cried out loud, flooded by a grief so great that I felt I couldn't understand or bear it. It was grief for the love we had once had, for all that our relationship had once been, for the soul I felt I had lost to Victor, and could never recover.

And, too, I cried for the hopelessness of my relationship with the child we had had together, that if she had known of her father's death, she had been so heartless that she had not told me. How could a child I had loved so much so easily forget me?

I cried, too, when the doctor told me I was pregnant with her. I was at work in the cataloguing department of the university library and I excused myself to phone the doctor for the results of my pregnancy test, since once my day's work was over, his office would have closed. When I was told, I went into the ladies' room and cried, not sadly, but I believe for the momentousness of what was happening to me and my inability to comprehend it.

Victor was noncommittal when I told him, although he didn't seem to mind particularly. If he didn't like it, I knew he wouldn't say much because it was his fault. This was just before birth control pills came into general use, I had warned him it wasn't a safe time, but he hadn't wanted to listen to me, hadn't minded taking a chance. And anyway, hadn't it always been taken for granted that we would have children? Although, already I knew I couldn't be sure of his reactions, that our once perfect harmony of opinion was a little askew.

"You lied to me!" he had shouted, when I had protested in tears about his being out so many nights each week with his friends, leaving me at home. "I asked you about this before we got married, and you said it would be all right with you!"

"What did I know about marriage then?" I pleaded with him, unable to say what I really feared, which was that he preferred being with his friends to being at home with me. But that was how it remained, that I was guilty of deceit, and for years I bore my guilt with humility.

Rose paid us several visits over the years. Each time something strange happened and she packed and left abruptly, without explanation, refusing to look at either of us as she mounted the steps of the bus or the train. Once we gave a dinner party and Rose drank two glasses of wine and then, after talking softly and intimately for a long time to the woman sitting next to her, began to cry, still sitting at the table in the midst of the remains of the meal. When she showed no signs of stopping, but only cried harder, our dismayed guests finally decided the best thing to do was to go home, leaving us to comfort her, although Rose never took comfort, not anywhere or from anyone, and Victor and I knew that.

Another time she took Julie to the playground in the park four blocks from our house and got lost bringing her home. They were gone hours, I was getting frantic, and when they finally arrived, four-year-old Julie in tears, Rose dishevelled and sweating, with tears in her eyes and grime in the lines her face had already acquired although she was only twenty, I hugged Julie and without meaning to, ignored Rose's disjointed attempts to explain.

"The houses all look the same ... the streets are all dead ends or they run in circles ... "

I could imagine the two of them toiling down the sidewalks in the sweltering summer heat, past the curious women sitting on their front lawns, the small children dropping whatever they were holding to stare, Julie and Rose growing more and more grubby and despairing as they passed one small, pale bungalow after another, each one familiar, each the wrong one.

When I didn't respond to her quickly enough, Rose locked herself in the bathroom and no amount of cajoling or entreaty from me would make her open the door. When she finally came out after Victor got home, she made him drive her to the bus depot so she could catch the last bus of the day home to her parents' house in the small town where they lived, and where she and Victor had been raised.

Each time she returned to us it was as though nothing had

happened the last time. She arrived smiling, carrying small gifts for each of us, and within a week something stupid or silly or incomprehensible would have happened and she would depart, her desolation left behind hanging in the air. I don't think that one of her visits lasted the appointed length of time.

"Oh, someone should have told me," I whispered to the silent room. The magazine slipped off my knees and fell to the floor. "Someone should have." But who else would have known who also knew me? Victor and Rose's parents were dead and I never knew any of his other relatives, all of who lived in the East. And our divorce was more than a decade old, perhaps they had all forgotten me, although Victor was as alive to me as when we had been so much in love and married.

One night when we were lying side by side in bed reading — by this time we had graduated to an apartment with a real bedroom and a double bed instead of a fold-out couch — I remembered that I was supposed to do my breathing exercises. I was about five months pregnant and that afternoon Jim Hearne had given me the instructions for the ones I was to do during my labour and delivery.

I set my book on the floor by the bed, we didn't have bedtables yet, I lay flat on my back and began to go through them. I don't remember anymore how they went since this was all more than twenty years ago and I never had another child and so never repeated them, but they involved controlling my breathing in a strict way, while counting. I had to concentrate very hard to get them right, but I was enjoying working on them since I liked the novelty, and I did want very much to do everything, the pregnancy, the delivery, right.

Victor lay beside me, perfectly still, sunk in the book he was reading, while I breathed in slowly and counted, held my breath, let it out, took so many short breaths, let them out to a count, and so on.

After a while I began to feel myself suspended, floating above the bed. It was a peculiar, pleasant feeling, and surprisingly, it didn't scare me, I barely noticed it, or rather, it had happened so gradually as I concentrated, that it must have seemed normal and not strange at all.

But as I hovered, I knew something that I hadn't known before, something I hadn't even guessed at, that was at once so terrible that I didn't see how I could live knowing it, and yet that had an inevitability about it, as well as a certainty so absolute that I didn't, not even for a fraction of a second, doubt it. The knowledge came suddenly, whole, and irrevocable.

"Victor?" I said.

"Hmmm?" he said, turning a page. It was not even hard to say since I knew with such finality that it was true.

"You don't love me," I said. "You don't want this baby."

There was a long silence. I lay beside him, by this time I must have been back in myself, and I didn't even wish that he would deny it.

"Well," he said, in a resigned tone, then paused, and seemed not to know what to say next. I risked a glance at him. He lay staring straight ahead and the sadness in his eyes and in the lines around his mouth would have given me hope if I had been inclined to look for it.

"Why is it you haven't left?" I asked.

"I've thought of it," he said, and paused again. "But I didn't think I should." He closed his book and set it on the floor by the lamp. For a second I thought he was going to turn out the lamp and go to sleep.

A few moments passed during which we continued to lie side by side. Then he said, "I'm hungry. Are you?" as if nothing had happened, or ever would. He got out of bed, dressed, and went out. An hour or so later he returned carrying some cartons of Chinese food, which we sat up in bed and ate in silence.

I knew also that night that he still might leave me. I thought of leaving him, despite how much I still loved him, but how could I? I was pregnant with his child, I would have rather died than return to my parents' home. I felt I could only wait for whatever he might decide to do. The months lay ahead of me as if I would be pregnant forever and at the end, with the birth, lay only blackness, a falling off, a void.

I wanted to call Rose and tell her not to come, that we no longer had anything to say to each other, that we need not bother with any kind of pretence of being a family anymore, or that we were bound together in any way, but I had no idea where she was staying, and besides, she was probably already on her way. I was tempted to lock the front door and pretend I had gone away.

But now, strangely, I found I was eager to see her, not because I had ever liked her, or because we shared any memories I wanted to relive, but because I knew how hard it would be to go on not knowing about Victor's death. I was sure she would be only too glad to answer any questions of mine: What had Victor died of? Where was he buried? Where was Julie? What did she know? Had Julie been at Victor's funeral?

I looked at my watch. As nearly as I could tell, more than an hour had passed since Rose had called. Maybe she wouldn't come at all, had changed her mind. Or maybe she had had a seizure and had forgotten her plan to come. I stood, parted the sheer curtains and looked out into the sunshine-drenched street. Rose was getting out of a taxi in front of the house.

I saw at once how thin she was. She had always been, not fat, but a big woman, and now she looked tall, bony and thin. As she came slowly up the sidewalk keeping her eyes on the path ahead of her feet, I saw in the way she moved, slowly, a little unsteadily, that she had aged more than she should have for her years. She shifted the small shopping bag that I recognized as from a woman's clothing store downtown, then rang the bell. I went to answer it.

We greeted each other, then went into the sitting room. She was wearing a neat grey linen summer suit with a gay yellow blouse under it. The frill at its neck was incongruous under her solemn, even sad face. She set her pink plastic shopping bag carefully on her lap and placed her feet in their neat white pumps side by side. This reminded me of her careful demeanour when she had first arrived for one of the visits that always ended so disastrously. She was facing the windows and in the afternoon sun that shone through muted by the white sheers, I could see clearly and was shocked by the lines of suffering in her face.

"How are you?" I asked, chastened.

"I'm never well," she said. "I have to take more and more medication. It disturbs my sleep, it upsets my whole system, there are side effects I don't dare tell anyone about."

"How terrible for you," I said.

"Yes," she said seriously. "It is terrible. I wish my mother were alive to help me." She had never married and Victor was her only sibling. He had, as long as I had known him, refused to take much responsibility for her. He claimed she had been favoured by their parents all through his childhood, that she had had tantrums if she didn't get her way, he even claimed she used to fake seizures, though I doubted that. But the result was he couldn't like her much, much less bring himself to care much about her plight which, during our marriage, wasn't really a bad one, since both her parents were still alive.

"Victor is dead, too," she said, and she rocked slowly forward and back once, as if in a dim memory of some ancient keening.

"Yes, I know," I said, and realized that Rose thought I'd known, hadn't thought of notifying me, but had assumed that I came to know things like that in the same way she did, because they hung in the air or one dreamt them and woke knowing.

We sat in silence for a moment, me not knowing what to say to her, Rose staring at a spot on the rug, her mouth working as if she might be talking to herself, although she made no sound.

"Where was he when he died?" I asked.

"Where?" Her head shot up and she stared at me so intently I was taken aback. "In Toronto where he lived, of course," she said. "In the hospital. He had cancer. He hadn't been sick very long." She paused, then stared at the same spot on the rug and said, "Not as long as I have. All my life. As long as I can remember." She lifted her head again. "It always starts with this," she said to me, and I recognized that old, pained, intimate tone she had adopted when she told me of the wrongs she constantly suffered. "It always starts with this," and she passed a hand slowly in front of her face, the fingers spread, fanlike.

Disconcerted, not knowing how to respond to her remark, I asked, "Where are you living now?" She drew in her breath slowly, not looking at me.

"With Victor, of course. But he's gone now."

I hesitated, hardly knowing how to go on. If Victor had been looking after her, where would she go now? The thought that she might want to live with me passed quickly through my mind, but I dismissed it at once. It would never occur to her.

"And ... Julie?" I ventured, not sure she would remember who I meant.

Her face cleared, for a moment she looked almost young again, and the lines in her face melted as she smiled.

"Julie!" she said. "Of course, Julie!" Her voice wavered. "I have trouble remembering, I ... " She swallowed, then started again. "I came to ask you to tell Julie something."

"Doesn't ... didn't Victor know where she is?" I asked, trying not to show that my heart had begun to pound and that my breath wouldn't come. I could feel my face turning red and perspiration was soaking my blouse. Menopause, I reminded myself, it was passing already.

I don't think I blame Julie for loving her father more than me. It must sometimes happen that way in a family. He always had a love of adventure which Julie shared, while I have wanted above all things, assurances, routine, simplicity. I do not want things catching me by surprise, although it's true that despite my efforts to strip my life to the simplest form, they seem to anyway. And I don't think of Julie as troubled. She's not a troubled girl, it's just that she had this indifference that I can't understand.

"Oh, yes," Rose said in that same, bright tone. "She stayed with us until Victor died. And then she said she was coming out here to see you."

"I haven't seen her," I said, relief swelling through me. She knew her father was dead, she had been there with him. Knowing she was all right and had been there made me feel as though I could go on living my life again.

After high school Julie went to Europe with two girlfriends. The girlfriends returned, one after six months and the other after eight or nine. Julie went to Australia instead of coming home, and then to New Zealand where she stayed a year. Then she went to Singapore, Bangkok and Hong Kong. Over two years passed before she returned and then I knew about it only because she phoned one night from Colorado where she was working.

Her letters always came infrequently, until finally they stopped altogether and she began to phone, but the phone calls were even less frequent than the letters. I grew used to her

absence and to the perpetual distance between us. It had its own
kind of peace. And between us there was not enmity, but rather a
restraint that we had come to cherish, that seemed to us — to
me, anyway — the healthiest possibility.

"Well," Rose said irresolutely, and reminded me abruptly of
her brother, so like him was her intonation and the expression
on her face. She fiddled with the plastic bag on her lap, smoothing it carefully, her lips moving again.

"Would you like some tea?" I asked, embarrassed because I
had forgotten to offer her some, and fearing she would see it as
another of the inevitable slights she found herself subject to each
day. "I'm sorry, I didn't think of it sooner. This has been a difficult day." I thought she might ask me what had made it so
difficult, but she said only, "No, no tea. I wanted to see Julie."

"If she comes I'll tell her to phone you," I offered. "Does she
know where to find you?"

"I'm still in Victor's apartment," she said. "Tell Julie that, and
that she should come back and live with me."

"She might not come here," I suggested tentatively.

"She is on her way," Rose said. "She is sure to be here soon."

It wasn't long after we sat up that night in bed and ate
Chinese food, before our marriage began to deteriorate. He
stayed out late, I didn't know where he was. He had an affair,
then ended it, we criticized each other, we were no longer
happy together, yet I continued, despite everything, to love him.
That long ago realization I no longer thought of. It was as
though it had never happened, and I now expected to remain
married to him forever. Still, our relationship grew worse and
worse, he was away more, he ignored me when he was home,
devoting himself to our daughter. We grew further and further
apart till I could no longer reach him at all, and in fact, had
stopped trying.

"I'll tell her as soon as she comes," I promised. "I'll tell her to
phone you at once." It seemed that Rose had forgotten that Julie
was my child, that there was any possibility that she might want
to stay and live with me.

When my miscarriage was over I bled a little for a day or
two, and that was it. Even today I feel no regret over losing that
child, only regret that I was so unaware that I didn't cry out from

my bed of pain, "Husband, I am having a miscarriage. I am miscarrying our child." I wish I had known. I wish I had lain there feeling the inexorable pull of the lunar tide in my womb, feeling the full weight of loss and death.

Rose stood up, bouncing the little plastic bag uncertainly against her skirt. The lines had settled back in her face and the darkness in her eyes.

"I'm taking the plane back at five o'clock," she said, "so I can't stay and wait, but it was nice to see you again, Jeanne."

"I'm so glad to have seen you," I said, thinking of all the things I would never know about Victor's life and his death. Looking up into Rose's face, I thought of her suffering, and I wanted to ask her if she was taking her pills. But the *distance* of her, the weight of her pain and the lightness of her *knowing* silenced me.

I called her a taxi and stood with her out on the sidewalk in the sun, where she insisted on waiting, until it came. She got into the car and didn't so much as give me a backward glance as it moved away, even though I waved and called, "Good-bye, Rose, good-bye."

Victor had a mistress, he barely spoke to me, nor I to him. Our daily life together, what little there was left of it, had become a horror of cold, silent anger. In the month which ended with his leaving me, I woke from a deep sleep into the blackness of our bedroom to find that I was being kissed. My first thought was that I must be dreaming since, although we still shared the same bed, we never touched, and we had not made love in months. But I could feel his soft breath on my face, and the slight, warm pressure of his body against my arm and hip. Victor was touching my hair and shoulders gently and covering my face and neck with light kisses that were filled with tenderness

I lay motionless, hardly daring to breathe I was so bewildered, and I thought, in my surprise and aching disbelief, that he must be asleep and dreaming he was kissing someone else. I pretended I was asleep, too, and suffered his caresses, which were more painful to me than blows because they stirred in me echoes of our once perfect love. I didn't move.

If he was awake, it was plain he didn't want me to know that there was a part of him that still loved me; if he was asleep, woke, and realized what he had been doing, he would probably say something to me or do something that would cause me even worse pain. I lay in an agony of doubt, wondering if this demonstration of love was for me or not.

And all these years later, as I watched Rose's taxi disappear down the street, I realized that I would never know. I would never know if Victor truly loved me, or if it was all only a dream of his, or, of mine.

Healer of the Earth

To have come so far; to have found life so full of joy; to have seen the visions he had seen. The light on the wall opposite his bed was fading not into greys, but into pinks. He knew his room faced the west so perhaps he had got it wrong and it was dawn, the colour having turned more lemon now than pink, and morning, and he was waking and not falling into sleep.

He sank into a sleep full of forest, for everywhere there were shadows and light, and the scent of pine and cedar rose up and ferns waved their thick fronds at him; he sank onto a carpet of rich green moss, felt its softness press against the palms of his hands, felt the cool damp of the earth against his cheek where the trees protected the soil from the sun. He lay and felt himself cradled by the thick, aromatic roots that crept beneath his body, stretching out, searching for nourishment. He slept, and the forest dreamed him.

Someone was speaking to him. He opened his eyes and saw a young male face looking down on him through gold-framed spectacles. Another doctor, he supposed, or the same one as before.

"Yes?" he said. "Yes," hearing his own voice once so robust, now fading to a quaver, an old man's, a dying man's voice. He blinked and saw the light moving over the white wall behind the doctor's head.

Dr. Mowbray looked down on the dying man, a great man, sometimes famous, now old and dying. He could hardly speak through the sadness that had seized and held him, not that he had known this good old man. He hadn't even known of him, until the old man had arrived days before, a patient, weakened by and gasping with his pain. Even brought in on a stretcher the old man carried a few of his small books pressed against his thigh, and Dr. Mowbray, overhearing whispers of his fame, had claimed them and read them. Now he wanted to speak to the old man, to question him, to listen in intent silence to the answers.

For everywhere he looked Dr. Mowbray saw only death. He had an urge to kneel beside the narrow bed and beg the old man to tell him what it was he knew that had impelled him and then sustained him on his life-long journey through the forests of the earth. Instead, he drew in his breath, straightened his glasses over his thin nose and leaned forward again.

"Mr. Baker, are you having any pain?" he asked. "Are you ... " He stopped, having given up, fell silent, thinking of the book the old man had written that sat at home under the lamp on his bedside table: thin, frayed, its simplicity of language.

The old man was bending again, turning sideways to make his way through the green and lucent light of the bamboo forest, the bamboos so thick that there was no other way to pass through, and they were lost, had been lost for days, God knew, might never find their way out again, for the bamboos, more than fifty feet high, couldn't be climbed to get one's directions and the bearers wanted to lie down neatly, side by side, to wait for death to come and claim them.

"Not ones to waste energy struggling against the insurmountable. When death comes, one knows it, one dies in peace." The doctor repeated to himself the old man's words, for he was tired, sick of science, sick of his white coat and of the pain he walked through every day and the talk of golf in the doctors' lounge. He dreaded even going into the lab where his senior students worked, loathed the steady hum of the fluorescent lights that seemed to pierce his very being and set his body vibrating with it. He loathed too, the smell of the chemicals, the disinfectants and preservatives and the drugs, even the white fingers of his own hands and the hands of all the men he worked with. No more of this, he said each morning, and every night, going to bed exhausted.

"Get me his chart," he said to the nurse who stood beside him. She looked surprised, pursed her lips, picked the heavy chart up from the bed where he had just laid it.

"Oh — yes," he said, took it, then in the act of opening it, failed to.

And there it was — the light. He had persevered, he had not given up, had walked four days and four nights, urging his bearers on, wouldn't let them lie down to die, made them carry their packs onward around the steaming, waist-high mounds of elephant dung, listening breathless with fear to the distant rumblings of the herds, knowing how swiftly they could move, trampling everything before them. It seemed to him that the watery, greenish light filtering down through the tops of the bamboo canes was changing, growing light, a cleaner, whiter light. He had found the edge of the forest.

"He keeps drifting in and out of consciousness," the nurse said softly, not that it wasn't obvious, but because she wanted to call the doctor's attention to the task at hand. So very old a man, she could see that he would die soon. She felt no regret, wished to go home as soon as her shift was over and change into her new red bathing suit and sun herself in the hour left to her, on the lawn of her apartment building. She could feel the sun on her face, how its heat would melt her bones; hoped he wouldn't die near the end of her shift, keeping her late with paperwork.

The doctor thought of all the other patients he had to see, but still he didn't move. The air conditioning hummed insistently, its icy, artificial breath touching the top of his head where his hair had begun to thin. He thought for no reason of the small farm he had come from fifteen years before, of its dusty brown fields, its thin, short crops of wheat, failing again this year in this heat, he supposed. He would send his father money.

The old man was crossing the Sahara in his jeep under the stars, the air so cold his teeth chattered. The sand was orange here, packed hard and slippery as ice. He shouted for his companion to stop, they jumped out, they dug and unearthed a small piece of petrified wood. Joy soared through him, claimed him: it was the petrified remains of an ancient tree. You see, he shouted, you see, *there was once a forest here!*

They got back in the jeep and drove on, skirting the dirty white pools of quicksand, running the hard-packed ridges, racing into the rising sun, into the hundred and thirty degree heat of noon, for days and days, suffering the bitter temperatures of the clear, hard nights, finding here and there more bits of petrified wood.

His dream grew, lying in the hospital bed; dying, his dream overtook him once again, one day to reclaim two million acres of the Sahara Desert, to plant trees and more trees where his evidence showed there had been forest, where today there was only hard-packed sand or giant, glittering dunes that shifted and changed even as he watched. A forest: tall green trees, the cloud of cool, moist air which the forest created and in which it lived, the lessening of the terrible cold and the terrible heat; the trapping of water, then the return of birds and small forest animals. He couldn't remember how or when, but his dream of a reclaimed Sahara was born long ago, and now he had the evidence to show others. He moaned with joy and turned his head fretfully on his hard, white pillow.

The young nurse had been glancing with a puzzled look at the doctor as he stood at the foot of the bed staring down, not really seeing the old man, seeing instead the thick, sighing forests of the old man's dreams. The doctor turned toward her. At last, she thought, we can move on to the others, to Philip Monroe, who had arrived the night before. But again the doctor paused, forgetting her, and stood still.

"I'm going to watch him for a bit," he said, without looking at her, aware of the mixture of bafflement and irritation emanating from her. She turned and rustled quickly out of the room. He heard her say something to someone out in the hall, but couldn't make out her words. He moved to the high-backed leather chair at the side of the bed and sat down in it, leaning back tentatively.

The old man's cheeks were mottled, the skin reddened and

leathery from eighty-odd years out-of-doors in all weather. The doctor was again reminded of his father. The trees are dying, his father wrote, and the creek's dried up, we can't get enough water from the well or the dugout to water them. It's too bad, his father wrote, to see them die.

Dr. Mowbray knew he was no longer kind to his patients, out of absent-mindedness rather than ill will; he had become abstracted, caught himself not listening when they spoke to him, forgot to give them medicine that would help the pain, until he was reminded by his nurse or they asked for it. Doctor, how much time has she left? What? he'd say, vaguely, his mind somewhere else, though he couldn't have said where if he'd been asked. I can't tell, I don't know, and he'd tap his fingers on his desk, his eyes gone vague again.

The old man had come back to his redwoods. So many years away from them in Africa, New Zealand, England, in northern Canada camping in the Peace River district. All of it fell away, was as if it had never happened, to be walking again, to be nearing, to be here in his sacred grove of *sequoia sempevirens* that stood three hundred and more feet high.

He paused, stood, the silence of the grove settled around him, seeped even into his bones, his blood, stilled his heart, calmed him, cleansed his spirit. Here was his cathedral, his temple of the gods, here he communed with the ancients, the trees themselves a thousand years old, growing already when his native England was ruled by the great king Athelstan, and the Mayan temples were being built in the jungles of Central America. And these trees had sprung from stool sheets thrown up by a parent tree back and so on, back as far as nine thousand years ago. The trees were so old that he saw that as living things, they reached toward immortality.

He walked among the shoulder-high lilies and wild irises, the violets and wild roses and the bracken. The trees stood tall, straight, slender, silent, the light striking them, here illuminating trunks and foliage, here leaving in rich forest shadow clumps of ferns, patches of treed distance. He walked slowly, gathering strength from them, sending out his spirit to mingle with their holiness.

This old man had saved the giant redwood trees of California that Dr. Mowbray had never seen, but vowed now he would the next time he took a vacation; he would take his wife and two teenage children to see them. No, he hardly knew his family anymore, he would leave them behind. He would walk alone in the groves, trace the old man's footsteps, try to feel his ecstasy, and maybe then he would learn what the old man knew, that he had failed to learn from his practice of medicine or from his patients, or from the other doctors in the lounge or the operating rooms with their bloody, irreverent interrogation of the human body.

He sighed, looked down at his hands again, despised them, so delicate and white. He thought of his father's hands, thick from hard work and brown from the wind and sun. Even in the midst of the coldest winter his father's hands were brown. His father who had never gotten past elementary school, whose reading was a few farm newspapers. His father who would lose the farm this year almost certainly. And what then? And the trees his grandfather had planted, the poplars and the maples, even the hardy carraganas dying in the drought.

The nurse walked briskly past the door and saw the doctor sitting motionless in the chair. She hesitated, annoyed, God knows there's work to be done and a dozen more patients for him to see and all he does is sit there moping. Leave him, come and see Philip Monroe who only needs his appendix out or his bowel attended to and then he'll be all right again. But Dr. Mowbray didn't lift his head and she went on so quickly that the man in the stiff, khaki shirt and trousers mopping up some spilled medicine from the shiny floor hardly noticed that she'd hesitated.

"Nurse?" the old man said, not opening his eyes.

"I'm here," the doctor said, "is there something I can do for you?"

"Nurse?" the old man repeated, more faintly this time.

The doctor placed his hand on the old man's forehead as if testing for fever. The old man relaxed visibly, could be seen to sink back into dreams.

He was a small child again playing around the skirts of his

nurse who was scrubbing clothes in a washtub on the grass at the edge of the forest near his childhood home. The forest beckoned to him, he longed to walk in it, to lose himself in its green shadows, to feel its coolness on his face, to touch the rough bark of the oaks and he wandered off, leaving his nurse to her scrubbing, and entered the forest on a narrow path that grew narrower till it vanished. He made his way among the ferns and lilies and trod on mosses, soft and brilliant green, he wove among the solid, greying trunks of the oaks, yews, chestnuts, until he was lost.

The forest grew darker, the sunshine retreated, he could find no path at all. Shadows leaped at him, tried to swallow him. He ran, pushing back scented underbrush, ducking under branches, catching twigs in his hair, tripping over roots and falling headlong on the spongy forest floor. Panting, sweating, no longer searching, but running madly, tears smearing the dirt on his scratched cheeks, he broke through the underbrush and stopped suddenly in his flight.

He had found the sunlight; it was captured in this glade. It made the tall grasses that grew from its floor glow with soft green light and it softened and greened the leafy branches of the old trees that formed the glade and intertwined overhead. He had never in all his five years seen anything so beautiful.

He fell to the ground and sat in the grass, his small back cradled by the root of a giant tree, he breathed in the beauty of the glade; he saw then how the trees lived even as he did; he understood their age, that they had lived longer than his father, or grandfather, or even great-grandfather; that they were time itself and he was a fresh, new spirit, cradled by the spirits of other ages, an infant rocked in history of which he was himself, small and insignificant as he was, a part; he saw how he and the trees and grasses were one.

Time hesitated, stopped; perhaps he slept. At last he rose to his feet and found that the glade no longer quivered with sun, had collapsed back into itself, and that now he knew the way directly back to his nurse. I shall dedicate my life to trees, he told himself, and the knowledge that this was so and would be so for all his life wove itself into the fabric of his being.

"Nurse?" he whispered again, and Dr. Mowbray leaned closer to him.

A patient was being wheeled past the door, returned from surgery, judging by the caps and gowns worn by the two nurses pushing the stretcher and by the bottle of plasma one of them was holding aloft as the patient sailed silently down the corridor, the only sound the whisper of the wheels, the rustle of the sheet as it brushed against the wall. I have work to do, the doctor reminded himself, and half-rose from the chair, halting in a crouched position as though his back had caught in a spasm or he was at the starting line of a race.

He hesitated, not knowing whether to sit down again or to go on out of the room and down the corridor to see Philip Monroe who would greet him cheerfully enough, though with frightened eyes. He thought of the man's lean, athletic body, his thick, dark hair — he was only thirty — and of the yellowish tinge his skin had taken on. Dr. Mowbray had known at once it was cancer, although there had been no tests yet to show it, and no one else seemed to think so. Perhaps it was dread of seeing Philip Monroe that made him hang by the old man's bed.

The old man had written so many books, simple books, so simple a child could read them. Perhaps he had written them for children, having given up on the adults of the world, who cut down trees and exposed the earth to the sun so that it grew parched and feverish, couldn't hold the rain and thus no longer produced anything. So that climates changed, precipitation dwindled, the land became desert and the people crowded into cities where they starved.

Dr. Mowbray thought how St. Barbe Baker had walked through the Douglas firs of Vancouver Island, through the poplars, birches, and pines of Saskatchewan, the scented orange groves of Palestine, the mahogany forests of Nigeria, and how wherever he had gone he sang the praises of trees, he planted trees, persuaded others to plant them, tried to save them from the loggers, the farmers, the developers. He had understood that winning out over nature is a hollow victory, one that leads only to the death of the planet, and its people.

While I have been concerned with microbes, bacteria, viruses, the systems of the body, with the tissue, the blood, the bones, and have found only disease and death and more death. He pondered, rising to look out his patient's window over the roofs of other wings, other buildings, to the multi-storied, steel car park beyond.

Philip Monroe would die. Thinking about the old man and his trees, he knew it was so. He would open that flat belly and find again only deadness and disease. All my science, he thought, seeing white-coated people pass the windows of the floor across from him, all my science won't save this old man or Philip Monroe. He put his hands in the pockets of his trousers and felt the coins he carried there, their hardness and how they had taken on the warmth from his body. He tried to understand what he had read the old man believed. He imagined himself walking with the old man through the redwood trees of California. He closed his eyes and concentrated, letting the coins drop, sinking into his imagining.

In it the forest lost its particularity, became merely a forest somewhere on the earth and he was walking in it by the old man's side, feeling first the sun and then the cool shadow on his face, smelling the sweet, clean scent, listening to the silence that seemed always to be filled with something, so that he caught himself always listening, as if when he held himself still enough, he would finally hear.

The spirits of the Maori leave this life to travel to the Underworld through the pohutukawa tree, the old man told him. And when the Maori have to cut down a tree, first they ask permission of the tree's spirit, and after, they cover the stump with branches to protect it. When the Kikuyu of Africa cut down trees they always leave one tree standing to collect the spirits of all the other trees so that they should not wander about and be uneasy. I have seen three thousand warriors dancing around one sacred mugumu tree. Shinto teaches that spirit — *kami* — resides in nature and especially in trees, and thus practitioners of the religion revere trees.

I will give you a vision, the old man said to Dr. Mowbray. I will tell you what I have seen ... Once I saw a broad highway lined with trees which radiated all the colours of the rainbow. Each of these trees bore fruit. I saw every fruit known to man hanging from their boughs and many I had never seen before. And at the end of this long avenue of trees, I saw a park, and a garden with many rare trees from all over the world growing there. And in the centre of that garden, dominating it, stood ... The Tree of Life.

The doctor sighed. Where can an old man go when he dies, he wondered, who has already seen the Tree of Life? Who already understands what I never have, that the earth lives, that the trees, the sky, and humankind are one?

He turned away from the window and saw that while he had been dreaming, looking out over the rooftops and the walls of the hospital, the old man had died.

When death comes one knows it, one dies in peace, he remembered.

He thought of his father's farm, drying up, blowing away, of the dying trees, and the empty creekbed behind the house, of the stench of the slime-covered weeds in its bottom, the white bellies of the dead fish, the waterbirds dead on its banks, the dryness of the air and the white-hot sun burning the pale, barren soil.

Drought had come, the trees were dying, the old man was dead. Soon, in a minute now, he would have to go down the hall and try not to show Philip Monroe by the look in his eyes that he was condemned. Although, it seemed to him, that in his heart the man knew this already.

And it seemed suddenly to Dr. Mowbray that he was the one who brought the death that surrounded him, that he in his white coat with his instruments and his head full of science, with his skillful hands and his remote eyes, it was he who carried death with him. He thought of throwing himself from the window to the concrete far below.

Shuddering, he turned to the nurse who was taking the old man's pulse.

"He's gone," he said, and she padded out of the room angrily, then with resignation, relinquishing her red bathing suit and the sun, to go and write things down, to telephone, to prepare papers for the doctor to sign saying the old man was surely dead.

Who will redeem me? the doctor asked. Who will make me again that innocent farm boy I was once so long ago? Who will journey with me through the forests of the world, into the heart of the universe?

No one, the old man said, no one, take your courage in your hands and go alone. They were covering the old man's face with a sheet and wheeling his body from the room.

And Philip Monroe? the doctor asked.

Go to him and hold his hand, the old man said. And somehow, that was enough.

The Vision of the Hohokam

The publicist checks them in at the desk, then leads them down a narrow corridor and up a flight of stairs. Alexis follows her and Jamie brings up the rear. They reach a small lounge with worn sofas on each wall and a coffee table between them that is so low a midget would have to kneel to use it. The outside wall is glass and looks out on the dark harbour and the rain. The opposite wall is glass too, but it looks into the studio where the host of the radio show with the biggest listening audience in that half of the province is smoking, gesturing with his cigarette, and talking into the haze to a male guest who is seated with his back to the three of them. Although they can't see the guest's face, they can hear his voice over the speaker system that is tuned to the show. They sit down, Alexis with her back to the harbour facing Jamie and Sheila, whose backs are to the studio.

Alexis can't concentrate on what the two men are saying. She has no idea what their conversation is about, it is that kind of radio, although she is aware that they seem to be enjoying themselves. She turns and looks out at the rain running silently down the thick panes of glass. Jamie, her son, says something to Sheila, who stands and waves mutely to the host on the other side of the glass wall. The host nods back and sticks up seven fingers. Sheila nods agreement and sits again. The voices of the two men, broken now and then by chuckles, murmur on.

Alexis turns again to look out to the black expanse of water spreading itself out below and behind her. Through the rain streaking down the window she can see the lights of a small vessel crossing the harbour and by its steady, angled course, she recognizes it as the sea bus nearing the downtown side. She had ridden on it a couple of years before when she had come to Vancouver to see Jamie in a play at his theatre school. Once they were under way the lights were shut off and they could see the north shore growing smaller behind them, and ahead of them, the lights of the downtown skyline approaching. With Jamie seated beside her, tired after his performance and now remote and thoughtful, the few passengers scattered silently about the cabin, it had seemed as if they could ride forever in that muted, gently rocking capsule across the black waters and through the endless night. Night sea journey, she thinks now, remembering, and grows silent.

"I thought you'd like it," Jamie said, smug, and grinned at her, not shy anymore as he had been at the airport when he'd said he wanted to bring her here. He had been standing at the top of the escalator waiting for her, smiling both eagerly and shyly as she approached. She could tell at once that he really was glad to see her and a small knot that she hadn't realized was there inside her let go. He had a small gold earring in one ear that hadn't been there when she had last seen him a year before, he was wearing a baggy, crumpled cotton shirt and pants that had been washed to near white and his hair was so short that she had wondered, startled, if his head had been shaved. But none of this mattered to her, she was so glad to see him again. "Isn't it big?" he said. "You can see why it's called Casa Grande. Come on."

The path the guidebook led them along wound its way among the mesquite and cactus. At each marked point Jamie stopped and solemnly read aloud what the book had to say about it, while she drank in the sight of him, knowing she was probably smiling like a fool and not caring. It was so hot that sweat beaded his forehead, trickled down his neck, and dampened his chest.

He took off his shirt, balled it, and used it to mop his face and torso.

Casa Grande, the big house, had once been at the centre of a walled village, although now there was nothing left of the other buildings or the wall but foot-high ridges which they stepped over casually. The big building looked as if it had been made out of the sand it was standing on, compressed somehow and baked to a lovely, warm, pink-brown colour.

"This stuff is called *caliche*," Jamie said, placing his palm flat on its granular surface. The building's highest remaining points rose thirty feet above the ground, much of its top storey had eroded away, and the walls were a good three feet thick. She leaned against the foundation at an opening, chest-high on her, which led into a passageway on what was the building's ground floor. How cool it must have been inside, she thought. When she had gotten off the plane in Phoenix and the hundred degree heat had rolled over her, she had thought, this is unbearable, I'll never be able to stand it, but here in the desert, even though it was much hotter, the heat seemed more natural.

"It says they don't know for sure who built it ... " Jamie paused and turned a page, "maybe some people called the Hohokam who are extinct now. And they aren't sure what the building was for." He glanced up from the book to the huge structure looming over them, and she saw that he had forgotten her, was absorbed in the mystery. She thought how it would have been the biggest thing within the knowledge of any living creature, how its size, towering over the desert, must have impressed the people who saw it. "They figure it might have been a sacred building like a temple, or that maybe it was for astronomy." He wiped a trickle of sweat off the end of his nose. "You see those rectangular openings near the top? I guess they line up with the sun on certain days or something."

"What happened to them? The people, I mean the ... Hohokam," she asked, hesitating over the name. Jamie flipped back a couple of pages, searching.

"They don't say. They don't know. They just disappeared."

Alexis peered into the narrow, shadowed passage as if she were looking for something. Impulsively, she said, "I'm so glad you brought me here," although this was not quite what she meant, and even though she knew their visit here was for Jamie a way of delaying what she had come all this way for and which both of them, for different reasons, dreaded.

And the heat, oh the heat, she was from the prairie herself, she knew dry heat, but not like this, never like this. It was incredible, it was a marvel. She wanted to lift her face to the sky, but she didn't dare, the sky was all sun, it would burn her to a cinder, and she thought of the Diving God of the Toltecs, or was it the Mayans, the red sun sinking into the sea at the end of each day. She turned to Jamie again.

"Do they know how old it is?"

"About 1300," Jamie read. "Not so old, but still, isn't it amazing to think that a building made of sand could last almost seven centuries?"

"Caliche," she said, raising one finger to make him laugh. "The elusive Hohokam," deepening her voice, making a joke of it.

"This is all that's left of them," Jamie said, serious, gesturing to the building. "This and a few broken pots and baskets. Incredible, isn't it, that a whole tribe of people who ... believed something, who must have had a vision of what things are, should just disappear from the face of the earth." His voice was perplexed, she thought she could hear the hint of something deeper.

But Alexis wanted to stand still, to touch the building with the length of her body, to hold herself motionless, to clear her head of all thoughts or ideas, to open her consciousness to that knowing blackness till something always just out of her reach finally came: a vision, a word, a feeling. They stood silently side by side, not quite touching.

"That their God would let them die." He said this softly, as if to himself, and in the midst of the appalling heat, Alexis was, for an instant, chilled. He turned away suddenly, speaking over his shoulder to her. "Tomorrow the Grand Canyon."

"No," she said, smiling so he wouldn't think she was being harsh, "tomorrow the ashram."

Across from her the man whose face she hasn't seen is standing, shaking hands with the talk show's host. They're laughing, it seems to her that she can feel the male camaraderie oozing through the panes of glass between them. She steels herself to face what might well be the host's hostility, for she suspects there is undeniable audacity in what she and her son have done and it was her idea and her energy that had kept it going in the initial stages.

Sheila is rising now and Jamie is too, and she follows them into the studio as the previous guest squeezes past them on his way out. Alexis feels prickly with uneasiness, not knowing what to expect, suspecting, from the interview she has watched but not heard, that this is the wrong venue for her and her sensitive, actor son. Or at least the wrong venue for her. 'I an artist,' she repeats to herself, and can't help but grin one more time over what is a joke so old — a line Mickey Rooney once said in a movie — that nobody would still get it but she and Jamie's father. But as the publicist introduces them, Alexis sees she is pleased with herself for having gotten them on this show. And well she should be, Alexis reminds herself, it's no mean feat.

Alexis has done her share of three-minute interviews she suspects were never run, over rock-and-roll stations, with interviewers whose carefully honed styles made them sound to her merely crazed, and not one of who, she doesn't think, had ever read one of her books. Once she had walked into a station for a scheduled interview and found the reception area empty and loud, muffled voices coming from behind a closed door. Then the receptionist had appeared with tears still streaming down her face and said only, "It's off, it's all off," and waved Alexis away. Later that morning, at another station, the man who was to interview her told her that the first station had been sold to a new owner who had decided to go country-and-western and had walked in that morning and fired everybody. She remembers wondering if she would ever be well enough known not to have to do that humiliating and, it seemed to her, fruitless round.

"Do you remember that radio interview we did at CK-some-thing-or-other? The one with the huge listening audience — in Vancouver, I mean? Let's go this way." Jamie followed her past the pen where the calves backed away, wide-eyed, before they turned and ran away, tossing their heads and kicking up their heels. With Jamie's help she kicked the snow away from the bottom of the gate and took off her mitts to unhook the chain that held it closed. Together they pulled back the gate, it creaked with the cold, far enough for each of them to squeeze through, and shut it behind them.

"Yeah," he said. "I still listen to him sometimes. He's pretty good at what he does, if you like that kind of confessional radio." They crunched over the snow-covered rocks to the edge of the riverbed. Ever since the latest cold spell even the shallow spot where she crossed in summer and which was the last to freeze over, was frozen solid. She could imagine that by now the river had stopped flowing under the ice cover, was frozen solid down to its bed. Her cheeks had begun to burn with the cold, but she didn't want to go back in yet, and knew he didn't either. He was the one who had wanted this walk, eager to see the place he was rarely on, even though it had been his mother's home for almost fifteen years now.

They turned and walked side by side along the bank following the path the cows had made in the snow. The air was very still, the only sound their feet crunching on the hard-packed surface of the path or, if one of them strayed off, brushing through the loose snow banked beside it. The sky rose on all sides around them, high and a perfect, clear blue, beginning to deepen now at the horizon. The sky made her forget the cold; on good days it made her feel she was soaring even if she was only walking along the riverbank.

"During that whole interview I felt off-balance. I couldn't get a grip on what he wanted from me, I couldn't seem to connect." She kicked at the snow beside the path, slipped, and would have fallen, but coming up to her, he caught her elbow and steadied her. "But you caught on right away. I felt that you understood because you're a different generation. I mean, I thought it was an example of the generation gap at work."

"Naw," Jamie said easily, his exhalation sending out a thin white plume against the blue-white of the snow. "It was the style of the show — speedy, that's all."

"He really liked you," she said. "After a while he only talked to you. It was just as well. I didn't know what to say anyway."

"It was a hard thing to talk about," he said. "After a while I just started saying whatever came into my head." He laughed and stopped in the path, turning to her. "Now *that* was what he wanted. He wasn't interested in the truth."

Alexis laughed with him, but she was thinking how she couldn't get the interview out of her head, how she still thought about it. And what puzzles me, she thought but didn't say out loud, is what it was that I missed. What I didn't know about you, what I didn't know about us. That what he wanted me to say was that I was guilty. But I'm not, she said to herself. Then, maybe I am. Maybe I really did abandon you, my only child, and I could never admit it. Can't, even now.

When the interviewer stands to shake hands with them, Alexis sees he is a big man, taller than Jamie. He has a rumpled, comfortable look and cigarette ashes have left a trail down his shirtfront. The big, flat ashtray by his microphone is full of crushed cigarette butts. She is surprised to find there is anybody left who smokes so unselfconsciously and so heavily.

"We'll do twenty minutes or so," he says, "depending on how it goes." Alexis doesn't like the sound of this and for some reason he doesn't make her feel easy despite his affable air, the dim lights in the studio, the comfortable-looking sofa at one end where the publicist has seated herself, or even the blue haze of cigarette smoke that gives the room a cozy, intimate air. They sit down at microphones across from him and wait. He listens to something in his headset, draws on his cigarette, nods, and begins.

"I hear this play is full of blood and murder and so on. Is that right?" Alexis is taken aback, as he meant her to be, and she laughs and says, "All of the above, but metaphorically, not literally," and knows by the look the interviewer, Bill is his name, gives her, that she has caught the right spirit. He turns to Jamie.

"Now, I understand that this play is autobiographical. It's about you and your mother — it's your story, right?" Alexis turns to look at Jamie, nervous for him, a little frightened suddenly at what has been unleashed here. And, she reminds herself, it's all her doing. Jamie swallows, then leans forward, a look of resolve that she's known as part of him since he was a four-year-old, crossing his face.

"Not entirely, but to a large extent that's true. My parents did divorce when I was eleven or twelve and when my mother remarried — she doesn't remarry in the play — I went to live with my father."

"That's pretty unusual, I think, isn't it?" Bill asks Alexis. "That a child should live with his father instead of his mother? How did that happen?"

Alexis pauses, wondering what she should say, she hadn't expected to have to talk about their real life, but only about the play. They aren't the same thing, she wants to point out, but doesn't, since they had decided ahead of time that in order to get the publicity that would bring the play an audience, they would play up the mother-son, autobiographical angle. Bill is looking impatient, so she speaks.

"I was going to live on an isolated ranch." She keeps her voice matter-of-fact, but she is caught between bewilderment and anger, that she should find herself telling this, the truth, because she has been caught off-guard. "As the time for the wedding approached I could see Jamie getting more and more unhappy. Finally I asked him what was wrong. He said he didn't want to live in the country, he didn't want to leave all his friends, he especially didn't want to leave his father." She swallows, then goes on. "So, I had to choose, and I chose to go, and to leave him with his father." How she feels must be written on her face, because Bill doesn't look at her, but turns to Jamie.

"Is this how you remember it, James?" he asks, and Alexis is surprised at the question.

Jamie shifts his gaze to the tabletop, frowns, then says, "Well, I don't remember ... " What? Alexis thinks, what? "But, anyway, that's not what happens in the play. In the play the mother is an artist and she leaves her family so she can pursue her life as a writer." She hears this with only a part of her mind. My god, she is thinking, if he doesn't remember that, that critical moment that is so clear to her, that she has clung to all these years, what does he think happened? "The son feels betrayed and abandoned," Jamie says. "He can't get over it."

For the first time it occurs to Alexis that she and her son might have different stories about what happened between them.

The ashram was situated on a hilly ten acres, the road up to it narrow and winding with a sheer drop off one side. From the small parking lot she could see a big, two-storey, ranch style house with a blue-painted roof. She said, "Do you live there?"

"No," he said, she thought he was avoiding looking at her, "only couples live there. I live in another, smaller house with the other single men."

"It sounds like there's lots of you."

"Sometimes there's too many," he answered. "But right now there's about two dozen of us." He led her from the parking lot up an asphalt path past the back door of the big house. A thin young woman, twenty years old or so, was standing near the door watching two toddlers who stood silently and watched Alexis and Jamie pass by.

"Hi, Lucinda," Jamie said, cheerfully, but didn't introduce Alexis or stop. The girl nodded her head, but didn't speak or even smile. When they had passed out of earshot, Alexis said, "Are those her children?"

"Just the little one," Jamie said. Alexis looked back over her shoulder and saw that Lucinda had picked up the smallest child and was holding him on her hip while the other child was still watching them. It seemed to Alexis that an air of unhappiness hung around the woman and she felt sorry for her, seeing perhaps echoes of herself years before, and then for the curiously silent children. It was the children who worried her, but, she thought, trying to shrug off her uneasy feeling, I'm probably just imagining it. It's a bad time, just before lunch, the kids are probably cranky because they're hungry.

To her right, down among some stunted, gnarled trees that she couldn't identify, she saw what looked like an Indian teepee with bright paintings decorating its canvas.

"A place for the kids to play?" she asked, remembering a tent that had been pitched on the grounds of a school Jamie had once gone to.

"No," he said and smiled at the idea, but she could see how nervous he was, growing more so every minute, his face pale, a slight sheen of sweat on his forehead, although here near the mountains it was not hot at all, was cool even. She wanted to stop him and say — whatever you want, anything you want, if you choose this, I accept it — but these were words that were not sayable, and emotion had risen up so hard in her throat that her eyes had begun to water. She took off her glasses and wiped them with the back of her hand, then yawned ostentatiously.

"I never sleep well when I'm travelling," she said.

"I know what you mean," Jamie said, "I'm the same way." He went on a few steps further, then stopped at a point on the path where they had a clear view of the tent below them. "That's where Irina lives. She's a clairvoyant." He said this last carefully, after an almost imperceptible pause, and she recognized that he had determined, as was his way, to lay everything bare before her, to hide nothing from her. When she said nothing, his honesty had silenced any comment she might have made, he went on almost eagerly. "She's gifted. She just has to close her eyes and she's in another space."

"Surely she doesn't live there in winter, too?" Alexis said. "What about snakes and scorpions and black widow spiders?"

"She says there's never been any insect or snake or anything like that in there. She's lived in it a couple of years now, winters too, she has a little heater she uses when it gets cold." They moved on up the path, Alexis again casting a last glance over her shoulder at the teepee down among the trees.

The ground around them was bare and stony between the few cactuses, other dry, thorny-looking bushes that she didn't recognize, and the clumps of sage. He had told her that this was once Apache country, the scene of much bloodshed and death and that people said the souls of dead Apache warriors still roamed the rough, ancient-looking countryside. Again she wiped her cheeks below her glasses, casually, as if she were only brushing something annoying away.

"This place was once a private school," Jamie explained and showed her the small swimming pool where no one was swimming and the tennis court where no one was playing tennis. She could hear the sound of hammering and sawing and the whine of power tools coming from a low, log building to the right of the tennis court.

"That's the workshop," Jamie said. "It's where I work most of the time." Alexis knew that the ashram survived on its cabinet-making business and this still surprised her somehow, it was so mundane, as if she had thought their spiritual interests should be enough to feed them.

The workshop had once been a stable, its wide doors were open to the sun, but now it was full of wood-working equipment — saws and lathes — and heaps of sweet-smelling, curled, white wood-shavings lay about. A muscled young man, his long, thick hair held back with a red headband, stripped to the waist, was bent over the white wood of a new cabinet, sanding it by hand with careful attention.

"Mom, this is Jeremy," Jamie said, stopping.

"Hi, Jeremy," Alexis said, smiling. Jeremy stopped sanding only long enough to lift his head and say a quick 'hi' to her and to flash her a smile that she saw at once was far too bright to be genuine. She saw then that everybody in the ashram felt on trial because she was there, a parent, somebody bound to disapprove, even to scoff. Jamie led her quickly away without taking her inside where other young men were moving about.

"It's still an hour till lunch. Would you like to see where I sleep?"

"Oh, yes," she said quickly. They followed another curving, gravelled path through the trees upward to where an unpainted wooden, dome-shaped building squatted in a clearing, its shingles weathered and grey. They went inside and Alexis saw the bare boards of the unfinished interior, some cupboards along one wall, a Franklin stove, a sofa in a corner and a ladder leading straight up to a loft. Jamie sat down on the sofa, and she was about to sit beside him when he said, still smiling, although she thought he was beginning to seem tired, "Why don't you go upstairs and see where I sleep?"

Alexis hesitated, looking at the ladder which was set perpendicular to the floor, wondering if her sandals would slip on the narrow rungs. But no, she decided, I've come all this way, I'll see everything, I won't hold back now. She went to the ladder, gingerly putting her foot on the first rung, then turned to Jamie, laughing, and said, "You know, in Borneo the shamans climb a ladder to the sky during their ecstasies." She began to climb and went up through the rectangular opening in the ceiling.

The roof upstairs was low and angled, the walls unlined. Pallets, that was the word that came to her mind as she saw the foam pads with sleeping bags or bedding stretched over them. She stared around, trying to think, trying to be reasonable, but the thin pallets on the bare wooden floor, the absence of bedding on most of them, the books left open beside them, the frayed remnants of carpet placed on the unfinished board floor beside a couple of the beds hurt her, gave her an actual pain in her chest. Her eyes were blurring again and she took a few deep breaths, then called downstairs, keeping her voice light and strong-sounding, "Which one is yours?"

"Third one on your right." It was one of the ones with a flannel sheet and a blanket spread on it and folded neatly on it, she recognized the quilt she had given him when he had left after high school eighteen months before. She took off her glasses and bent over to wipe her eyes and cheeks using the hem of her cotton skirt, put her glasses back on and began to climb carefully down the ladder. When she reached the bottom, she went to sit beside Jamie on the couch. Neither of them spoke. Her eyes and cheeks needed wiping again, but she resisted.

She noticed then that framed, colour photographs hung here and there around the walls and she got up, pretending to be interested in them. When she got close, she saw that all of them were pictures of the same man, a dark-skinned, frizzy-haired man with a big nose. In each picture he was dressed in a flowing white robe, staring intently at the camera, and in most of the pictures his image had been artificially blurred and softened to give him an otherworldly appearance, a sort of halo around him. Shocked, she began, "But what ... " Jamie broke in quickly, in a voice she could hear him struggling to keep casual, and she felt such pity for him, that she was here, requiring explanations he knew she would never be able to accept.

"They're just here to remind us of what we're supposed to be doing here, that's all."

"But, who is it?" she asked, although once again this was not at all what she wanted to say.

"Michael, our ... leader." She had a feeling he had been going to say 'guru.' But so what, she told herself, she knew they had one, knew even that he lived upstairs in the big house in a private apartment with his wife and child, that he didn't even eat with the others. Her carefully tamped anger was rising, but before she could say anything, Jamie said, "Those pictures upset most people who come here." Again he wasn't looking at her and she could hear how hard he was working to keep his tone even. "But they're just supposed to ... remind us of things," he repeated, now sounding as if he knew it would be useless to say anything more.

She could not help herself, but turned to look at him, and seeing how pale he was, paler even than he had been all morning, she found it impossible to speak and went instead to sit beside him again, taking his hand in hers, holding it loosely at the wrist, his fingers spread out across her palm. She wanted to hug him hard, to tell him she loved him, that she loved him so much that even her fingertips ached with her love for him, but these weren't things that could be said and it occurred to her that she mustn't ever let him know how much she loved him, that it would be too much for him, for anyone to bear.

She thought about all the people who had urged her to come here and take Jamie away, to rescue him by whatever means, to kidnap him if necessary, anything to get him away from this place which they were sure was evil and where he was surely being kept by coercion, however hidden.

She had argued with them, saying first, what better thing could a young man do than to go out in search of answers to spiritual questions? Then, but don't you see, he chose that, it's his choice. And finally, he has to find his own way. That much she knew and clung to, but in the end, she had had to at least come, to see for herself.

Despite all this, which she went over silently, she heard herself say, "If you want to go to college or to theatre school, I'll find the money. If you just want to take some time and travel, I'll give you the money." She looked into his face, she knew he had been looking at her, but he turned away quickly.

"Oh, Mom," he said, irritated, "don't you know everybody's parents' offers them money and trips?"

He took her then to the big house for lunch where the members of the community ate their meals together seated on benches at long wooden tables. Jamie sat on one side of her and Irina, the clairvoyant who lived in the tent, came voluntarily and sat on the other side. She turned out to be older and very intelligent and articulate with a quick sense of humour and she made Alexis laugh so that even Jamie relaxed a little and joined in the conversation which was mostly about what Alexis had seen and done since her arrival.

Alexis's eyes wouldn't stop watering though and every once in a while, even while she was laughing, she had to take off her glasses and wipe away the hot fluid that kept seeping from them, steaming up her glasses and wetting her cheeks.

Embarrassed, she offered her excuse again, "I couldn't sleep last night — my eyes always water when I haven't had enough sleep." She pushed her brown rice around her plate and picked up a carrot stick, sniffing and laughing a little at herself at the same time.

"I bet it's an allergy," Irina said to her, while Alexis mopped her cheeks again with a thin paper napkin Jamie had given her. Her hand over her eyes, Alexis replied, "It probably is. It's probably just an allergy."

The interviewer changes his tack, thinking perhaps it would be taking the two of them further than even he wants to go in the intimate perusal of their lives.

"If that's the case," he says to Jamie, "that this is autobiographical and you even wrote some of your own lines, how did you find working on the play? It must have been hard for you, all things considered."

"As a production it wasn't particularly difficult," Jamie replies, then plunges in in the way Alexis hasn't been able to. "But considering that it was at least partly my story and my mother's and that in working through the part I had to try to understand what happened, I found it cathartic."

Alexis stops listening. Cathartic? How could that be? As far as she was concerned much of the play was a fabrication they had built based on a few grains of truth. Or was this just what he had decided ahead of time he would say?

"Alexis, if this play was cathartic for James to act in, was it cathartic for you to write?" She supposes she has to say yes to this and so she does, although privately her mind is racing, wondering what the real answer is. "Was it hard to write all this down?" Bill prompts her, crushing out his cigarette and lighting another one. No, she is thinking, no, not cathartic, it was ... but what was it?

"It was good for me to try to understand what happened," she allows, her voice trails off, she has forgotten the radio audience. Bill, impatient with her, turns to Jamie, says something, and Jamie is off talking.

One part of her thinks how well he is doing, how he understands the pace of the show, while she, used to a different kind of interview, is lost. She sees how charmed Bill is with Jamie's quickness and his good looks. She finds it both strange and delightful to realize that she gets more respect because she is the mother of this handsome and talented young man. But all the while she is thinking, hard to write? Yes, in the way that everything is hard for her to write, never knowing if she is going in the right direction or not, never sure she hasn't hit a note that is merely maudlin, struggling to bring what is really only another sordid divorce story to a level that would redeem it, trying to explain what she thought it meant to be an artist. Had she understood what it was she had done? Had she, inadvertently, stumbled on the truth? What was the truth, and what was only the play?

The field on their left ended in low hills a mile away and she saw the pair of golden eagles that lived to the north in a deep coulee, one ridge of which was studded with the remains of ancient medicine wheels, flapping onerously to rise out of it, then following the line of the hills, blurred now with blowing snow, searching for prey. She and Jamie had reached the point where the river curved past them to go south, and the fenceline was in front of them. Instead of going to the gate, she put her foot on the bottom pole, slipping a little on the crust of ice, and climbed it. Jamie waited till she was over, then climbed it too. Plumes of grey smoke rose from the tractor her husband was running in the feedyard in the next field.

Although it was hardly past two in the afternoon, already their shadows were lengthening. Soon the day would grow dark, would turn to night. In a few days it would be the winter solstice, the death of light, and of the old year.

"It's wonderful to have you home," she said.

"It's really nice to be here," he answered, looking across the field to the distant hills. She was struggling to say something, but not sure what it was.

"I didn't have a happy childhood," she said, "but I think you did, at least, till you started school." But no, that wasn't it, and he didn't reply, or made some sound that might have meant anything or nothing, meant only that he was listening. Since the day he was born she had had the compulsion to speak to him, but she had never been able to translate that barely contained tide of feeling into words. She wondered, hope rising in her chest, is this the time when I will finally speak to him?

"Do you ever wonder if our luck is tied together?" she asked Jamie.

"What?" he said.

"When we did that play together, when we used my writing and your acting — we're mother and son. Do you ever wonder if in some way that neither of us can know about, at least not in this daylight world, that we're linked together? If one of us has good luck, so does the other, and if it's bad, it's bad for both of us?" But this isn't quite what she meant. She had a quick vision of him and all the members of his ashram with their guru seated cross-legged in front of them, leading them all through a long evening of chanting and meditation. But, frightened of it, when he had invited her to come, though she had wanted to, she had refused.

"It never occurred to me," he said, thoughtful. "I don't know."

Seeing his perplexity, afraid she might have gone too far,

assumed too much, Alexis decided to let the subject drop. But, she thought, I wonder if on that same level that nobody has words for, I wonder if that is where one person can help another, if maybe that's the only place that makes any difference. Not through money or jobs or gifts of food, but somehow, by thinking hard enough about the other person.

Or maybe I'm only talking about prayer.

"Well, really," Alexis interrupts, impatient now. "I decided to write the play because Jamie was just out of theatre school and it's so hard for a young actor to make a start. Like any mother, I wanted to help him, but since I have no influence in the theatre world, I couldn't think what I could do. Then I thought of writing a play, one with a good part in it for Jamie, and with second stages springing up all around the country, I was sure we could find a venue for it."

"And this has nothing to do with your having," he is careful with the word, "left him?"

"No, of course not, not at all," she replies. Then, "Maybe."

"I felt it was a gift," Jamie says suddenly, without being asked. "And when I performed in it, it seemed to me that I was giving back my mother a gift."

Alexis is astonished. Warmth floods over her. Then, staring at Jamie she wonders, does he think I wrote the play to give him back some of what he lost when I, of my own free will, went away and left him? But I didn't, it wasn't free will, I had to go, my life was unbearable the way it was, I had no choice.

She has missed something, she isn't sure what Bill has asked, but Jamie is replying in a manner that is almost too patient, "But you see, we changed the story so that the woman in the play abandons her children." He pauses, and for once, Bill waits. "But I never felt abandoned," he says. "I wasn't abandoned."

The snow in the field they entered was knee-deep in places and, shorter than Jamie, she found it hard going. Seeing her floundering, he said, laughing, "Here, I'll break trail," and strode ahead, his strong legs plowing back the deep, fresh snow.

It had turned even colder since they'd left the house to go for a walk. The wind was rising and she pulled her parka hood around her face to break its force. With so much snow lying about, she thought, it's bound to blizzard, but with two days left before he had to leave to begin rehearsals of the latest play he was in, a storm tonight wouldn't hold up his departure.

They reached the other side of the field, both of them panting, and climbed the fence into the feed yard where her husband was clearing away snow drifted up against the balestacks using a small snowblower mounted on the tractor. Mutely, over its roar, using her eyebrows and a gesture, she offered him their help. He shook his head no, opened the tractor door and called to her, "You might as well go in. I'm just about finished here." They went gratefully to the house.

On the deck as Jamie bent down to brush the snow off his pantlegs, she stepped around the corner to see how the weather looked to the west, the direction the wind was blowing from. Snow scudded across the fields, blotting out the line of hills in a blur of swirling white. For a second, all she was able to stand, she stood and let the stinging snow strike her full in the face. I should have stayed. The thought rose up unbidden, and left a gap behind, a white space. It's true. I've never accepted the responsibility for what I did.

She dropped her head, putting up both her mittened hands to shield her face. She would ask him to forgive her, but she knew he wouldn't want to hear even that. Not now, after all these years and their various attempts to talk to each other, to put things right. In his busy life in the city he had shrugged the past off, while she, moving each day through the wide fields, under the limitless, pale sky, was enshrouded in it.

Early that morning they had parked the car on the edge of the narrow road with the Atlantic, or at least an arm of it, on their right, glistening that deep blue that only the Atlantic is. On their left, before the forest starts, is an empty field. The balloonists have put up a big, blue and white striped tent at the edge of the field on a slight rise of ground close to where the cove ends. Beyond it is only ocean and more ocean and then the British Isles. They have come to watch the balloonists take off in an attempt to cross the Atlantic.

Already other cars are striking up the muddy little road, going slowly to cushion the bumps, and Jamie steps behind her as one comes too close and almost splashes him. She reaches down and takes his hand.

"Let's walk in the field," she says to him. Jim strides ahead, not waiting for them till Jamie shouts, "Daddy, wait for me!" Jim pauses, looks back at Jamie, and waits while Jamie runs up to him and grasps his hand. She lengthens her step, just a little, so as to grow closer to them without appearing to hurry or to have been left behind. More people are arriving all the time and beginning to park in the field.

It's a perfect Nova Scotia day, the sky above the spruces and over the flat, dark blue ocean is a pale blue and cloudless and there is a light wind blowing, but not so strong as to cause trouble for the balloonists. The sea smell rises, strong and salty and she remembers the first time she smelled the ocean, the Pacific it was, and she had been faintly shocked by the odour.

Jim and Jamie are walking around the tent and she follows them, feeling silly, but what else is there to do? The two balloonists are working on the far side of the tent, facing the ocean. A small crowd has gathered watching them, and more people are coming all the time. The tent is filled with huge iron cylinders, the kind that are filled with gas of some kind and the balloon itself lies collapsed and wrinkled, spread out over the damp grass. The balloon is striped too, red and white, in a spiral from its red base to its white top. It is huge. One of the balloonists calls to them to keep back from it, not to step on it.

People crowd around and from then on Alexis catches only brief glimpses of whatever it is the balloonists are doing. There is a poof, and after that, until the balloon takes off, there is the steady, muted roar of a propane torch at work, doing what, she doesn't know, but the balloon, very slowly, almost imperceptibly, begins to fill over the next few hours. She sees only glimpses of this, only partial views, before someone steps in front of her. Little Jamie goes as close to the front as he dares, but if she and Jim lose sight of him, it is always Jim who pushes his way through the crowd to find him. Jamie asks question after question, his hazel eyes wide and full of wonder, and neither of them knows the answers.

Nor does the rest of the crowd. Most of them are young, men mostly, and many of them are drinking beer which they offer to the balloonists, who refuse it. The balloonists are intent on their preparations for their flight; they move around with their heads down, their hands always busy, serious, steady expressions on their faces. Nobody understands what they are doing or why, and members of the crowd of watchers turn to each other and ask each other questions and receive shrugs or murmured, puzzled phrases in reply. Alexis supposes that if the balloon fails the two balloonists might drown, although they are using a wooden fisherman's dinghy for a basket.

All day long Jamie, Jim and Alexis and the crowd watch the progress of the balloonists. There are several setbacks, once a heavy cannister of gas falls against one of the balloonists who is kneeling at the time, and knocks him unconscious. Or so she hears, the crowd has grown so huge now that only the top of the tent is visible to her, but soon the word passes back that the balloonist is fine and things continue as before. Once Jim wants to leave and get something to eat, but Jamie is outraged at the very idea.

"I'll wait for you here," he says to his father, who laughs.

"You're only four years old," he tells their son, "I can't leave you alone here."

"Mom will stay with me," Jamie says, confident, but although Alexis would never say so, she is always afraid that if Jim leaves without her, he will never come back. In the end a rumour moves back through the crowd that the balloonists are almost ready to take off, so nobody leaves. Another hour passes, then two. Alexis is seated on the wet grass now, and Jamie is leaning against her, his little elbow in the crook of her neck. She puts her arm around him. Jim has disappeared in the crowd.

Then a low murmur starts among the people, gathers volume, people near the tent press together and those who have wandered away come quickly from all over the field and even out of the forest beside it. The crowd around the tent swells and Jamie says, "They're taking off! Let's go, Mom!" and tugs at her.

Jim appears and lifts Jamie up in his arms and strides away so that once again she is forced to follow him. He skirts around the wide perimeter of the now huge mass of people until they are at the shoreline. The tide is out, there is no sandy beach here, only rocks that are wet and slippery underfoot. She follows him, her shoes sliding off the rocks. The distance between Alexis and her son and husband grows wider. Her shoes are wet and she keeps slipping on the rocks and has to stop to find better footing, she gives up trying to catch up with them and now they are out of sight around the curve of the shore. Others following come between Alexis and her son and his father.

Over to the left the beautiful red and white balloon bobs over the heads of the crowd. Voices grow louder, excitement is rising.

"Look!" someone behind her shouts, and yes, the balloon is rising, ever so slowly, wavering uncertainly, almost dropping, it rises above the crowd, dwarfing it, at the same time moving slowly on a diagonal path toward the end of the cove far ahead of her. She stops where she is and and watches its progress.

Now voices are hushed, the crowd grows silent, everyone's face is turned upward, eyes fixed on the red and white balloon. It rises in a slow ascent above them and to the right where the water glistens so invitingly, but as dark as the fathomless water in her dreams.

It rises higher, but its sideways movement is faster than its rising and now she is getting her first clear view of it, the heads of the balloonists just a suggestion above the sides of the fishermen's boat they are using as a basket. It is above the heads of Jim and Jamie who are somewhere ahead of her, lost in the crowd on the ocean's shore.

Nobody is moving now, nobody is speaking, the upward, onward rush of the balloon holds everyone's attention, it is as if a string is tied to the heart of each one that connects it to the upward rise of the balloon. Alexis feels its rise in her stomach, her chest, her throat. She is dizzy with its rise. Up, up it goes, up and out over the water, the red spiral growing lighter in the late afternoon sun. It dips, the crowd sighs, and then it rises again, a massive upward surge and now it has passed the cove, is beyond it, the red and white spiral with the dark dot below it is far out over the open ocean rising higher and higher, and growing smaller with each passing second until at last it melds into the sky and she can't make it out anymore.

SHARON BUTALA

A native of rural Saskatchewan, Sharon Butala writes about life on the prairies. She has published five books, and her short fiction and articles appear frequently in North America's best magazines. Butala is the recipient of numerous grants and awards, and her first collection of short stories, *Queen of the Headaches*, was nominated for the Governor General's Literary Award in 1986.

The text of this book was set in Weiss, a typeface designed in 1926 for the Bauer Type Foundry in Germany, by Emil Rudolph Weiss. Emil Weiss was first a poet, but when he was praised more for the originality and beauty of his calligraphy than for his poetry, he began to study type design. Weiss Roman was the first of his typeface designs.